'Follow Me, David!'

ISBN10: 1-931807-61-2
ISBN13: 978-1-931807-61-6
Library of Congress Control Number: 2008942459

Peter E. Randall Publisher LLC
Box 4726, Portsmouth NH 03802
www.perpublisher.com

Book design: Grace Peirce

'Follow Me, David!'

Jonathan Russell

☙

PETER E. RANDALL PUBLISHER LLC
Portsmouth, New Hampshire 03802
2009

Reviews

"This serious story of love and loyalty, which is also at times quite humorous, should be on every reader's list.

"This book chronicles the life of an adopted greyhound by a well-to-do widow, Jennifer, and her devotion to this docile, loving, handsome, giant dog whom she names David. She attributes her absolute devotion to David's near-human nature. David, in turn, returns her love with extreme loyalty.

"The author also weaves into his story Jennifer's relationship with bachelor Reverend Golightly, who not only helps her in training the greyhound to climb stairs, which is a very difficult task for a dog with such long legs, as well as assisting the widow in walking the dog, when she is not able to do so. In the course of time, Jennifer and the Reverend marry, and David finds himself unwelcome by the hostile housekeeper at the Reverend's manse, even though the housekeeper is well aware of the Reverend's love for David.

"Jennifer has a serious problem that she alone must solve since neither her husband, the Reverend, nor anyone else is in agreement with her wishes — wanting David, at the time of his death, to receive a Christian burial and to be buried in the family Mausoleum."

—from an advance review by Louise Montclare, editor, Martinelli Productions, and widely published in a chain of New York newspapers.

———————

"This is an unusual and thought-provoking book, it is not easy to characterise, but is broadly to be perceived as a comic novel with considerable popular appeal.

"The novel has some special characteristics as well which I liked. Russell makes many of his effects by understatement; thunder is in the wings, not in the audience's face; there are some great comic moments, but the all important element of the reader's imagination is engaged; he never drops into the error of being over explicit and leaving nothing for the reader to work over. Some of the incidents that are particularly effective are the jeweler's heart attack resulting in the fiasco over the engagement ring (some rather black humor there and the scene of the china crashing around Mr. Harding). There are also some genuinely poetic moments (the seaside picnic). The funeral oration over "David" is a scenic comic masterpiece: the description of the unfortunate canine as "shy and reserved, speaking little of himself" is memorable.

"Language is used effectively; the author has a real feeling for words, and a handle on their use. The story is richly inventive, the writing is smooth and unhurried, and this underlines the strength of the narrative and characterization.

"Almost incidentally, it makes some valid points about our own relationship with, and interdependence upon, the animal kingdom, and while it is a scenario of fantasy, there is nothing impossible in it and nothing that could not, or perhaps has, happened.

"'*Follow Me, David!*' is a real tour de force to achieve the essential suspense of disbelief within a particular world of the author's creation; and Russell succeeds in this—an original and highly individual book."

—*Mark Sykes, British literary critic, editor-in-chief, Athena.*

"We at Grateful Greyhounds would like to congratulate you. The adventures of David are very heart warming and a definite hit with all of our adoptive greyhound parents. We would like to thank you for your very generous contribution to Grateful Greyhounds from the sale of your book and are wishing you great success with it.

"Your donation will be used to help defray the costs to our foster families as they care for these magnificent ex-racers until they reach their forever homes. Also this funding is used to pay any medical bills for care of the greyhounds when we first receive them off the track."

—*Jane Pantaleo, Grateful Greyhounds Inc., Oakdale, NY*

Dedicated to Shirley

*This serious, yet oft-times humorous, love story, that
includes animals and their thinking,
is also dedicated to the
Greyhound Rescue charities, whose munificent
endeavors continue to save so many innocent lives.*

*The author also wishes to express
his profound gratitude to
Deidre Randall, Grace Peirce, and
Skye Wentworth, of Peter E. Randall Publisher LLC
for their tireless and willing efforts to ensure the
success of the work of a legally blind author.*

Parts of the profits received from this book will be donated by the author to organizations working to help rescue Greyhounds who are discarded and left to die after they are no longer profitable to the racing organization.

We rise like a sun from a beautiful dream
In the sunset of sleep no face can replace,
Yet the dearest most loving face recalled
Could belong to all creatures great and small.

Chapter One

"Jen, darling," said Giselle, staring into the mirror of her compact and studiously retouching her make-up, "you'll never get away with it! No pastor will do what you expect of him for David. It's too outrageous! Dogs don't go to heaven. No barking in heaven, period!"

The two well preserved middle-aged best friends were sitting in Jennifer's vast lofty living room in her Greenwich, Connecticut mansion. Resplendent potted palms, opulent furniture, oil paintings, Persian rugs and huge oriental jars (converted into halogen lamps), portrayed her as being a fine lady of taste and means. One who could feasibly command ways for succeeding, even in a bizarre obsession. And danger lurked in her beautiful cougar-like eyes when they flashed their blue fire.

"How do you know dogs don't go to heaven – you of all people who never go to church? Don't tell me you've suddenly become holier than a sacred cow! Have you got yourself informed on your hotline to God?"

Her confirmed hedonist friend ignored the cutting remark. Church to Giselle meant little more than a marriage and funeral shrine, where one walked down the aisle carrying roses and finally got carried out under lilies. There should be lots of sex and cocktails to fill in the gap between!

"No need for a hotline, darling. Everyone knows that dogs haven't even got a soul."

"How do you know?"

"Ask any priest."

"I have," declared the fifty-three-year-old widow, with triumph lighting her remarkable timeless face, "I asked a Franciscan friar and he said he couldn't see any reason why they shouldn't have, 'They are all God's creatures, great and small,' he said."

"Ah! But would he allow a dog into his own church?"

"Who – God?"

"No, your Franciscan friar of course, you idiot!"

"Yes, he would, as a matter of fact."

"And you expect me to believe that?"

"You may laugh but you are quite wrong, Giselle," said Jennifer with a swish of her girlish blond ponytail. "The Franciscans actually do admit animals into their churches every year, as a matter of fact."

"Are you out of your mind?"

"Check it out for yourself if you don't believe me. You can take your Doberman if you like – on the Feast of St. Francis of Assisi on October the fourth. You can have him blessed at the alter rail and sprinkled with holy water."

"Did your Reverend dog-walker tell you that rubbish?" asked Giselle, with her long green quills of fingernails scratching her erogenous legs in black sheer silk stockings.

"No, he didn't actually." There ensued an awkward pause while Giselle gathered her thoughts. Meanwhile, twin ropes of lustrous Tiffany pearls clicked over her skintight black silk dress in elegant contrast to the other, casually dressed in a Japanese dragon quilted kimono. (She had been interrupted while having breakfast in bed when her friend had called early to see the marvelous new dog expected soon from a check-up at the veterinarian.)

Giselle, a sophisticated agnostic flirt, was unabashed. Fingering her clicking pearls, she resumed her admonitions in her husky, sexy voice.

"I'm only saying it for your own good, darling, I hope you are not thinking of trying to persuade your new Reverend dog-walker to go along with that foolish scheme of yours. You'll only scare him away if you do. By the way, how's the relationship coming along, Jen – what's his name again? The Reverend Bernard something or other, isn't it?"

"The Reverend Bernard Houndsditch," replied the other icily.

"Sounds familiar and very woofy-woofy and probably very groovy since you seem so moonstruck on the guy. Could I have met him some-where, do you think?"

"Since you never go to church, Giselle, I would say it's most unlikely." Again the latter ignored the cutting remark.

"Then describe him to me, Jen – is he young and handsome?" inquired the other, with hand cupped under chin while sitting in her favorite excep-tionally low armchair across the coffee table. Her thighs were shamelessly splayed, revealing an absence of panties, and a most indiscreet intimacy! For she enjoyed shocking prudish people and in particular Jennifer. "Let's hear the breathtaking scenario, sweetheart," she demanded, seizing the chance to get her religiously inclined friend off the thorny subject of her dog's last rites.

"Nothing, you minx! All very proper with Reverend Houndsditch."

"Such a pity! What, no laying-on of hands?"

"Sex, sex and sex on your one-groove mind! Giselle, give me a break, why don't you change the needle sometimes? Bernard is not what you imagine – he's a genuine, Good Samaritan only."

"Only? You are very naïve, darling, aren't you? Surely you must realize you can be a real honeypot whenever men are buzzing around. You are too modest. It's about time you took a serious look at yourself in the mirror."

"Like you, Giselle darling – inspecting every second's damage in your compact. There are more important things in life. It's not all reflections, sweetheart!"

"Meow!" mimed Giselle, scratching the air with studiously painted claws. "Steady now pussy pussy – you could hurt someone who loves you."

Jennifer repented. "Sorry, I didn't mean to – just slipped out, forgive me."

"I'm not in a forgiving mood."

"You should be."

"Not when you make those cutting remarks."

"Sorry!"

"Okay, no bones broken." Instinctively the two friends leaned over towards each other and slapped the palms of their hands together, as in their college days. The clock spun back in their minds at that instant – two bright young sprites laughing and joking on campus. The chasm between them was for the moment bridged.

Then Giselle recommended fishing in her usual flippant style.

"Seriously though, Jen, isn't there anything beyond the holier-than-thou between you two saints? Damn monotonous, if that's really the true scenario. You've been a while now without a man in your luxury nunnery." She stretched up to touch one of the many tall potted palms. "It reminds me always of Palm Sunday. And you say this holy guy who walks your dogs every day is just a Good Samaritan? Don't tell me he still calls you Mrs. Trewlove and goes back to his church to kneel in prayer!"

"Now, Giselle, don't be sarcastic. You are sticking your neck out again. It's not what you in your infamous little mind suspect – he's a respectable Reverend like I said. Not one of your slippery lounge lizards."

"A holier-than-thou, eh? Or is he a gay perhaps?"

The blue fire flashed from her eyes. "Samaritans do exist without necessarily being gay, in spite of what you think – genuine concern for my arthritis is possible. You know I can't possibly walk my great big pulling bearded collie and now I've rescued this even bigger greyhound from the racetrack. You can't expect my lame, fat duck Maria who can't even waddle very far from her kitchen, poor creature. So he took pity on me I suppose when I told him. It was on a Sunday when he stood shaking hands with his parishioners outside his church."

"Pity for your arthritis? Jen, wake up! Pity is akin to love, remember. I bet I'm not hearing the truth."

"Which is, my gypsy of the crystal ball?"

"I see all crystal clear that he calls you 'sugarplum' and you, my love, go all goo-goo and say, 'Bernie, how sensitive of you to notice my arthritis. I can see you are a perfect gentleman – I can see it in your eyes!' Come off it, Jen! Who do you think you're kidding? Ah, you hesitate. When you hedge there is usually a reason."

"No, he's a perfect gentleman, I tell you, so don't go reading something into nothing, you minx. And for God's sake, Giselle, I know you don't go blabbing it all around Connecticut. It could put the cat among the pigeons. Or rather, among the parrots of the parish." She leaned across the low table and grasped her friend's hand, which was caught straying back to her compact.

"Gizzy, I can count on your being discreet, can't I? Promise me."

Deep in their green eyeshadows Giselle's dark brown eyes focused tenderly on the other through their contact lenses. Meanwhile Jennifer, with her habitually swishing long blond ponytail, augmented by well rounded cheeks akin to puppy fat, coupled with her gentle voice, created an illusion of imperishable girlishness and naïveté. She seemed too gullible, so in need of her more worldly friend's care and protection.

"What's there to be discreet about? You say there's nothing going on between you two saints."

Jennifer was silent and cast her habitual brooding gaze upon the poignant photograph in a decorative silver frame which stood on the grand piano. It was a snapshot of her beloved son and late husband, taken only weeks before the fated sports car in the background had so tragically consumed both marriage and motherhood in an instant of horrific implosion of twisted metal on the highway.

Seeing Jennifer's eyes fixed upon the enlarged sacrosanct snapshot, Giselle said intuitively, "He's become a surrogate son, Jen, hasn't he – this so human and understanding David of yours? Strange coincidence he should be called David as well."

"Actually 'Dave' was his racing name but he answers to the extra syllable now. Not much difference in his ear I suppose as I emphasize the first syllable always."

"And it's all happened so quickly – I was stunned when you telephoned me in London at the Ritz to tell me. You seemed so over-the-moon about adopting another dog – and one called David at that."

"Strange coincidence, I repeat – isn't it?"

"Yes indeed. Very strange the way it all came about. But you must not let it become an obsession. I'm warning you, it could lead to trouble. For your own sake, you naïve, innocent dreamer, I repeat, don't mention that subject to his doggie holiness, Saint Bernard!"

Once more, a chasm in communication cleft them apart. Jennifer remained staring at the photograph. Like a stricken animal, the widow was licking her wounds. In whom could she confide if not her best friend? The stark loneliness of bereavement having gradually dissolved over the years, now recrystallized in all its bitter poignancy. For Giselle was untroubled by, and unapproachable about, any future beyond the grave. While Jennifer cherished her faith and prayed nightly to be allowed to be reunited with her most loved ones in heaven. She believed implicitly in the power of prayer.

At times, as now, she felt lonesome and isolated. She craved for sympathy and understanding. But she had only a shoulder in nostalgia to cry upon. That of her revered dead father, a handsome naval chaplain, then happily married to her mother. Both parents, she felt, would have understood her predicament. She still missed them both profoundly.

Her mother had been a delicate, beautiful socialite, whose wealthy, bigoted sister had adopted Jennifer when her niece became orphaned in her teens. Often she would recall her aunt's sharp features and prim attire. Seated in the bay window of her Victorian mansion, she would be crocheting and ladling out matronly wisdom, more tart than her renowned cranberries which had supplied the income for running her vast estate near Cape Cod.

As she dreamed away, Giselle fell back into her everlasting preening. She knew that Jennifer was consoling herself by reliving the past. In fact she had gone back to being a little girl again and suddenly the other broke out giggling.

"What were you thinking of just then?"

"Oh, nothing, it wouldn't interest you."

"Never mind, I demand to know."

"If you really want to know?"

"I do."

"Well, I was seeing the expression on my aunt's face when she looked down during the sermon and saw that I was taking chewing gum out of my mouth and using the sticky stuff to mark my place for the next hymn. You see I was rather a naughty little girl in chapel in those days and my aunt was not amused."

"Still, she wasn't a bad old buzzard, your maiden aunt. She spoilt you terribly, from what I gather. And you wouldn't be able to keep up all this great indoor palmy oasis of halogen moonshine if it weren't for your inheritance. By the way, it was rather an unorthodox bookmarker she must have thought. A bit tough on the old gal if you were like that all the time. Where did you get rid of the muck finally? In your sticky pocket I presume?"

"No, I parked it under the seat as a matter of fact when she wasn't looking. I wasn't going to sacrifice recyclable gum. So you see I was far from being the little saint."

"Good for you. Saints are out of fashion this day and age," said Giselle, adding more grasshopper green to the startling hollows of large, piercing, dark eyes. As Jennifer watched, fascinated, lashes began to be curled, lengthened and thickened, while bits of mascara began to pepper the tiny mirror of her smart crocodile-skin bag. Afterwards the pageant continued, with lips being reinforced and made lush, eyebrows made sinuous and slim. It was her uninhibited way of expressing her sexuality – akin to the courtship of exotic birds.

At last, all done, for the moment at least, she looked up to find her friend's eyes misting upon the photograph once more.

"I caught you!" declared Giselle, as if she were on stage and every word had to reach the back row. Her husky, sexy voice implored, "Let's not fight, Jen – you know deep down we couldn't do without each other. Remember Vassar, darling – how you used to turn to me when you thought all the world was against you?"

Giselle watched the boomerang of memories return.

Suddenly the cougar-eyes were glazing and Giselle's own brown ones softened in their prowling green jungle of eyeshadow and mascara.

The arms of both women flew up and palms kissed – exuberantly forgiving.

"Together forever! Remember?"

"How can we ever forget! You haven't changed. Still green as a girl guide, and you still swish your ponytail like a horse shooing flies!"

"And your face is still like an artist's palette!"

"Touché!"

Jennifer studied for a moment that brilliant sunset of a face. Its well-formed natural features, crowned with close-cropped black shiny hair, were not unenhanced by the deluge of cosmetics.

Jennifer's bright cougar-eyes had ceased their fascination with the photograph on the grand piano, as she relented. She realized the contro-versial matter must remain her unshared secret, until such time as she could find perhaps the one and only ally compassionate enough to listen objectively, then having done so, be sympathetic enough not to reject her proposal outright.

"Oh! What the hell! We've been best of friends all our lives, through thick and thin, let's not quarrel now."

And Giselle responded warmly, "Well, I won't if you come clean with me, as my attorney womanizing husband is fond of saying."

"There really is nothing to come clean about regarding the Reverend – cross my heart – together forever, remember? We don't lie to each other, do we?" replied Jennifer, flicking her ponytail.

Giselle's remarkable eyebrows soared above her well-powdered nose, before she admitted most charmingly, "Well, I think that once or twice in a teeny-weeny little while we do! – Only the whitest little lies naturally."

"Well, I'm not lying now when I say Reverend Bernard is a perfect gentleman – no hand below the Plimsoll mark, as your yachtsman hubby would say."

"So your spiritual guru must be a saint – saint who? Let me see." She became mockingly inspired. "Why of course – Saint Bernard, the patron saint of dogs! – No wonder he wears a dog collar! Does he carry brandy underneath as well?"

"Very droll! Now can I finish?"

"Please be my guest."

"You are very unjust, Giselle, and when you meet the man you will realize it for yourself. What other man so heavily burdened with commitments would get up early in the morning just to walk my dogs and nothing else? Just a cup of tea and a chat – nothing else besides – just a cup of tea and be on his way. And in the evening come again rain or shine just out of the natural goodness of his heart. And you scoff at this? I think it's very mean and despicable!"

"Are you sure it's not tea and sympathy?"

"Not in the sense you mean – you little trollop!"

"I assume he's mortal?" said Giselle unabashed, with a winsome smile.

The cougar-eyes dilated and blue ice returned in their stare.

"Why don't you poke fun at your own Saint Peter, fisher of men – oh, yes, and not forgetting women? Quite a few you must admit to your cost!"

Giselle went very quiet. The bold mask was but a vulnerable façade. She had been deeply wounded, but she tried hard to hide the pain. She knew Jennifer had not been referring to her husband Peter but to another Peter in the past.

"It's not a crime, darling, to fall in love," said the subdued husky voice after a long castigating pause. "It's not even a sin, unless he's married, of course. Is your own Samaritan by any chance?" she slipped in slyly in retaliation.

Jennifer felt those dark hypnotic eyes reflecting a deep inner wound and regretted now her own cruel remark concerning that Peter in the distant past who had jilted her friend. "No he's not married," said Jennifer gently, "my Reverend is a bachelor."

"That's good – you need someone safe – it's been a long time, hasn't it?"

Now it was Jennifer's turn to resent the innuendo.

"That's all you can think of in relationships – hopping in and out of bed!"

Giselle giggled with unconvincing gaiety, but was saved by her elastic wit.

"You make me sound like a flea."

"You must admit, you do hop a little, and you do bite the host! I caught several of your hot pursuers with one of your infamous red sucking marks on their necks – you're incorrigible! Fancy wanting to flaunt your dirty little escapades in public!"

"At least I'm honest," she answered, casual and quite unperturbed. "Got any emery boards handy, Jen? I've got to do a very quick touch-up. One of my glue-on claws must have come adrift and I'm meeting one of Peter's VIP clients for lunch – my Peter in case you're thinking anything!"

"I'm not," replied Jennifer, whilst stretching for her own purse on the mirror shelf under the table, to oblige her claw-flawed friend. As the latter took the proffered emery board, she squinted at her minuscule marcasite wristwatch.

"Holy cow! I'm afraid I'll have to shove off if this veterinarian of yours doesn't show up within the next ten minutes or so. Pity, because I can't wait to see your beautiful David. Jen, sweetheart, what do you think's keeping him? Why don't you give Dr. Bigden another buzz?"

Jennifer leaned over and picked up the telephone.

"His line's engaged. Busy as a bee I suppose. His waiting room is like a zoo. I can never get him on the phone; I can't understand why he hasn't got a beeper in this day and age. You can never reach him on the road. But hang on, I'm sure he must be on his way. The receptionist called just before you arrived. She said he's picking up some sick parrot first. Should be here any minute now – probably before you've finished trying the impossible on that false claw. Why don't you carry a spare? I always imagined you to be so sophisticated that you carried a spare everything."

There was a brief dramatic pause, while the cougar-eyes studied their prey.

"In fact a spare everything, including a spare conscience and a spare husband or two – including mine!"

That fated last word galvanized Giselle into looking up in alarm. "That time at your place while Peter was away sailing, remember? You told me my David was advising you on the sale of some shares. Don't try to kid me by looking so mystified. To refresh your amnesia it was one hell of a long bit of advice my husband was giving you. In fact it lasted all night. Until 3 A.M. as I remember! But I won't speak ill of the dead. I still love my husband David you know."

The nail-filing ground down to a halt as Giselle's thick eyelashes dropped, revealing their garish lids, while her thin brows almost closed their gap. "So you knew?" she whispered. "But why now for crying out loud – after all these years? For fuck's sake why did you bottle it up? Not fair you know to hide a grievance."

The brown eyes opened and in a hurt tone she repeated the last emotive question.

Jennifer regretted her disclosure immediately. She hesitated awkwardly. "Truthfully, I cannot be sure. Sorry Gizzy, it just slipped out. Forgive and forget – I'm sorry I said that about Peter Craven – something to do with what you did to me that long ago I suppose."

"Now we are quits! But you know, Jen, you really did hurt me terribly – and Peter Craven wasn't at all like that. He wasn't your wisecrack fisher of women – just shit scared of his parents. That's why he ditched me – just hadn't the guts to face his father, the senator. Thought I wasn't good enough for their precious son Peter."

"But he quickly picked up quite a few hopefuls afterwards, as I recall."

"I was a hard act to follow I guess. He kept trying without much success. And you know, Jen, I was very different in those days. In fact, I was almost a virgin!"

"You got to be kidding!"

"Oh, in your fashion? Like in Dowson's poem you mean? The one called 'Cynara in my fashion.'"

"How did you guess?"

"We used to read that poem over and over together at Vassar, don't you remember? Plus that other beautiful one of Dowson's. Do you recall still, Gizzy, after all these years?"

"Yes, Jen, I remember like it were only yesterday." Again Giselle paused in her nail filing while she recalled the lost but often recalled happy days.

"How time flies, Jen," she sighed. "It was called *The Days of Wine and Roses*. It was in the Oxford Book of English Verse on the next page. You showed it to me in the library, do you remember? It preceded the movie of the same title by about a hundred years. So we know who took what from whom."

"Yes, I even remember what you were wearing – it was that funny sweater with the heart on it, plus 'I love Pete' – as if everyone down there, including the faculty, had to know when they couldn't care, sweetheart, even after – how many years is it? Let me count – at least twenty-seven."

"You know, Jen, it's still 'in my fashion' when my husband thinks he's sent me to the moon with an orgasm! That's clue enough, isn't it? You know whose face I see when he's puffing away on top of me, don't you?"

"I'm not sure."

"Bullshit!"

"Peter Craven, then?"

"Bullseye!"

"You embarrass me, but I'm glad you got it off your chest. You are crying on my shoulder, aren't you? I truly am sorry now that I've heard the truth about Peter Craven."

"No need, I'm a survivor – Ha! Ha! Who am I kidding now – myself or you?"

"I understand fully – together forever, don't forget. Carry on – don't bottle it up – release the tension. It will make you feel better," coaxed Jennifer, as the clicking pearls invoked their nostalgic echoes.

Giselle took a quick gulp of vodka and leaned forward into the halogen haze, as if hiding from those cougar-eyes while asking the delicate question of her prudish friend, "Did you ever, Jen? You know what I mean – did you ever do a 'Faithful to thee Cynara in my fashion' *à la* Dowson yourself? I mean see another face while doing it? You know? – That boy your husband was jealous of, for instance?"

Jennifer blushed and looked away. One of those little white lies that Giselle had accused her of was beginning to form on her lips in protest, but she was rescued from her dilemma by Giselle intervening.

"No need to spell it out in chapter and verse but did it help orgasmically, I mean?"

"Let's change the subject. You know I don't like engaging in your shameful little sexual postmortems. But why don't you divorce him, then you wouldn't have to do your deceitful Cynara act, would you? Poor Gizzy, yes, why don't you divorce him? Surely you can get proof enough from one of those private eye photographers?"

"Divorce a slick divorce attorney? You must be joking! I actually did engage one a long time ago. But when I burst into his office one day and confronted him with my private eye's compromising photographs, what d'you think he did?"

"He had a fit, I suppose?"

"Wrong! Cool as a cucumber, the clever little bastard suggested exchanging them for some that his own shitty little closet-creeper took of me!"

"Poor Gizzy – but you do lay yourself open, darling. You can't say I didn't warn you."

"I know, I know, but we aren't all born saints like you, Saint Jennifer. Anyway, Jen, we came to an arrangement – his! A kind of 'Nelson's eye *entente cordiale*', as he calls it. I think he picked that one up at his yacht club."

"At his yacht club?"

"You know? At the bar. Men sticking together laundering their dirty jockstraps in public!"

She broke off to squint again at her wristwatch, while Jennifer began counting the sepulchral gongs of the grandfather clock in the hall. In the middle of the booming sounds, they heard the scuffing of gravel in the driveway followed by the unmistakable clicking of the handbrake of the veterinarian's jeep.

Giselle got up excitedly and flew to the window.

"Jen! Oh, Jen! It's David! It's David! – What a giant handsome show dog! Your David's absolutely fabulous!"

Chapter Two

"Yes, isn't he fabulous!" exclaimed Jennifer, proudly rushing to share the experience with her friend at the window. Giselle felt the other's hand pressing affectionately upon her shoulder, as both women glued their faces to the glass.

"Oh Jen! I knew he must mean more to you than just another dog. It had to go deeper. When we lose our very worth living for, we find a surrogate, don't we? In my case, a Doberman like Peter's. I look into those soulful eyes and see you-know-who. It's Peter's dog all over. He was nuts about the creature! I mean of the one he had himself. That's why I had to have a Doberman."

"I guessed as much. Don't I know! Same with my new David – when he stares at me I see my poor dead son."

With Jennifer breathing down her neck, so proud, Giselle could not take her eyes off the wonder dog towering over Robert, her bearded collie, who was an impressive, big, shaggy dog in his own right. Now they could see him vociferously tugging tall, burly, Dr. Bigden across the spacious lawn. The big veterinarian, with white coattails flying, was being hijacked towards the front doorstep by the powerful dogs!

Upon arrival, his ringing of the door chimes was an unnecessary activity. Robert's exceptionally loud voice was enough to alert heavy Maria, Jennifer's live-in maidservant.

Meanwhile, the white and tan beautifully marked giant greyhound stood beside his noisy companion, panting down at him with smiling dignified superiority. His beautiful large eyes were glowing and his long tongue was hanging out and dripping saliva onto the red brick doorstep.

The great moment was approaching. Giselle was excited. Maria had her orders, which were to lead Robert straightaway to the kitchen to be muffled with ice cream. She was afterwards to deal with the veterinarian, then release David to them in the living room to be introduced in peace to Giselle.

Meanwhile, Jennifer warned her, "Back to your chair – quick! Or he'll have that dress shredded in seconds! He's all over the ladies! But men he backs away from – especially men wearing those peekaboo caps – remindful of something in his past – it's pathetic to see him so cowed."

Once they were seated again, they heard the no-nonsense Maria placing Robert under house arrest, and whisking him off to her kitchen to be silenced with his delicious bribe.

Dr. Bigden, left holding onto David in the hallway, suddenly let go! The released greyhound instinctively leaped forward, as he was trained to do at the start of a race. He skidded to a halt at the screen dividing the entrance hall from the vast living room. After taking a quick cautious sniff round it, the giant male greyhound, as tall as a female Great Dane, came striding into them to bury his docile doe-like head in Jennifer's kimono, where she sat welcoming with her arms outstretched.

"Oh! Jen! He's so handsome!" exclaimed Giselle, leaning over to stroke the dog's long, velvety, beautifully marked tan and white back. Meanwhile in the hallway, Dr. Bigden, having bent down on one knee to tie a shoelace, caught sight of the two ladies from his extremely low vantage point beyond the edge of the screen.

"Peepo! Dr. Bigden," cried out the irrepressible Giselle, "Come and join us for a tipple – we're drinking vodka – but we've got practically everything else, so come and take your pick."

"Yes, do come in for a drink," invited Jennifer hospitably, one hand modestly clasping her kimono with David irremovably wedged therein. "Please forgive my friend Mrs. Carboni whom you must know already. Her Doberman is your patient. So you must know his mistress is a bit of a clown. Take no notice. Thank you for bringing back our lovely dogs. You'll join us for a drink before you go, won't you?"

"That's very kind. I hope I am not disturbing you ladies, I was only—" apologized the embarrassed big man in a white coat, rising swiftly onto his feet and pointing to his trailing shoelace.

"You can see I wasn't playing Peeping Tom, though I must admit my name by coincidence actually is Tom," he admitted with a laugh, as he hovered awkwardly near the cocktail cabinet just inside the room. "You'll have to excuse me, ladies, I'm not dressed for socializing."

"Don't worry. We are very informal. Hang on, I'm coming over to play hostess, Dr. nonpeeping Tom," said Giselle, mischievously playing the coquette. Shamelessly, she was tacitly encouraging the man to gape down her revealing bosom. Viewed from his considerable height as she positioned herself at his side, it was inevitable.

"What will you have, Tom? Have a look around – don't be shy," said his self-appointed hostess impishly, as Bigden hesitated.

The burly veterinarian was obviously a trifle overpowered by Giselle. He stroked his neat ginger beard, then scratched his thinly thatched giant's head, feeling a little out of his depth, yet pleasantly so, in the presence of the two attractive ladies.

The galaxy of scintillating labeled decanters and bottles beckoned. Plucking up courage before the dazzling, facetious Giselle, he said at last, "I think I'll have a dry fly sherry, Mrs. Carboni, thank you very much." Flirting with her eyes, she poured from a labeled deep cut crystal flask into one of the noble renaissance Venetian goblets.

"Gosh! That's a beauty!" remarked the man in a stained white coat and smelling pungently of his profession. "It's a long time since I drank from one of these!"

"Genuine Venetian, Tom – made in Tennessee!" teased Giselle.

"You are putting me on, Mrs. Carboni, aren't you?"

"Don't take any notice of her, Dr. Bigden. As you rightly noticed, they are the real thing, bought in Venice on our honeymoon."

The exquisite glass, during repeated revolving under the appraising veterinarian's scrutiny, caught the sun. A flash of brilliant red startled David, who had come out of hiding and promptly gone back into it again.

"Like a red rag to a bull, I suppose?" said Giselle in her husky, sexy voice while looking up at the connoisseur for corroboration.

The gruff veterinarian smiled discreetly at the suggestion.

"Close, Mrs. Carboni but no cigar! You see dogs are color-blind! They see everything in monochrome. All this talk you hear about bulls going berserk over seeing anything red is all bullshit! – Oh! Sorry ladies it just slipped out," he apologized sheepishly, behind his huge hand.

Giselle giggled.

"We're not blushing, Dr. Bigden, it's not the first time we've heard that expressive word. Bullshit is bullshit whichever way you look at it. If you say it's bullshit, Dr. Bigden, we believe you. After all, as a qualified veterinarian, you must be an authority on animal stools!"

Dr. Bigden looked unsure how to take the compliment and glanced at Jennifer who said reassuringly, "Take no notice of my incorrigible friend.

Please sit down and explain why my poor David was scared of the red glass."

Giselle pulled him by the sleeve and sat him down at their table.

"Not at the red glass, Mrs. Trewlove, but at the reflections – it reminded him of something cruel, no doubt, in his past. For instance, when he growls and slinks away from men wearing peak caps. Perhaps they did things to him during the night – probably suddenly appearing on the scene carrying flashlights. A flash of sunlight from the glass would bring back memories."

Jennifer was now sitting on the sofa with David sprawling on his side, his long legs sticking out from the wide sofa and touching the table, while his head lay again on her lap. At last he was peaceful once more.

Watching David cautiously for any incipient sign of reaction, Bigden retrieved the goblet from under his white coat, and placed his drink beside Giselle's on the protecting glass over the low table's lovely walnut grain. David's eye – the one which was not blinkered in his mistress' kimono, glowed at the man's ginger beard and when it moved the stare followed, as do the eyes in some oil paintings by the masters.

The veterinarian leaned over to fondle one of David's strange rose-like floppy ears.

"Oh! Jen, he's beautiful!" exclaimed Giselle, joining in the petting. "I never knew greyhounds could be as big as Great Danes! And he's so wonderfully mottled – just like a deer. If he had antlers he could be mistaken for one. He's so velvety – and so docile and cuddly – and those glowing eyes! Just like my luminous watch. You know, Jen, what he reminds me of?"

"No, what?"

"One of those long-eyed Egyptian Pharaohs we see pictures of in their burial chambers."

Jennifer went very quiet. The mention of tombs invoked her secret thoughts on the subject of her own family vault, wherein she planned one day to be reunited with her loved ones – the three inseparable Davids in her life – awaiting the promise of eternal life!

Suddenly Giselle, seeing that her friend was daydreaming, winked at Bigden, then cut off her raptures to examine David's curious rose-like ears, which twitched and rolled back to reveal their pink skin. She brought her friend down to earth by suddenly exclaiming, "Jen, look! Those funny folded-back ears he's got – oh, look! You must have seen these horrid numbers tattooed inside on the pink skin. It's pathetic. It reminds me of Belsen!"

"I know, I know, poor thing!" said Jennifer, bending low to kiss the passive greyhound's head. "But that's nothing to what goes on down at those unspeakable racing kennels."

"How could human beings be so cruel?" continued Giselle. "No wonder greyhound racing is banned in New York State. I watched a program on TV showing what they do to the poor creatures after their short racing career is over. After only two years, the man said, they run out of steam. Then they are slaughtered. I had to switch off. I just couldn't bear to continue watching – it simply turned my stomach!"

"David is one of the lucky ones," interposed the veterinarian, sitting back in his comfortable armchair. "The Rescue Society stepped in just in time. He was found crammed into a cage hardly big enough for a Pekinese. A barbaric leather muzzle was strapped on tight, and he was about to be left with several others to be starved to death without food or water. Cheaper than euthanasia by us veterinarians!"

"Don't, Dr. Bigden – I can't take any more! Spare us the details, I beg you," interrupted Giselle, pulling a face. "No more please – when I see this beautiful gentle creature and think of all he's been through—" She broke off to squint at her tiny wristwatch and then looked up, feeling herself being drawn by the dog's remarkable, glowing, hypnotic eyes.

"I can see now what you mean, Jen. It's as if he can see right through you – into your very brain – know all your secret thoughts. It's most uncanny! I never saw a look so knowing! Certainly I've never seen a look like that from my Doberman, or, for that matter, from any other dog."

"Yes, David is different," said the burly veterinarian, wedging himself into the conversation, because the strange dog fascinated him. "Yes, David is different," he repeated, "very, very different from any other dog I've handled. I can't explain what that difference is exactly, but sometimes – it was during the week I had him with me to recuperate – he used to stare at me just like he were psychic!"

"So you noticed it too, did you, Dr. Bigden?" interposed Jennifer, growing excited at having her own more questionable belief confirmed by a pragmatic professional like the burly, earthy veterinarian.

He took a sip of his dry fly sherry, then put his goblet down. "Yes, indeed. I've been handling dogs for over twenty years and not one of them gave me that queer feeling before. And I never heard him bark

– most unusual. That is, until once he saw something, something invisible to me – and then he gave out one single – I don't know how to describe the sound. I can only say it was a blood-curdling, helluva high-pitched kind of yell! Nothing like a dog bark. It scared the daylights out of me, coming from him, because he's so docile. And never barks. Most unusual."

"Oh shit!" said Giselle under her breath, upon squinting at the time once more. "Sorry Jen, I've got to fly – Peter will be furious! You'll have to excuse me, Dr. Bigden, Jen."

Whereupon she rose suddenly, letting out a string of, "Sorry, sorry, sorry you lovely people" flung to them over her shoulder, and fled with her pearls clicking like faint castanets. Bigden half rose from his chair out of politeness, but she was gone before he could say anything. There followed the briefest pause while she snatched her mink coat from its peg in the hall.

"Catch up with you later, Jen – bye, darling – see you later!" she shouted, half an octave higher than her natural low voice. They heard the heavy door slam.

There goes a minx in mink, thought Jennifer to herself. *Yet one I can't help loving just the same.*

But Robert Bearded Collie, locked in the kitchen, celebrated her departure exuberantly.

"That's a typical collie bark, if ever I heard one," remarked Bigden, getting up again from his chair and glancing at his own impressive wristwatch.

"I bet," he continued, looking at Jennifer through the halogen haze (*preventing her from catching the expression on his face*), "I bet he wakes the whole neighborhood at times in the early morning – when the Reverend takes them out!"

Jennifer was startled. Could he be discreetly warning her that tongues were already wagging in Bernard's parish?

It made her uneasy. She watched him take a small package from his coat pocket and lay it on the table.

"Those are the stool containers. Please tell Reverend Houndsditch to let me have them back as soon as possible for the lab reports – they may both need worming. And don't forget the heartworm pills, Mrs. Trewlove – one a month – most important."

But Jennifer was not concentrating. Her mind was disturbed at the veiled insinuation concerning what could be damaging to the shy rector's reputation and consequently threatening their very relationship. She was still trying to pluck up courage in order to find out more on the sensitive issue, when he suddenly took one more glance at his watch and plucked away the opportunity, exclaiming, "Oh my gosh! I've got a sick parrot I must take a look at. It's been such an interesting morning, Mrs. Trewlove. I almost forgot. Duty calls. Thanks for the hospitality. Much appreciated. Have a great day, Mrs. Trewlove! And don't forget the stool samples," he reminded her on the doorstep when she saw him out.

"Give my regards to Reverend Houndsditch and tell him Reverend Golightly's poodle is doing just fine – just fine. And thanks again, Mrs. Trewlove! Great personality, your friend Mrs. Carboni, and very glamorous. I can just imagine her on Broadway."

"I'll tell her you said so. I'm sure she'll be thrilled. Good day then, Dr. Bigden, and I won't forget the pills and the worming."

Now she had plenty to reflect upon, as she climbed up to her bedroom in order to shower and dress.

Soon, through the sound of the water cascading, she became conscious of David whining pitifully at the foot of the stairs. It stirred her heart. Poor thing, he had never been taught to climb.

Jennifer got out of the shower. Snatching a towel, she ran to the banister and leaned over the rail to shout down to Maria.

"Maria, quick! Give David a bowl of ice cream."

"Yes, Missus Jennifer. Maria make David happy puppy. David come quick kitchen! Come David, come! Good puppy – ice cream, ice cream." The words worked like magic. David followed her immediately.

Her therapy produced more barking from the bearded collie who had finished his own bowl and now loudly coveted his companion's.

But the universal canine panacea worked on David too. After Robert's bowl had been replenished, suddenly all fell quiet in the kitchen front. Jennifer returned to shower and afterwards to dress and make-up with painstaking moderation before her dressing table's flattering pink mirror. It convinced her that Giselle was right: she truly was a "honeypot" and that dog-walking was the shy cleric's way of "buzzing around"!

Later, when she was in the middle of trying on one dress after another in order to discover which suited her best for modestly seducing a timid bachelor cleric, she heard Robert barking again fit to send Maria into hysterics.

Both dogs were in the hallway, with muzzles raised like howling wolves and their tails beating the radiator cover and making a fearsome noise.

Visitors were rare. What could it be? Beneath her unfastened brassiere, Jennifer's ample bosom stirred. Evidently something dramatic had been seen or heard by the dogs.

She scurried to peer through the bathroom window. All seemed quite normal below. The driveway was clear as far as the road beyond. No one was in the garden or on the doorstep, while neither animal nor bird was in sight to account for the dogs' most scary reaction!

Scouring in vain for the mysterious cause, she leaned far out of the open window. Suddenly David let off his terrifying, high-pitched, single yell that had so ominously impressed the veterinarian. It tingled through Jennifer like an electric shock.

Surely it must be God's way of giving one of His portentous signs? She knew He acted mysteriously His wonders to perform. He was often an abstract communicator, a fact to which the Bible bore ample testimony. He sent signs from heaven above in forms most mystical, including disembodied voices speaking in riddles from on high. Her teaching told her so. She had recently prayed fervently, this time upon her knees beside her bed, for the granting of an intermediary in the insoluble problem involving herself and David with regard to their indivisible future.

Jennifer convinced herself that it could be a sign from heaven to say that all was well! A sign from above, as in the case, say, of Joan of Arc, or, more recently, the "Angels of Mons" appearing to soldiers during the First World War!

She could imagine Giselle and her ilk with eyebrows raised but why should their skepticism prevail over her faith? She tried to picture what form the sign had taken, capable of electrifying both dogs.

In the Bible messages were occasionally reported as having been delivered by angels. Had one appeared before the bearded collie? She very briefly considered the startling possibility before dismissing it as being most unlikely! She could not conceive of the cowardly Robert barking at an angel! Surely he would be slinking away to hide, as he invariably did at the first clap of thunder!

Moreover, she decided, he was much too ordinary a dog to possess transcendental perception, like David did, in the opinion of several people who had dealings with the strange dog. So then, what? Surely the apparition must have taken on a more familiar and less frightening form, otherwise the cowardly beardie would not have barked so bravely!

But David – well, there was something very unaccountable about his behavior – she even had the word of Dr. Bigden for that. She recalled how all signs from heaven did not always take on the form of angels. Sometimes, according to the Bible, they materialized in more mundane guises.

Jennifer was convinced that the strange greyhound letting out his rare blood-curdling "un-doglike yell" was somehow involved. It was a matter for her faith to interpret intuitively.

Could it have been a visitation in the familiar shape of Rev. Bernard? This would explain why the cowardly bearded collie had not gone into hiding. Both perhaps had either seen or "felt" their dog-walker's familiar presence.

After all, was Bernard not the Lord's ordained representative and messenger on earth? Therefore, could he not be predestined to become at some future auspicious time, not only messenger but the merciful intermediary she was seeking for her cause?

If so, all would, no doubt, be revealed in good time. Or was God trying to tell her something else? In one of His most mysterious ways? Was it perhaps a warning of some danger? Perhaps nothing to do with her obsession, but more perhaps to do with the malicious gossip at work behind their backs in the parish – which could scare the minister away from continuing their relationship. This also, after a veiled hint from Dr. Bigden, could be the explanation for any warning sign for her to tread carefully.

Thank heaven she had been able to throw Giselle off the scent regarding the true developing relationship beyond that of Good Samaritan. The incorrigible flirt could have started the parish gossiping, and she was also not above trying to seduce him herself! For had her friend not, behind her back, had an affair with her own late husband David and once even tried seducing David, their son? Recalling the fact, the reflection of her own face in her dressing table mirror betrayed the underlying uneasiness of jealousy and suspicion.

This, in the face of the fact that Bernard would be coming again that very evening not only to walk the dogs but to come in for a chat and a drink, all nice and cozy together in the romantic halogen haze beneath the shade of the potted palms.

All was quiet again, now that Maria had herded the disturbers of the peace back to her kitchen. Jennifer fell into dreaming. Dreaming of what wishfully could happen after dark in the roseate halogen haze.

She had a vague feeling that somehow David could become the catalyst – make it all happen. The strange dog had already forged a tight bond between them and would lean heavily and possessively against his legs as well as hers. In this show of possessiveness, it was difficult to imagine who belonged to whom! Even the pragmatic Dr. Bigden had found cause to believe that the strange greyhound had about him something paranormal.

Suddenly, although she knew it was impossible (both dogs being in the kitchen), yet she became conscious of David looking up at her with his intense glowing eyes – hypnotic eyes which had made even the worldly Giselle feel that they could see into her very mind. Jennifer peered down as if half expecting the dog to be there. Simultaneously, she began to experience a vague prescience deep inside her and beyond her natural woman's intuition. In a vague yet intense way, which she could not have described properly even to her best friend, she felt certain that something out of the ordinary was about to take place. Something momentous concerning herself, David and the rector would transpire that very evening – when the Reverend Bernard Ignatius Houndsditch arrived to walk the dogs.

Chapter Three

"Come in, won't you, Reverend?" cooed Jennifer over Maria's shoulder, as soon as the latter had opened the door. Thereupon, to a fanfare of barking from the bearded collie, the shy cleric found himself being pulled into the confined tiled entrance space between doors by the powerful dogs. His reply was swallowed by the noise and commotion.

Stooping to unleash the boisterous pets, he found himself, to his embarrassment, being buffeted against the rotund Maria and her mistress. The scramble instigated a round of apologies.

"Forgive me, Reverend, for subjecting you to all this hassle," apologized Jennifer, reddening. "They are such powerful dogs – especially David when he gets excited – let me take your coat, Reverend."

As David jumped upon Jennifer, almost knocking her down, the rector replied as he handed over his coat, "David's very affectionate, isn't he? – And so docile for so powerful a dog."

"Yes, he's an angel," said Jennifer, recovering her balance and wiping David's great lick off her face as they stood cheek to cheek, the giant dog on his hind legs with his forepaws resting upon her shoulders.

The gangling rector's cadaverous features beamed down to her their renowned beatific smile, during which Jennifer noted that in doing so his narrow lips stretched almost into two thin parallel lines, which a sudden leaping shove by the bearded collie finally succeeded in stamping upon her own surprised forehead!

Both in shock spontaneously exclaimed, "Oh!" and recoiled. Jennifer suppressed a titter, while the Reverend froze awkwardly. At this point, Maria sensibly bulldozed her way in to arrest the offender and escort him, vigorously resisting, to her kitchen to be put on probation with ice cream.

Now the Reverend Houndsditch could regain his natural dignity. His dark beady eyes were sunk deep below arched brows soaring high into a balding dome, and together with his high-bridged aquiline nose, suggested a classic intellectuality, mitigating his somewhat off-putting pomposity.

Upon the bearded collie's ignominious departure, David descended from disgrace and insisted upon leaning heavily against Uncle Bernard, whom he had grown to respect as an amiable walking companion.

"I'm afraid Robert is a bad influence," remarked Jennifer, "But he's such an angel really!"

"Angelic, I think you mean, Mrs. Trewlove. Even David would look a little misplaced in heaven, don't you think?"

"I don't see why he should be misplaced, God loves all His creatures, doesn't He?"

The Reverend dog-walker was put on the spot. Being infatuated with the attractive widow, he wanted to avoid any controversy at this fragile stage in their relationship. So he put on his famous smile to disarm with sweetness. "Yes, indeed He loves all creatures great and small."

Jennifer, too, wished to avoid controversy, and not put in jeopardy their inchoate intimacy; so she too smiled and said no more on the subject. Although she was sorely tempted to ask why the Merciful Creator of all creatures great and small should be excluding His innocent animals, especially those who had become part of the human family. This seemed to her a contradiction. For was He not proclaimed "All merciful and understanding?" How could the Good Shepherd abandon the innocents among His flock? Dogs surely were more faithful, less cruel, less sinful, more vulnerable creatures of His own creation? Wherefore such a sacrilege, she reasoned, if a beloved dog who had become her inseparable truest friend were to accompany her to their just reward in heaven?

But intuition warned her that now was too early to risk questioning the church's baffling obfuscations on the matter which so disturbed her naïve faith. Therefore, upon the threshold of great expectations to be realized (she was still all keyed up and just waiting and wondering what could be forthcoming), she must tread very cautiously. Not do anything to prejudice the outcome. Fate must be allowed to set its own occult course.

If she aimed at safe passage to her delicate goal she must be patient and not rock the boat. For she had strong "vibes" that somehow this was going to be a momentous occasion. She had dressed for the part in a low-cut mauve silk evening gown. With matching finery, it had been borrowed from Giselle, the Delilah of *haute couture*, who was now ostensibly reading magazines in the big living room within earshot.

Unfortunately, Jennifer was stuck with her presence after the lending of garments and the giving of advice based upon long experience in the art of seduction.

With the beardie's silence bought by Maria's ice cream in the kitchen, Jennifer was free to usher Bernard into the luxurious living room, where the vanishing orange winter sunset was augmented by the romantic roseate halogen haze.

There, the Good Samaritan was promptly introduced to Giselle. Her remarkable eyelashes lost no opportunity in commencing their coquettish psychedelic fluttering.

Indeed, the effect produced upon the shy bachelor was visibly electric. Jennifer was not slow to note this with a jab of jealousy, which she quickly struggled to suppress.

As usual, Giselle trailed over to the cocktail cabinet in her gorgeous black silk evening gown in order to play hostess, while her friend beckoned their guest into one of the leather armchairs facing the low walnut coffee table.

Like some species of long, spindly, human praying mantis, the gangling, shy rector jackknifed himself awkwardly down upon the low sumptuous leather cushions and wriggled into a seated position, with his hands clasped round his knees under his jutting bony chin. A placid David moving synchronously at his mistress' heels, sprawled at her feet as she sat down on the settee on the opposite side of the table.

She could see how, she also had made an impression upon the shy, frustrated bachelor. At least for this she had to be thankful to Giselle, her own wardrobe being far less eye-catching.

"Yes, darling – you've got to look the cat's pajamas," Giselle had said earlier to her best friend. "Think of the stunning effect of your wonderful legs in my mauve silk stockings plus that you-know-what slinky mauve gown of mine – the one you said made me look ten years younger. I can just imagine you in it with your Little Bo Peep kind of looks – Jen, you'll be sensational! Trust me, you'll be a knockout! I know my matching shoes could be a trifle too tight for comfort – but darling, you can always kick them off under the table, can't you?"

Now those shoes were killing her and this particular low table was quite unsuited for such covert acts with a susceptible male guest sitting opposite. She began wishing she had not listened so slavishly to her devious mentor.

At the time it has seemed sound advice from an accomplished predator, but now she felt like a little shy dove in her friend's fine borrowed plumes. They fitted her ample curves like the skin of a peach.

"Name your favorite tipple, Bernard?" inquired Giselle with her undauntable familiarity. Her voice sounded husky and sexy from across the big room.

"Brandy, rum, ouzo, you name it, we got it – Scotch on the rocks – multiple malt, single malt, rye, absinthe – we're a bar-none kind of bar."

"Don't get the wrong impression, Reverend," Jennifer interposed alarmed. "Giselle, of course, is greatly exaggerating – she's an incorrigible tease."

With a further stab of jealousy, she watched the inimitable smile latch onto the seductress, whereat her own hopes in competition for his preferred attention blew away like flies in a gale.

"I understand fully, Mrs. Trewlove, girls will be girls! No doubt, same as boys will be boys!" replied the staid rector, "Scotch on the rocks will do fine, thank you."

His voice was as resonant and mellifluous as if he were delivering a sermon, and he continued staring as if infatuated with Giselle. Jennifer struggled to hide her own feelings.

Taking advantage of the distraction from herself she now managed to ease her feet out of the garroting from those painfully narrow shoes, while still keeping them half on, ready to don at a moment's notice. David stirred but did not give the show away.

Now she was adorned by the lender's ropes of Tiffany pearls and the agitated fingers of the borrower began making them click, as they habitually did when worn by their owner.

What could the brazen temptress see in this pious, slightly pompous, seemingly confirmed bachelor? But, more pertinently, how could such a wet blanket fan back into flames under her own widow's long unpoked smoldering ashes?

But suddenly, upon Giselle turning to face her and inquiring if she would like her usual dry martini with olive, Bernard also turned and lowered his eyes to Jennifer's cleavage and held them there long enough for her to feel her ear lobes burning.

So, she was wrong in imagining him to be a pious, wet blanket Good Samaritan dazzled by irresistible charm and nothing more! Obviously, he had now shown himself capable of rising to the occasion! For her own eyes began wandering and did not fail to note. So he was not all starch, carbon and holy water, but hiding hot flesh and blood! It warmed her to a degree she had not experienced since the man she had met years ago on a Caribbean cruise, but who in the end had turned out to be already married!

Bernard, on the contrary, was a bachelor. If he made overtures there could be no trap for her to fall into. So in that comforting knowledge, she threw all caution to the wind and returned his lingering look with all her awakening heart. Surely it was destined to happen now?

When Giselle had finished pouring their drinks and had trailed back, voluptuously, bearing a silver tray laden with three magnificent Venetian goblets, she found the pair deeply engrossed in conversation. She sensed the lit fuse between them, and she was greatly put out by Bernard's sudden cooling off in his manner towards herself, whom she imagined to be irreplaceable as the focal point of any male presence!

"And he worships you," she heard him say as she put down the goblets. He leaned over to stroke David, his eyes caressing Jennifer!

Giselle, momentarily floundering like a fish out of water, affected a most artificial little cough.

"Your whiskey, Reverend – twelve-year-old single malt. I hope it's to your taste," inquired the sexy and suddenly even huskier voice, as its owner irritably fingered pearls that were no longer there because they were being worn by her friend.

At last Bernard took his eyes off Jennifer and looked up with polite, exaggerated attentiveness.

"Oh how nice! You are spoiling me, Giselle," replied Bernard charmingly (she had been introduced only by her Christian name). She noted for the first time how pale he looked when caught directly under the halogen lamp's powerful beam. Almost, she thought with sour grapes, as pale as his clerical collar! Overly sickly, she consoled herself – not healthy enough for evoking special interest on her part any longer! Jennifer was welcome to him – there were more virile beasts for stalking in her own lascivious jungle!

"Man's best friend," said Giselle, leaning over again while stroking David, and in so doing accidentally touching Bernard's hand caught doing the same. She was disappointed when the intimacy did not produce the desired response, but appeared to have passed unnoticed. It was a great blow to her sensitive ego. Jennifer intervened, "No wonder they say if you wish to be a king, choose a dog; you'll never find a more loyal subject."

"How true! How true!" agreed the rector at once "Did you know—" said Bernard, putting down his drink and with a fond look beaming on Jennifer, who had her head in the clouds. "Did you know, ladies," he repeated, looking round with perfunctory politeness to include Giselle, "David descends from the royal dogs of the pharaohs. Not too difficult to imagine in his case, do you not agree?"

"Absolutely!" said Jennifer, clicking her borrowed pearls and with her cougar's brilliant violet-blue eyes shining upon Bernard warming to his subject. "By the Egyptians they were treated with great kindness and reverence. They were paraded like gods around those ancient palaces. These gentle creatures weren't subjected to all the cruelties associated with greyhound racing as they are today – it's unspeakable! – Reminds one of the slave trade. I'm sure you will be rewarded in heaven for rescuing poor David, Mrs. Trewlove." (Why didn't he call her Jennifer? He had demonstrated that his eyes could stray, so why could he not defrost?)

Aloud she said only, "I wish I could have done more – taken on more if I could."

"Unthinkable! Mrs. Trewlove." (She thought perhaps she should drop the "Reverend" and call him Bernard? That would be a hint. Like Giselle was always telling her, she should be more "forward" and less formal herself.)

"You have taken on too much already," said Bernard. "—God understands. So He sent you, a Good Samaritan, to walk your wonderful dogs. You undertook the burden of rescuing one of His suffering creatures without giving a practical thought to your own crippling arthritis. So it would not be in character with our Heavenly Father to have turned His back on your compassionate deed."

"And yours, don't forget—" she hesitated, then lost her nerve in front of Giselle – to drop saying "Reverend."

"I'm sure He is watching us both – by the way, I didn't notice you in your usual pew last Sunday?"

Jennifer quickly managed a sniffle and took out a lace handkerchief from Giselle's borrowed matching mauve purse.

"I had a cold – I'm only just getting over it."

"I knew there had to be a good reason."

But she was hiding the true cause, namely, that she had been avoiding those wicked tongues whispering behind her back and mixing calumny with their prayers!

Giselle suddenly stopped sucking her olive. She had at long last skillfully caught the rector's eye and Jennifer saw that there was mischief in the way she looked at him.

"I don't know if you are aware, Bernard, but poor Maria's going berserk still having to clear up the stinking mess. You can't blame the poor dog. Coming from those monstrous kennels, he's hardly to the manor born! But I gather from Jennifer that once he is able to climb up to her bedroom and join Robert at the foot of her bed to sleep at night, he'll get civilized and the nightmare will be over. I understand you told my friend it's as simple as that."

"Yes, it's what Dr. Bigden told me," he admitted.

"So how come you haven't taught David to climb those stairs then, Bernard?" she asked triumphantly.

She was reveling in seeing the Good Samaritan profoundly taken aback. An awkward silence followed. Sweet vengeance! It was his inevitable comeuppance for stinging Giselle's inviolable vanity earlier!

But her mischief backfired when the man she had put on trial suddenly sprang from his low armchair like a towering gladiator ready to do battle!

"Well, ladies, what are we waiting for?"

Jennifer was euphoric. At last! At last she felt, here was the happening about to begin!

"Jennifer!" (not Mrs. Trewlove this time, thank God!) "Are you ready to help?" inquired a most uncharacteristic cleric, displaying most comic athletics. He began by wildly flexing his muscles, as if limbering up for some strenuous feat. Being so tall and his arms so long, and dressed so conservatively, he presented a remarkable spectacle, which sent Giselle into a fit of giggles.

Jennifer, however, took the matter most seriously and responded enthusiastically. Giselle, still giggling, was forced to do likewise. She had made a rod for her own back!

"Come on Gizzy, let's help Bernard perform the miracle!"

In the contagious excitement all restrictive formalities went by the board and they had suddenly become a team on Christian-name terms, all committed to the formidable task of teaching a scared greyhound to climb stairs. Very soon all four – Bernard, Jennifer, Giselle and Maria from her kitchen, were gathered in an atmosphere of tremendous excitement round the fateful staircase.

Each had been given her instructions by the miracle worker. The slim, muscular David, held by his mistress at the foot of the stairs, was trembling like a reed in a gale!

The poor creature was looking up terrified at the steep flight he intuitively knew he was about to be made to climb.

He looked from one to the other of his tormentors. Uncomprehendingly, despairingly, at the turnabout in treatment, his pathetic skeletal ribcage rebelled in his mistress' frantic grasp. On the face of it they had suddenly turned into his enemies – and, most distressing of all, so had Jennifer. For so it must have appeared to a dog well acquainted with torture in the past. Instinctive animal self-preservation thereupon took over and to the humans he seemed no longer able to read their minds and know that their intentions were only good. Thus, he began to struggle and whine pitifully. It needed all four of them to restrain him from bolting.

In the background, Robert was barking furiously and making matters worse. So Giselle broke away to throttle the disturbance with kisses, as soon as Bernard had got a firm hold on the bulging great hard muscles of the greyhound's most powerful hindquarters. (His gait when he walked was reminiscent of the ambling power of a weightlifting "Mr. Universe" albeit when he ran he had the grace of a cheetah.)

Suddenly a commanding voice rang out, "Jennifer! I want you to place the two front paws very, very slowly, very gently on the first step, just to give him confidence. Whisper something soothing into his ear," concluded the canine instructor on his knees behind his trembling pupil, and anchoring him with bony fingers locking as in rigor mortis. "Easy now David, you can do it – good puppy! Listen to your Uncle Bernard. He'll take good care of you. Don't be frightened, that's a good puppy!"

"Follow my directions, Jennifer," he continued later, "and do what you can to calm him down."

With her own heart in her mouth while hearing the dog's in her ear pressed into his thumping fur, she obeyed. "David, my dear one, don't be afraid. Uncle Bernie is not going to harm you – only showing you how to climb to your new place to sleep beside Robert and me. Then you won't be alone anymore – see, my angel? You'll be able to sleep all nice and cozy beside Robert and your dear mommy."

She kissed him repeatedly on the head between his rolled back ears – to seal the bargain. The dog went quiet for an instant.

"Keep it up Jen," said Giselle, greatly impressed, "I can see you're getting through to him – it's really amazing. I knew he can read our minds. It's really uncanny, isn't it? Only fear is a powerful emotion, he's bound to react."

"If anyone is reading our minds, it is God, not the dog," said the miracle worker piously. "Don't underestimate the power of prayer, Giselle." For a second Bernard had stepped back into his clerical collar.

"Were you praying then, Bernie?" answered Giselle, cheekily.

"Of course I was! You can see me on my knees, can't you?" countered the rector, revealing an unexpected sense of humor accompanying his charismatic smile.

"What next, Bernard?" inquired Jennifer over the long back of the momentarily becalmed greyhound.

"Just manage the front paws, will you, my dear, and leave all the tricky part with the back legs to me. I have been well briefed by Dr. Bigden, so you need have no fears on that score – and with God's help—" His final words were swallowed by another bedlam of barking from the bearded collie and David evinced terror once more. He began struggling violently, threatening to break free with his front paws. But fortunately Maria's hand thrust through the banisters, managed to hold on to the dog's collar.

"Pull hard Maria – up we go when I say pull! Not before – wait till I say, then get him onto the next stair and stop, and hold him there. Do you understand me – no – I mean *comprenay*, Maria. You are Hispanic – not Italian, aren't you?"

"Yes, Reverend, Maria Spanic understood good."

"Good, at last we are getting somewhere marvelous! But wait till I give the order to pull – you understand, Maria?"

"Yes Reverend, Maria understand good."

"Marvelous! Then pull hard!"

"Yes, Mister Reverend, Maria wait till Reverend give marvelous order. No up we go till Reverend say marvelous pull!"

"Ready Maria?"

"Okay, Mister Reverend, Maria ready." She oozed her considerable bulk over the handrail and tightened her grip on David's collar.

"Pull!" roared the Reverend, letting go at the same instant.

Giselle sneaked back to hold a bowl of ice cream to the bearded collie's mouth.

Maria strenuously applied all her strength, yet could not get the powerful greyhound to rise one single inch.

But the Rev. Bernard Houndsditch was not daunted by the setback.

He peered up the staircase, as if looking for a sign from above, before dispersing the rotund Maria's doubts with his renowned lightning-like smile.

"You believe in God, don't you, Maria? You are a good Catholic, aren't you?"

"Yes, Reverend, Maria good Catholic. Mass every Sunday. Holy communion, leetle bit leetle sin only confess."

"Well," conceded the Episcopal rector, "that doesn't matter – what counts is faith, of course. We are all under the same Christian roof. You know why it's so important for David to be able to climb upstairs, don't you?"

The big woman looked perplexed. "Maria not know?"

"Well, Maria, God is helping us make David a clean dog. When he is able to sleep beside Robert in your mistress' bedroom he will not mess downstairs any more. After that, Maria – no more big jobs for you to clean up. Isn't that wonderful?"

Maria's round face shone like the morning star.

"Yes, God make Maria 'appy – no more Maria clean big jobs. God make David clean puppy. Maria say prayer thank God make David clean puppy sleep Missis Jennifer bedroom."

"Precisely!" said Bernard, feeling that he was gradually breaking through the language barrier at last. "Well, we have to help God first to make David climb stairs, Maria. Dogs do not make a mess if they sleep in the same room as their mistress. That is why God is guiding us in helping David to climb. We must try again. We must not give up. Reverend *hablo tray simplahmentay por* Maria *comprenay – comprenay yoosted* Maria?" said Bernard in his terrible Anglo-Spanish.

"Maria understand. We try again, Maria pull, Missis Jennifer pull, Mister Reverend pull – pull everybody when Reverend give marvelous order – everybody give big pull."

"Excellent! But Maria, wait till I give the 'marvelous' order!" said Bernard, covertly winking up at Jennifer who was greatly enjoying the comic exchanges between the two below.

"Maria understand. Maria wait Reverend give marvelous order – then Maria big pull quick quick!"

The satisfied miracle worker now addressed a concerned Jennifer hanging on to a becalmed greyhound, for the time being seemingly resigned to his fate, while nothing more deadly than talk was going on between the incomprehensible gathering of humans who professed to love him.

"I'm afraid, my dear, it's now a matter of push comes to shove. I'll get right down like I used to do in my college football days, and with my shoulder literally catapult him up! He'll scramble up the rest of the way by himself. He'll do it – instinct for survival will take over. It's the law of the wild inbred," said Bernard confidently.

Jennifer's smooth brow puckered with concern.

"Are you quite sure, Bernard, he won't trip or anything and he won't get hurt?"

The beatific smile beamed.

"Quite sure, my dear. He's a highly intelligent agile dog and knows how to take care of himself whatever the circumstances. His reflexes are instantaneous. Like coil springs you might say. Trust me, he'll come to no harm, and once set in motion he'll soar up those stairs. It's fear of the unknown that freezes him."

Thereupon Bernard began preparing himself for the demanding feat. First he let go with one restraining arm to jerk about into the air to limber up, while holding the suddenly trembling greyhound firmly with the other.

"Bernard," she called out with mounting concern. "Can you really be so sure he won't slip or anything? He could get seriously hurt."

"Trust me, my dear, the Lord is with us – I am His minister, don't forget."

This comforting assurance being said, the Lord's ordained minister got into the appropriate low position, behind the animal's hard, bulging, tremulous buttocks. Then as Jennifer watched with her heart in her mouth, he gave one tremendous heave. It hurled the frightened animal upward by several steps, as Maria on target let go.

As Jennifer quickly climbed to be at David's side, Robert celebrated the miracle at the peak of his wall-shaking bark!

"Giselle," shouted the Reverend Houndsditch, "Get that dog out at once! He'll ruin everything!"

"No! Maria," he continued, "For God's sake grab him! And don't let go! Jennifer! Hold down those two front legs. Maria your good work is done now—" the miracle worker suddenly countermanded when he saw the fat woman clawing at space. "You can't reach any higher, so keep back! Keep back! Thank you, leave us now please! Go with Giselle."

When the beardie had been taken out of sight and sound and David had settled precariously in the middle of the staircase, Jennifer, coming up behind him, leaned close and whispered desperately into the trembling dog's furled-back twitching ear sweet words of encouragement.

"Excellent! Now Jennifer, one paw at a time onto the next step please and hold while I synchronize with the back legs."

Jennifer, still with her heart in her mouth, struggled to obey, but the opposition was catastrophic!

"Look out Jennifer! – Hang in there! He's slipping back – he'll break free – hang in there! Remember, God is on your side – look out! Quick! He's slipping back! Shoulder to the wheel my brave one – God is watching over us, remember."

With her whole heart anxious to please Bernard and her whole feeble body straining to keep David's front paws on the stair, she whispered more sweet words of encouragement into his twitching ears.

"Wonderful Jennifer! Keep it up – he listens to you," exclaimed Bernard, feeling the dog's great sinews suddenly relaxing.

"At last we're winning. Have faith. Trust in the Lord. He's watching over us. The Lord helps those who help themselves, remember. We must never give up."

Meanwhile, Maria, plus Giselle, throttling Robert with love, remained detached and impressed, and not daring to put a spoke in the wheel of their exciting entertainment. They peeped round the kitchen door.

"Both paws now on next step – softly, softly, gently does it! Continue whispering something reassuring – he listens to you, Jennifer."

Jennifer obeyed with modest success reinforcing distance gained with tender kisses and more loving words, and caressing with her lips touching the pink skin of the greyhound's velvety ears.

"Marvelous! Well done my dear," exclaimed the tall, gaunt, kneeling miracle worker, holding onto a now-reasonably subdued David. "We are getting somewhere. We shall overcome! Have patience – don't try to rush things – we have plenty of time. Let's take a break, but hold on still."

They both paused for breath and during the brief respite Bernard called up softly to her, "Don't you feel something at this moment, Jennifer? I have prayed hard for this moment."

Jennifer's heart stirred upon hearing those telling hopeful words delivered over the trembling greyhound's buttocks, together with that most devastating flash of beatific smile.

"Oh, yes, Bernard," cooed the lonely widow, "I do! I do!"

She peered round and ascertained that they were alone, for Maria and Giselle with the bearded collie having been banished to the kitchen, could not from Jennifer's position on the stairs be seen engaged in peeping.

The Reverend Houndsditch, kneeling behind the passive dog halfway up the staircase, then fixed upon her lit-up face devouring eyes as soulful as a dog's. His clerical collar gleamed softly in the romantic halogen haze as she euphorically looked down at him.

"Do you not feel the same as I do, my dear? Anything spiritual in all of this, I mean?"

"I do, I do!" sighed Jennifer, emotively. "Look at David now, Bernard – he's stopped shaking! He was so wild only a minute before. I believe in Fate bringing us three together, don't you, Bernard my dear?"

"I do so feel, Jennifer darling," confided Bernard, with impassioned piety (while still clutching the greyhound's passive buttocks with fingers locking as in rigor mortis). "Jennifer," continued Bernard looking up at her adoringly over the dog's long back, "I feel most strongly that our Heavenly Father is on our side and wants us to try again. Are you ready?"

"Yes, Bernard darling, but isn't he locked solid? He's dug in – he won't budge.'

"Never mind. Have faith and you'll see. I feel suddenly that God's given me the strength. One more mighty shove from behind and David will rise like a rocket by the power of the Holy Spirit!"

Chapter Four

Most embarrassing to the Reverend Houndsditch, the greyhound rocket was slow in taking off. In fact it took several more vigorously assisted attempts before David could make his solo flight! But a milestone had been achieved, with David as the catalyst, in bringing Bernard and Jennifer together. It was what she felt had to happen and now at last it had. Destiny was on course, leaving no doubt in her mind as to the power of prayer!

One only had to have enough faith, Bernard said many times, and mountains could be moved. Now that he had finally called her "darling" she felt that the future was full of promise for fulfilling her wildest dreams – including her controversial ultimate objective. Giselle and all her gloomy forebodings could go to the devil! What a happy thought! She went to bed singing as brightly as a lark.

The following morning, David Greyhound, now a full-fledged member of the human family, awoke beside Robert at the foot of Jennifer's bed. He began to sniff suspiciously. The air smelt sickly of flowers – not altogether a wholesome smell to dogs, while the aroma seemed to be coming from the direction of Jennifer's dressing table. Suddenly it dawned on the highly intelligent greyhound that he had reached the sacred place where Jennifer and Robert slept. At long last he had joined them in their sleeping partnership, thanks to the tall man in a dark suit. It was comforting to observe that he wore a dog collar like David himself. The latter had finally overcome his harrowing fear of stairs.

It was also exceedingly comforting to see Jennifer tucked up in her bed, so close, and cousin Robert even closer. The latter was making a loud sound in his sleep, like a carpenter sawing wood.

Robert was but a tangled heap of sound and density smothering any shape of a dog beneath. David, observing cautiously, and having already stretched his fine long limbs, was lying upside down again with his legs saluting the ceiling. He was only half awake and waiting for the day to begin not with the sun rising, but with Jennifer showing signs of life. However, the shaggy dog awoke before her and David felt his manner seemed most unfriendly when, after stretching profoundly, he passed by on his way to Jennifer's pillow. Taking a deep breath, he sounded the morning reveille!

Jennifer's blond ponytail flayed into life as she recoiled and confronted the loud herald.

"Quiet! Noisy dog. Quiet! Shut up, Robert! Quiet! Lie down. Lie down! Lie down!"

Robert growled himself into silence as a yawning figure in black flimsy sat up and gathered her thoughts. Slowly and painfully she eased her cramped limbs out of bed, revealing well rounded white nakedness as she tiptoed along hurriedly past David to vanish into the bathroom.

He pricked his ears at the sound of water flushing. Soon followed other mysterious, unidentifiable sounds. During their long intervals, David occupied himself by luxuriously stretching every rippling muscle of his long, handsome body, ready to welcome his loved one with a leap and a lick when she returned. For he knew she was not gone for ever because he could still hear her through the door. Meanwhile, the scolded shaggy Robert had sunk nose to pink carpet, sulking.

He studied David fiercely, peeping through his long, wispy, gray hair. David knew that in reality his roar of a lion was backed up by no more than the courage of a rabbit! There was nothing lion-like about him but his mane, and nothing wolf-like but his deafening bark and his howl when fire engines went by.

Yet he was cuddly and affectionate, and between growls would often unexpectedly flick at David's nose a quick flycatcher-like kiss.

Jennifer eventually emerged with a towel for a turban and dripping water, like a panting dog's tongue. Both pets leaped together to welcome their mistress, as if from a long absence. In doing so, they cracked muzzles together in midair, both crying out in pain – Robert vociferously, David faintly whining. Recovering from the impact and in need of reassurance, David went over to lean against his beloved Jennifer. The bearded collie, growling and barking, sank low, head down, hindquarters raised, simu-lating a threat of attack.

"Robert, don't be so jealous!" admonished Jennifer, trying modestly to pull down her brief, frilly, lace teddy sliding up her bare thigh under pressure from the leaning, nudging greyhound.

No stranger to the pangs of jealousy herself, she was not unsympathetic to what Robert felt, and consequently she tried her best to conceal how David (and not he) had become, in effect no less than a surrogate son.

She was often in need of a shoulder to cry upon and the bearded collie was too unresponsive, whereas the strange handsome greyhound would lean against her and look up with such understanding in his beautiful glowing eyes. She was convinced it was telepathy – from soul to soul! Even Giselle, the sophisticated skeptic, believed it was possible.

With consummate relief, Jennifer inhaled deeply and detected at last only the aromas of her perfumes. In her mind she could hear a delighted Maria's gobbledygook euphoria: David now clean dog good – Maria happy, Missis Jennifer happy everybody happy! Big job Maria no more time necessario clean.

But to her mistress it was also an enormous comfort to have David sleeping where he longed to be and to know that he was not pining alone in the darkness. When Jennifer returned to the bathroom to dab creamy milk over her beauteous complexion, Robert again challenged the usurper, this time with loud intimidation instead of icily staring through woolly stalactites.

David Greyhound stood his ground. He did not flinch. Instead, from his daunting advantage in height, proud long neck and slim muscular body, he stared down at his jealous challenger defiantly. The hard-earned right to sleep near his mistress he would defend with all his might. The gentle giant issued a warning – a single blood-curdling brief shriek. Not only did it scare the bearded collie out of his wits, but it brought Jennifer, with head still under towel, sweeping in to the rescue. "Now then you two!" she cautioned, "Kiss and make up, like good Christians!"

With David standing dignified and silent and with Robert cowed and growling, she quickly divined who was the inciter.

"Robert, you are behaving like a barbarian!" she admonished in a tender, conciliatory voice, and bent down to stroke her badly frightened pet, "We must be kind to our poor David – he has suffered so much at his cruel kennels. What would kind Uncle Bernard say, if he saw you squabbling like this?"

The bearded collie showed no sign that he had understood a word, but profited by an opportunity to lie on his back and have his belly rubbed!

Eventually Jennifer went over to sit at her dressing table, while both dogs having, like children, quickly forgotten their differences, took a sitting position behind her – each in his own peculiar fashion. They were mesmerized by their mistress at her make-up. To them it was a kind of *cinema vérité* for dogs.

Her bottles fanned breezes of blossom – though not as ravishing as a whiff from Maria's hot oven! Sitting close together, like a couple at a theater, they watched entranced while their mistress slowly drew something cylindrical along her lips, then made faces at a magic imitative moving picture of herself in a portable glass screen which she held in her hand. She grimaced with her mouth and swallowed her lips and the magic shiny picture did the same. To the uncomprehending canine beholders it was bizarre!

The curtain came down on the performance abruptly when the protagonist suddenly got up and untied her ponytail, her hair flying like wheat straws in the wind. They watched her dart back to the bathroom.

Staring into the bathroom mirror, the better to inspect the results of her endeavors, reminiscences meanwhile commenced their nostalgic kaleidoscope. How brightly she recalled the aftermath of David's destined climbing lesson. Giselle had gone home, leaving Bernard and herself alone together. Suddenly and surprisingly, how romantic he had become! Both of them had missed their dinner and only wished for a snack – Maria's famous home-made scones. With his hand leaving hers to spoon honey from the pot onto Maria's delicacies, he had said mellifluously – in words that melted in her mind, "Do you know, my beloved, if only I could replace this fading vase" (referring to one in the middle of the table), "with everlasting flowers, they would be called not marguerites or daisies or violets or roses, but jennifers!"

What inspired words flowed from his mouth! She saw him in the pulpit, the wide sleeves of his white surplice fluttering histrionically heavenward, like a soaring angel's wings; and hanging round his neck a chasuble as gorgeous as a peacock's tail. And instead of becoming the fire and brimstone preacher anticipated by his vigorous gestures, he became one of uncastigating eloquence, as uplifting as the altar itself or the stained-glass window.

His were hypnotic words to touch the hearts of his parishioners, among whom many, Jennifer imagined, were his worshipers in more sense than one! They were as jealous of her as she of them.

Her thoughts shifted back to the dangerous gossip that Dr. Bigden, she imagined, had brought to her attention.

"I simply must switch to Reverend Golightly's church and pray to put an end to those wicked tongues before Bernard gets cold feet," she told herself, as she watched the water slowly drain from the basin.

Returning to her bedroom stool and sensing David scrutinizing her, she looked round at him and said tenderly, "You can read my mind, can't you, David, pet?" And his lustrous umber and amber eyes seemingly confirmed this, while Robert's inveigling warm chestnuts remained hidden and blank.

She returned to dreaming as she powdered out telltale, trespassing faint crow's feet, while Robert got bored with their becoming lackluster *cinema vérité* for dogs and took a catnap. David began his habit of leaning against her legs. She became conscious of the warmth of the greyhound's long body, and feeling its poignant skeletal ribcage nestling against her thigh. Her hand went down affectionately to play with his curious, velvety, rolled-back ears. Then she cupped his head in her hands, while his beautiful Pharaoh's eyes, elongated at their corners as if by charcoal pencil, glowed into hers, as if eliciting her need to confide.

"David, your Uncle Bernard is not taking you for a walk this morning as usual, because something terribly urgent for his church came up. You remember? I held the telephone to your ear last night and you recognized his voice – clever dog! – Didn't you? – Because it made you all excited. So I shall be taking you both to the park instead. And you will be kind to your Jenny, won't you? – Not pull too hard – she is only a poor weak woman – not a big strong man like your Uncle Bernard. Perhaps we shall catch a glimpse of him as we pass by his church on our way back from your squirrel's playground in the park you both love so much. Now, you won't try to chase those poor creatures, will you? It will be very painful for me, trying to hold back a great, big, strong dog like you."

David released the pressure against her momentarily and then resumed it, as if to show that he understood and sympathized. His bright eyes waxed like soft brown moons and she felt their telepathic silent communication.

She began eagerly preparing herself for the possible chance encounter near the rectory. She must look her very best. She would be compared with Giselle who always did.

So, after careful comparing in the mirror the allure of several different outfits, she chose a sharp blue pleated serge skirt, white polo neck sweater under a rakish long black leather coat, complemented by knee-high matching zip-up boots. With blond ponytail hanging out of a burgundy silk scarf tied rakishly round her head, she looked most fetchingly a decade younger than her fifty-three years.

"Lead the way, Robert!" cried Jennifer, after struggling into her boots and at last pleased with her appearance.

"Show your new cousin how it's done!" she rhapsodized over her shoulder into the mirror for a last look to make sure nothing was forgotten.

The exhilarating tone of her voice rather than word comprehension spurred the show-off beardie into action. Here was a chance to shine, and he went tumbling to the tiles in the hallway like a barrel over Niagara!

"Go on, David, you can do it – look at Robert already at the bottom!"

She gave the hesitant greyhound the gentlest of shoves, launching him into breaking the staircase record set by the bearded collie in his puppy prime!

Anxiously she watched the long-legged dog skidding below on the slippery tiles and seemingly running out of floor space, inevitably soon to be crashing into wall or door. But his reflexes were phenomenal. Miraculously, like a tight keel ship knocked down by wave or wind, he would right himself endlessly. It was not a pretty sight, the graceful greyhound had momentarily turned into a dexterous yet clumsy-looking clown. The sturdy bearded collie did better. Unlike his rival, he did not have delicate catlike paws but instead possessed their very opposite, capable of doing duty as heavy anchors, while mighty proud was he of this built-in advantage.

However, he was in no mood to acknowledge David's impressive exhibition on the staircase, which greatly exceeded, in speed at last, his own not inconsiderable performance.

Ah! But Robert had one unbeatable trick under his collar. He could turn his nose into a billiard cue and spring the catch of the hallway double doors with a couple of deft clicking cannons! It was a minor wonder to behold!

He looked round to ensure that he had an audience. The bearded collie had. Jennifer in her knee-high boots and trailing a train of black leather, was slowly creaking down the staircase, her hand tightly gripping the banister, her heart subsiding in relief that David had come to no harm.

The greyhound himself, now fully recovered although standing by and looking principally at Jennifer, cautiously kept Robert also in his sights.

Robert now taking center stage, was in place, approximately two feet from the double door panels. He took consummate aim down his muzzle sight of tunnel vision, hampered further by hair over eyes, then finding his target, charged! The doors parted outwards an inch or two at the most. Now, the moment of truth! Expertly with one paw raised as a lever, he prized them wide open, first one panel then its twin. With incredible timing, as the doors squeaked on their hinges, he leaped clear in each case.

Afterwards, one could almost hear him say, "Beat that if you can, smarty-pants greyhound!"

Soon the trio were on their walk to the park, after being let down from Jennifer's little car. She soon found herself like a chariot harnessed behind a canine postilion! The air was brisk, the sun bright and their feet among the russet leaves began whispering.

Her heart beat faster as they turned the corner leading into the park and she could see Bernard's slim, dwarf, Episcopalian spire, pricking above skeletal trees. Would she get a chance encounter to show herself off, handling the big dogs and looking so young in her trendy black leather?

Chapter Five

They entered the park to please Robert who enjoyed shuffling through rustling dunes. Entering by way of some steps to the ground above was made easy now that long-legged David had been taught to climb, and he leaped up the few wide stones in Olympic style at the end of his extending long leash. A trio of crows perched judiciously on a twiggy bough hoarsely warned of impending danger on the ground. Robert barked fiercely as if to ward off a possible aerial attack, while the crows fluttered in a black cloud to a higher line of defense.

The trio on the ground passed children shrieking to the sky or toddling to and from sand, all happy in their allotted playground with its slides and swings. They were taking advantage of the warm spell of early winter warm sunshine. Their mothers and grannies from the surrounding donated benches kept a watchful eye. And Robert began sniffing the legs of strollers on the path and sprawlers upon the dry sunny patches of grass. The bright clear sky made winter seem as exhilarating as spring, and it did Jennifer good to see so much shared enjoyment among her fellow creatures.

Nearly all turned to gaze at the handsome David (and not passing unnoticed by a proud Jennifer), while Robert continued to pull towards his favorite haunts of leaves and redolent sniffing and watering places. David followed his leadership, relying on the bearded collie's greater sense of smell. The former was a gazehound rather than a smellhound – greyhounds being renowned foremost for their speed and sight.

Jennifer, with the world seeming at peace, fell happily into dreaming of the possibility, under a propitious star, of becoming a rector's wife. She realized she had fallen deeply in love with the man who could say such pretty things with such sincerity to a widow past her prime. It must be love! What else could it be? Rain from heaven had fallen upon her widowhood's thirsting cactus and it had burst into bloom.

But jealousy and over-possessiveness – somehow she must not repeat these mistakes with Bernard. It could smother a relationship, as well she knew, for she could learn from failures so painful in her past. There had been that only too vanishing kindred spirit she had met on a Caribbean cruise. Then later came that ephemeral romantic in Portugal who soon made love to her under the moon and as quickly vanished under the sun! Subsequently, on the rebound, the persistent romantic from the Prudential Insurance had knocked on her door and she had opened unto him and afterwards regretted it. His insurance had provided no cover against fornication!

Eventually, she was restored to a buoyant mood after recalling how she had been compared with an everlasting flower – what a pretty conceit! – Not a beautiful commonplace lily or rose had she been compared with by the unlikely staid rector of "All Souls," but a flower surpassing all others that he called by her own name – a jennifer. Surely it was cause for rejoicing. She must have found her kindred spirit.

So, with such pretty thoughts in mind, Robert was allowed to roll at his pleasure in his crisp playground of leaves. Meanwhile David, fully extended on his long wind-in leash, was busy at a large clump of bushes. When he had done, he came over to lean against his approaching smiling mistress. Both stood observing the bearded collie on his back in the leaves and paddling the air with delight.

"Tell me, David," said Jennifer into the greyhound's quaint rose-like small ear, as she warmed to his glowing eyes looking up at her when she was seated on a bench. "Are you happy sleeping with me in my bedroom, the three of us together? Robert has been sleeping next to me for nine years, you know, so you must forgive him for being a little bit jealous. I'm sure he doesn't approve of *menage à trois*! He's a bit old-fashioned – a throwback from his Scottish ancestry, I suppose. We must not let him think that you have taken his place. It would break his heart – I'm sure you understand. You do, don't you, my dear one?"

She was unaware that there had been a sprawler hidden within possible earshot behind a hedge! Later, as they passed him, the young man gave the intimate confidante of dogs on a leash a very embarrassing stare! Jennifer reddened to the roots of her ponytail and hurried on with Robert quickening his pace and pulling harder as he felt the restraint upon him being relaxed.

Soon Jennifer was running and her arthritic hip was giving her pain. She tried to rein in the now speeding Robert, who, fortunately, suddenly stopped of his own volition at a fire hydrant.

This enforced spirit served to impress on the middle-aged widow the fact that she could no longer continue the dog walks. It convinced her of their absolute dependency upon their tall, gaunt, athletic Samaritan. When winter really set it, the ground would be frozen over. A fall upon ice could fracture her susceptible hip. This she dared not risk.

With Robert now walking sedately, giving himself time to sniff and pay his respects en route, they continued on towards Bernard's church pinpointed by its spire. Her pulse quickened at the faint prospect of an accidental encounter.

She could just catch a glimpse of a figure emerging from the rectory. But it turned out to be not the rector but his organist, whom she later recognized and who waved to her as they approached one another on opposite sides of the road.

He crossed over to admire David, whom he said everyone raved about and whom he had not yet met.

Jennifer found it impossible to restrain the powerful greyhound from leaping onto the dapper little man in a dark business suit and almost sending him flying. Afterwards, when David was leaning heavily against the man's legs and being continuously petted, the organist interrupted his long stream of eulogies to tell a remarkable story.

"Oh, I must tell you, Mrs. Trewlove," he began solemnly, "I was sitting down at the organ playing *Buxtehude* – every note perfect till one pipe went flat on me and everyone looked up – most embarrassing! I didn't know where to put myself because there was that pipe again to be played several times in the music later on!"

He paused to ask Jennifer the question, "What do you think it was, Mrs. Trewlove? You'll never guess."

"I haven't a clue – what was it?" asked Jennifer, hauling David away with difficulty from the man's smart suit, now littered with the greyhound's shedding fur.

"Well," the little man revealed, while bending down to brush his trousers with his hand, "The Reverend Houndsditch phoned for the repair man this morning. That's why he couldn't walk your dogs. They were up in the loft, the rector and the young mechanic, making a lot of noise.

Suddenly about an hour or so later we heard them laughing together
– real loud it was – most unusual for the rector."

"Laughing about what?"

He ceased brushing and looked up with a twinkle in his eye.

"You'll never guess, Mrs. Trewlove. It's an entry for the *Guinness Book
of Records*. Soon after we heard them laughing, the sexton and I and Mrs.
Broomworthy the housekeeper, we all gaped and then we couldn't stop
laughing ourselves. It was when we saw Reverend Houndsditch holding
up a dead mouse by the tail in the organ loft and he told us it had fallen
down a pipe! No wonder my *Buxtehude* sounded flat!"

Chapter Six

Suddenly it was the gorgeous ghost of winter relentlessly returning to haunt the landscape in her frozen garb so white. She had touched the stark, bare trees with her magic wand and turned them beautiful overnight. But it was a bitter-lovely wonderland, where even the hardiest of creatures were at their wits' end foraging to survive, and somewhere alone out there David had gone missing. Jennifer was distraught.

In spite of Maria's protestations, a door had obviously been left open. But the identity of the culprit was unimportant compared with the tragedy. The greyhound possessed no thick winter coat like the bearded collie, so the scythe of the sub-zero air would cut through to his very bones. Moreover, he had no great sense of smell, like most dogs, in order to track his way home. He would have to depend on the breed's remarkable sight alone, while his knowledge of the locals was extremely limited and was handicapped further by the mounting dunes of blizzard snow.

The hours dragged appallingly for poor Jennifer, who hardly ever left her vigil, even for a minute, at the windows and by the telephone. Everyone who could possibly be of assistance – every neighbor and local animal shelter had been alerted.

All had listened sympathetically and had promised to do everything they could, although they were loath to admit to the frantic woman how they held out little hope of recovering the animal alive. He had no road training and the odds weighed heavily against him. How could he escape being run over? To the police it was just another unfortunate reported statistic.

But the Rev. Bernard Houndsditch proved to be a godsend in the widow's hour of need – literally a constant shoulder for her to weep upon. As she sobbed pathetically, he would pat her head and run his fingers down the blond strands of her bleached ponytail. Giselle also came over and stayed the night, and three of the four bedrooms of the luxurious villa were occupied for the first time in a decade.

Giselle thought she heard footsteps stealthily passing during the night between the Reverend's room and that of her friend, but she could not be sure. Long she listened for their return, but did not hear them before she herself fell asleep. She had left, hopefully, her own door unlocked, but as it turned out, in vain!

She awoke to the sound of Maria's heavy hand grinding coffee on the wall. When she came downstairs, Jennifer and Bernard seated side by side, were already taking continental breakfast.

Giselle, the experienced lover, scrutinized them both, looking for any giveaway signs indicating they had perhaps slept together, but detected none. Jennifer, with her croissant on her plate still untouched, looked up as her friend came in. Her smile was pathetically put on, her make-up was smudged by tears. She did not speak but beckoned Giselle into a chair, while Bernard sheepishly withdrew his hand from Jennifer's neck.

"No news?"

"None yet, I'm afraid, Giselle, but don't let us underestimate the power of prayer," replied Bernard brightly, as he patted Jennifer's arm and beamed his renowned beatific smile.

Suddenly they heard a sound.

"Did you hear that?" cried Jennifer most excitedly, while jumping up and rushing to the window. Her morning arthritic aches and pains were momentarily forgotten as she imagined David bursting through the barricade of the garden's fallen branches. But it was only a foraging raccoon.

Giselle and Bernard also rushed to the window. The latter put his arm round the bitterly disappointed widow and conducted her gallantly back to her chair. As they all sat down again in silence, the partly closed kitchen door swung open and Robert sailed in to his mistress' side. A bark signified no more than a loud jar upon their nerves. A relieved Bernard and Giselle watched her hand stray down to pet the shaggy disrupter. She brushed away the gray wisps concealing his face and long they gazed mournfully into each other's eyes. As if he understood her grief, Robert the dumb Scottish sheep dog resisted his mania for barking relentlessly. Meanwhile Giselle and Bernard exchanged quizzical glances.

It was Bernard who broke the awkward silence as an unusually somber Giselle helped herself to coffee. His words were well chosen for they were a quote from Jennifer's favorite harvest hymn. They sang – in Jennifer's mind to organ accompaniment – so uplifting and reassuring that David was not alone out there – not lost permanently. For the Good Shepherd was watching over him. One only had to have enough faith, as Bernard had reminded her so many times. The words of the hymn kept repeating themselves in her tortured mind and bringing a fragile relief. Bernard was declaiming mellifluously, as if from his pulpit. And Jennifer was infatuated with his voice. Oh, how he could sound her heartstrings when reciting, "His tender mercies shall endure, ever faithful, ever sure."

Giselle watched Bernard rise suddenly, and taking Jennifer by the hand, pull her gently out of the room.

Bernard's beautiful Christmas tree, still sparkling in Jennifer Trewlove's drawing room, welcomed them, as the minister dragged her in to kneel in prayer at its foot.

Jennifer smiled as she obeyed and an amusing reminiscence came to mind. Bernard had just brought in the Christmas tree, and while he was busy with hanging decorations, David sauntered in and to their consternation, mistook it for a magic pine, a tree planted indoors for canine convenience!

The idiopathic smile graced the rector's words intermittently – an intermittent light like the magic pine, as he led her in prayer. Jennifer felt that he too, despite his calming reassurance, was under a great strain.

She was now grateful for his comforting arm around her waist, drawing her close to him as they knelt. She felt the warmth of his body as she had so often felt that of her loved one, poor David who leaned against her constantly. Meanwhile, the hard floor beneath the carpet bit into her arthritic knees, but the discomfort was nothing as compared with the relief and thrill of kneeling so close to Bernard as he shared her grief. His arm never left her waist.

He squeezed her hand while looking straight ahead at the Christmas tree, now dried out and ever growing more brittle. Soon it would have to be put outside. But not before David returned. Memories hung from it brighter than the lamps, because it was his special magic pine. How his eyes, wide like a child's, had glowed in wonder at the careful unwrapping of the presents! Bones for David, treats for Robert, caringly wrapped in silver paper. Uncle Bernard had acted the part of Santa Claus. Now she heard his deep resonant voice, "Let us pray. The twenty-third psalm. The Lord is my Shepherd, I shall not want, He leadeth me into green pastures…"

When the rector had finished reciting he made the mourner repeat after him an impromptu prayer.

"I, Jennifer Trewlove, thy penitent sinner, do solemnly beseech thee, O Lord, to let the light of thy Heavenly mercy shine upon my poor straying David and deliver him back to me safe and sound, in the name of our Savior, thine own begotten Son, our beloved Jesus, the Christ."

Afterwards, Jennifer felt an immense relief – as if God's mysterious wonders had now been hopefully set in motion – that a greater Shepherd than Uncle Bernard was out in the cold white wasteland searching for David – a Good Shepherd that even the fleet greyhound David could not outrun!

If only she had enough faith, David would be returned to her unharmed. Therefore she had to think positively – it was David's very life at stake, dependent upon that precious act of faith, faith which could move mountains and allow feet to walk on water.

Somehow she must put her despair behind her and convince God that she really believed in Him and that His tender mercies, in her own most pathetic case, were still truly being counted upon to endure. Was He not the Good Shepherd – His crook long enough to retrieve David and send him home in answer to her prayers?

Therefore, if she outwardly showed signs of rejoicing ahead of time, what greater proof of faith could Almighty God expect? Therefore, to Jennifer it logically followed that for those mercies to prevail, David must be made to return.

Bernard was taken aback at the apparent instant efficacy of prayer! He had expected some sign of relief, but none so great as that which he now beheld. For suddenly, from the depth of despair, she had emerged bubbling with joy!

"How about a nice drop of sherry, Bernard? Thanks to you my faith is solid as a rock. Now I'm going to stay by the window till God makes David come running back."

She broke off to gaze up into his face, as if seeking reassurance.

"You feel, too, that God will return him to me safely, don't you Bernard?"

The Rev. Houndsditch hesitated and was about to make some noncommittal pious quote, but seeing her bright dewy eyes searching into his so desperately, he had not the heart, and the grandfather clock in the hall took the words from his mouth – was it a sign? Twelve resounding gongs – could it be one for each apostle?

"Did you count those gongs Bernard?" exclaimed Jennifer jubilantly. "They came exactly after I asked the question. Was it a sign, Bernard – not just a coincidence? You would know, wouldn't you?"

"I wish I did, my dear, but I am only God's minister not his mouth-piece, but if in your heart you feel it was a sign, then it could have been. But let us not look for signs but for David. If we prayed hard enough and I am sure we did, and we have faith, then David will return – for is it not written that 'His mercies shall endure'?"

Chapter Seven

Giselle, the agnostic, was amazed at how a few words said on one's knees could speed darkness into light. But immensely relieved, she could now escape to more congenial surroundings, namely her luncheon date, without feeling callous. At the door she kissed her friend compassionately.

"Bye then, Jen – keep smiling and don't forget to get in touch when you hear anything positive – let me know when and I'll be back to give him a hug." But she was only too conscious even as she spoke the words of the unavoidable hypocrisy, for how could she impugn her friend's comforting mirage of faith?

When she had gone, Jennifer and Bernard, still with their celebratory goblets of sherry in their hands, took up their vigil once more, Bernard in the kitchen and Jennifer in the halogen haze of the big drawing room with its several windows facing greater surrounding views of white garden, footprinted by hungry scavenging raccoons. She strained her eyes for David's delicate greyhound prints among them but in vain.

Bernard in his role of lookout was more perfunctory, alternating between the window and the coffeepot as soon as he had drunk all his sherry. Maria hovered in the background, just a silent, heavy shadow. But after an hour of uneventful non-happening, they both heard a loud crackling of twigs! They rushed to splay their noses at the windowpane, hoping for a miracle.

This time their heartbeats raced as David, all covered in snow like some dog ghost, suddenly sped into view from the frozen waste.

They exclaimed at once together, "David!"

"Come Missis Jennifer!" cried Maria, rushing into the hallway. "Come quick! David! David! Come missis quick – quick!"

But she had no need to repeat herself, for her mistress was on her way with her heart in her mouth.

Jennifer reached the kitchen as Bernard opened the back door and the greyhound came rushing in like a white lightning rod! He immediately jumped upon her and nearly knocked her down! He began licking all over her face and absorbing all her tears. It was a most poignant scene which moved both Maria and Bernard profoundly. The dog was all over his beloved Jennifer and she was obviously having difficulty in coping with the canine avalanche of euphoria, but they refrained from intervening. She was so evidently overjoyed that she was in the mood for bearing anything.

"I tell you, Jennifer!" cried Bernard, "We've witnessed an amazing miracle! You now have proof beyond all shadow of a doubt, in the power of prayer!"

The dog's boisterous behavior suddenly ceased and he jumped down and shook the snow from his saturated body all over the floor and over their legs. But nobody cared. All that mattered was that David was home again safe and unharmed – except for a trail of blood mixed in with the snow.

"Oh, David, you are hurt!" cried Jennifer in alarm. "Come to your mommy – let me have a look to see where you are hurt." But David, still shaking, expressed interest only in the refrigerator. His glowing beautiful eyes stared, mesmerized, at its door! "Oh, of course you must be starving, poor darling! Let me see that paw," she added, as she opened the door of the refrigerator and, taking out a frozen piece of beef, wrestled for a few seconds with the dog intervening while she was engaged in slipping it into the microwave to defrost.

"Just a minute David – you can't eat it like that – you'll break your teeth – wait! Let go! Let go. You'll break your teeth!"

But moments later and in ravenous possession of the great chunk of frozen meat, the dog had proven her wrong! With a sound like ice cracking on a pond, the delicacy was quickly disappearing before their very eyes which were still filled with concern.

"Amazing, Jennifer! Simply amazing! I think we ought to kneel and thank the Lord."

But the pious suggestion fell upon deaf ears, for she was on her knees and taking advantage of the dog lying down (and too busy eating) to examine the animal's crimson front paw. One claw was missing and blood had congealed and was matting the surrounding fur.

Jennifer fell into kissing the dog from head to tail. She was not listening to Bernard's pious utterances, only to the panting hound's pounding wet flank against her ear.

But she heard the devoted Maria intrude in her naïve fashion.

"Now all good time, Missis Jennifer. Maria see Jesus bring back David. Maria pray – all time pray; everybody happy now. Big puppy no more gone – good no more David leave house. David stay Missis Jennifer. Good! Good! Make Maria 'appy too."

Meanwhile, his meal devoured, David rose and leaned against his mistress – statuesque like a zombie and passively absorbing the excess of emotion and tears of joy. Evidently he was completely drained by the ordeal of survival in that frozen wasteland. When frantically trying to find his way home, his very limited sense of smell had proved itself the severest handicap. He had been wandering in circles until finally he had recognized the festive holly wreath on the back door of his home.

She bent down and clung to David with her arms round his long, wet, velvety neck and began sobbing profusely with ineffable joy and relief – in her ear his heart sounded like a muffled beating drum.

He had not in truth wandered very far from his home but had run around madly never recognizing any landmarks because they were either hidden or transformed by the blizzard's deep covering snow.

"Oh! David! David! Where have you been? You gave your poor Jennifer such a hard time! But never mind – you're back safe – that's all that matters – oh, you must be starving! Let me feed you some more at once."

She felt all round him and laid gentle pressure with her fingers to discover if he felt any pain anywhere else. The statue remained graven and stoical, evincing no sign of discomfort anywhere under pressure from her fingertips. Then, with a sigh of relief she said, "Thank God it's only a claw – how did you lose it, my darling? Got it caught in the wire fence, did you? It must have hurt terribly at the time, poor thing – Bernard get me down the first aid box, will you? It's in the top cupboard by the stove."

When he obeyed and handed it to her she said gratefully, "Oh, Bernard it's a miracle! Thank you! Thank you from the bottom of my heart for making me kneel down and pray beside His very own special magic pine. I felt it must have acted like a shrine, didn't you Bernard?"

The Rev. Houndsditch raised his eyebrows, and began rummaging in the first aid box, pretending he hadn't heard. "I think this one should do the job, Jennifer?" David, however, disagreed and started to whine as soon as his paw was introduced to the sterile gauze, and in the resultant commotion the thorny question for the cleric to answer concerning the shrine of the magic pine was forgotten.

Chapter Eight

That night David did not fail to note a disturbing departure from their normal routine. Uncle Bernard accompanied them up the stairs. Robert threw caution to the wind and behaved as if nothing unusual had occurred. He took the biscuit bone from the Reverend's hand and settled down to profound enjoyment of it at his customary place on the bedroom carpet beside a partially digested slipper!

But David was in no mood for chewing. He was very uneasy. He watched the tall, staid skeleton of a man, bereft of clerical suit and his dog collar, and now naked as the moon on a cloudless sky, slide into Jennifer's bed.

The greyhound kept a weather eye open, noting every detail while trying to make up his mind if all was well. He watched his mistress return from the bathroom and turn out the light. He felt the hem of her silk nightgown swishing silkily across his face, as she crossed over the room to join Bernard, who was making an entry for her into the pink luxury linen. Their bodies coalesced in a passionate embrace and soon she was naked too – writhing like a fish in a vortex.

David's keen ear drank in fully the whispers of a honeyed deep male voice, melting like dark chocolate in a dog's mouth. Then, a little later, followed the most unfamiliar happenings between those moving mountainous sheets! David's very keen eyes were straining to observe through the darkness lit only by moonlight beaming softly through a chink in the curtains. But his beloved mistress did not seem in any imminent danger, or he would have leaped to her defense!

The moon waxing and waning through that chink in the drawn curtains was beaming for a moment brightly onto the lovers' bed. David saw the rhythmic movements of the two bodies and his ears twitched to a spate of squeaking emanating from somewhere below and synchronous with the rhythmic undulations.

But first the dog noted a faintly familiar activity which he found reassuring. The sheet and counterpane had just slid off Uncle Bernard's hairy buttocks, revealing Jennifer's smooth white naked body with her legs splayed and hooked round that of their Good Samaritan, drawing him into her, while he licked her risen nipples. It reminded David of the kennel maids in the hayloft with the dreaded men who had treated him so cruelly – only they had been less than half naked. But otherwise the strange carryings-on, as they appeared to a dog, had been much the same, while no harm to either participant had resulted. So David had observed in their case.

But the licking by itself, a very canine practice, was a favorable sign which put his mind at ease. The rhythmic movements of the entwined bodies meant very little to David Greyhound – they rang no doggy bells in his canine mind! Thus he watched, now more out of curiosity than anxiety, while Robert, who had fallen asleep, continued to snore, sounding like a carpenter sawing wood, while the bed creaked on and rocked exuberantly.

David heard a great gasp from Bernard succeeded by a long drawn-out sigh from Jennifer. Thenceforward only the peaceful snoring of the bearded collie broke the stillness of the night. David heaved a sigh whilst scratching up the edge of the carpet with his long claws. Then he circled a few times head to tail, before settling down contentedly in his chosen place to sleep. Believing his protective duty done, he quickly fell into a profound doggy dream.

Robert, as usual, awoke at the crack of dawn and went over to his mistress' pillow to sound the morning reveille!

"What the hell!" cried Bernard upon waking with a start. "Robert! Quiet! Quiet! Lie down! Noisy dog!" admonished an embarrassed Jennifer this time, over the naked Reverend Houndsditch's shoulder. "Lie down now – be a good Christian! I'm ashamed of you in front of your poor Uncle Bernard!" And then softly to her lover, "Sorry, my darling one – I forgot to warn you. Robert is our alarm clock."

"Better set it for an hour later then in future," commented Bernard dryly.

David could see how all was back to normal, although he could see that there had been a slight change in the sleeping arrangements. However, there was nothing to fear. Robert still had his own favorite place and so had he.

The Reverend was the first to get out of bed. Snatching his clothes from a chair, he went back to kiss Jennifer tenderly before hurrying to the bathroom. David had never seen his tall dog-walker naked before and observed that he had copious "fur" covering his bony chest and round his genitals, and that he was minus his dog collar. He could be heard making a singing noise as he shaved.

His voice reminded David of the crows in the trees outside. When he reappeared he was dressed as black as any of them and his dog collar was back round his neck. Meanwhile, Jennifer had dozed off.

Both dogs received from the guest sleeper warm caresses from head to tail before he left the room, closing the door quietly behind him. With a finger to his thin lips he had whispered, "Shush!" to a now quiet Robert, who mistook the signal and gave it a bark for luck!

After a long interval, the dogs pricked their ears to a rattling of porcelain on the staircase. The door was flung open and a moment later, Uncle Bernard, having picked up a tray from the low table outside, came in with a laden breakfast tray with legs to place over Jennifer's lap, as Robert loudly again played herald.

"Oh Bernard darling, you are spoiling me. How wonderful to have breakfast in bed – I can't remember how long it's been since—" She broke off to admonish the bearded collie.

"Quiet! Quiet! Lie down! Before you frighten off our guest – sorry Bernard, it's the change in routine I suppose."

Her bright cougar-eyes swept the tray and then looked up to captivate its bearer.

"Oh, Bernard you are a darling! Such a lovely surprise, so thoughtful. But how did you know I simply adore muffins in the morning – and my favorite cranberry conserve, I see – how on earth did you know? It takes me back to my childhood. You know, I was brought up on a cranberry farm by the sea – Maria must have told you, I suppose?"

"No, she didn't, as a matter of fact," replied Bernard, generously buttering a slice of muffin and tossing a bit from it to the bearded collie. The silence that it bought made conversation easier. But, as double indemnity, he tossed another morsel to David who was beginning to lean heavily against his legs.

As Jennifer, sitting up, poured out coffee for two, she exclaimed, "It must be telepathy! We're kindred spirits, aren't we Bernard, my darling? It's just like what goes on between David and me."

"I trust it's a little more than that," said Bernard with a frown, as he took his proffered cup of coffee from her delicate hand.

"Oh, you poor man, of course!" laughed Jennifer, as she quickly read his mind. "You were absolutely wonderful last night! – More than I have ever felt before. I was only referring to the telepathy aspect."

"So I fully came up to expectations then?"

"Oh, my dear, you were absolutely – absolutely, oh, yes absolutely! Didn't it show? I was absolutely transported. I never felt it could be like that. I married my husband partly to please my aunt, who was my guardian and partly to get away from her domineering. I was not madly in love."

"Poor Jennifer, I'm sorry. You deserved better," said Bernard, squeezing her hand.

The act brought tears to her eyes and she responded with her free hand stretching out to the back of his head and drawing their lips together passionately into a ravishing embrace. Both dogs took advantage meanwhile of the unguarded muffins!

"And was it all right for you darling? Did I make you fully happy?" Jennifer inquired anxiously.

His ecstatic reply was partly drowned by Robert barking somehow through a mouthful of muffins, while David crept within range for stealing yet another after testing it for taste with his tongue. It was not buttered and he spat it out onto the carpet.

Bernard saw out of the tail of his eye and disengaged himself from their embrace, gently to push the thieves away, while Jennifer looked on in embarrassment.

"I'm afraid, Bernard, you are not seeing them at their best. David is usually so well behaved, but Robert leads him astray. However, I'm sure things will be a lot different from now on with a man about the house."

"I'm not so sure," said Bernard, cutting out a licked section of a remaining muffin and buttering the other half for himself. "Natural law of the wild inbred, my darling. They don't keep the ten commandments, I'm afraid. You see, they all descend from wolves," he added, while seated on the edge of the bed and handing out to the suddenly whining giant greyhound a piece of buttered muffin. "Sounds incredible when you see some of these flyweight specimens masquerading as man-eating micro guard dogs! Yet it happens to be true. They all descend from wolves, even the tiny toy dogs."

Jennifer warmed to his dry sense of humor. She was basking in post-coitus euphoria. She had not had sex for a very long time and at last she had succumbed to an honorable eligible bachelor who satisfied her in every way and whom she had set her heart upon marrying. It seemed inevitable, infatuated as he was, and with nothing standing in the way of him proposing one day in her seductive halogen moonlight. And she fancied herself as a rector's wife, doing good works and becoming an important, well-respected figure in the parish and a credit to her husband.

They would all live happily and comfortably in his fine big rectory. Moreover, both would be even better off financially into the bargain.

There was the question, of course, of her being ten years his senior, and that she had lied about her age, but only a little white lie which the mirror failed to give away. However, narrowing the gap between them, he appeared much older than his years.

"Do you believe in predestination, Bernard darling?" inquired Jennifer, taking the bull by the horns, as he squeezed her hand again and looked at her soulfully.

"Of course, my love, we are all God's creatures — all subject to His divine planning."

"Then it was God who brought us together, how wonderful!" said Jennifer, leaning forward and pursing her lips for another kiss.

While Bernard was obliging her passionately, the doorbell jarringly interrupted them.

The infatuated rector, who was far away searching his mind for memorized eloquence from the Bible to quote, was galvanized like Faraday's frog's leg! He was shaken from clerical collar to galoshes! A less concerned Jennifer quickly concluded that it could only be Maria's friend who often called up in the morning.

"Who can that be so early? I hope it's not my nosy sexton — most unfortunate if it is. I wonder what could possibly have gone wrong?"

"Don't worry, darling — you hid your car in the garage, didn't you? He wouldn't be looking through the window. So it can't be him. He can't know you're here. It's probably only Maria's friend, my neighbor's *au pair*."

"Thank God for that! Tongues are wagging in my parish already. Anyway I'd better fix my collar," said the scared man as he disappeared into the bathroom with the bearded collie hot on his heels and loudly telling the world!

Meanwhile David seized his opportunity to be at his mistress side, whereupon he looked up with sad eyes, convincing her that he understood the crisis and wished to be of comfort.

Jennifer was disappointed that her lover showed such signs of concern, before realizing upon reflection that he was naturally thinking in terms of all the gossip he was letting himself in for if his position as spiritual leader of his parish should be compromised.

Fortunately, he was fully dressed and could make an appearance quickly, if necessary! That much was in his favor if he had to invent some plausible alibi for his sexton to swallow, should the early visitor be the jailer of his rector's conscience – in his long black robe and jingling his great bunch of keys. He had appeared before unexpectedly. But fortunately on that occasion it had only been at his bishop's house.

Moments later, both hearts leaped, Jennifer's and his, when they heard footsteps on the stairs, soon followed by the dreaded knock on their bedroom door. They both prayed for it to be Maria's voice, but, alarmingly, it was unmistakably Giselle's!

"Stop that dog barking, will you, I can't get a word in edgeways!" shouted the latter through the locked door as she turned the handle.

"Quiet! Robert – lie down! Lie down!" screamed Jennifer with a leaping frog in her breast. In panic, she swiftly hid away Bernard's telltale cup and saucer, plus knife and plate under the bedclothes.

"Why so early, Giselle?" shouted Jennifer, as soon as Robert fell silent with a protesting growl. "Not bad news I hope, Gizzy?" she asked innocently with feigned concern.

"Don't keep me waiting, you hypocritical child of love. I've just brought a bottle of bubbly to congratulate you both – it's about time. Are you two lovebirds decent? Can I come in?"

"What on earth do you mean, you minx?" shouted Jennifer, still feigning innocence. "I'm all alone, come in, if you must and see for yourself, you Doubting Thomas."

"The door's locked."

"Is it really? Sometimes it locks itself. I've been meaning to get it fixed," shouted back Jennifer with feigned innocence.

"Likely story! You Little Bo Peep – who do you think you're kidding? Come on Jen – open up! I'm your best friend, remember, not your ruddy priest. I've seen a few jockstraps in my time. Open up! I'm shockproof, I'm no blushing Mother Teresa!"

Jennifer's adrenaline flowed to overcome her fear and appear calm. She glanced in the mirror for evidence of any lipstick smudges on her way to the door. Wiping her lips hurriedly beforehand, she turned the key. She tacitly cursed the fact that her lover had been so overly cautious as to have locked the door behind him after bringing in their breakfast tray.

Beautifully gowned, and clicking her famous Tiffany pearls, as if going to a ball, Giselle thereupon breezed in with a bottle of champagne. The bearded collie was on cue to herald the occasion!

Giselle scanned the room suspiciously, then, seeing the dog facing the bathroom door and continuing to bark, she stepped briskly over and rattled the doorknob. Jennifer froze as she was brushed aside when she tried to intervene.

"Come out Reverend Bernard Ignatius Houndsditch, I know you're in there! Doors don't lock themselves from inside, do they? And by the way, I saw you sneaking your Mercedes into my friend's garage last night. I happened to be passing on my way to the yacht club. Don't worry, I won't tell anybody."

The door suddenly opened, revealing the badly shaken dithering cleric behind. Giselle, with a sly wink at a speechless Jennifer, and beguiling with a most charming smile through a veritable peacock of make-up, exclaimed in her husky, sexy voice, "Oh, Reverend! What a pleasant surprise! How cute to be hiding behind a bushel! Don't be shy," she continued, holding up the bottle of champagne, "You see I've come prepared. And I'm so happy for you both. I always knew you two were as compatible as knife and fork – or, if you prefer, prayer book and Bible!"

Chapter Nine

Jennifer Trewlove, with sitting canine approval, studied the well preserved reflected face of a woman of exactly fifty-three years. A birthday party was being given for her in the Reverend Houndsditch's rectory at eight o'clock that evening. With the one exception of her inseparable David, she alone had been invited. Not even Bernard's housekeeper, the formidable Mrs. Broomworthy, would be present, even in a serving capacity.

Surely, Jennifer thought, *such a very private setting could only mean one thing – that the shy bachelor was about to propose.* How kind, thoughtful and understanding of him, she considered, in including her dear David – wonderful because it would save her from feeling guilty, thinking all the while of him whining and pining as he always did whenever she was out of his sight.

Of course, the thought of proposing had been precipitated by Giselle a few days earlier when she had rattled the handle of that locked door of her bathroom and lo and behold, he had been behind it! He had been forced to declare his honorable intentions! Otherwise the court-ship might well have dragged on indefinitely. Despite her questionable behavior at times, Giselle could reveal herself to be a true friend in the hour of need. The thought struck her as she made-up in the mirror: had the little minx really been passing on her way to the yacht club or had she been spying on them? But obviously her motives had been only good. So she dismissed the matter from her mind. However, it bothered her to think that Bernard had been chiefly thinking of his career and the havoc which could be caused among his parishioners by disturbing the next of those jealous female wasps among them with multiple stings.

Critically, Jennifer observed the work of the beauty parlor in putting back the clock by seven years or more at least, so she thought with satisfaction, to better coincide with her admitted age! She was glad that she had, as Giselle would put it, that Little Bo Peep kind of looks. The long, blond ponytail she imagined had a lot to do with it, plus the unlined fullness of her face, which she had inherited from her mother, rather than the genes of her maiden aunt which produced those sunken cheeks and aging wrinkles. Happily, she had overruled the beautician's choice of a formal short set looking permanent that hardened rather than softened the passage of time. She had agreed to the blue rinse but had kept her long loose curls of the little girl look she had never outgrown. Conversely, Bernard, at forty-three was balding, lined and cadaverous, looking much older than his years, so nicely bridging the gap between them. But his beaky high-bridged nose below a high-domed brow, to some gave him an attractive, distinguished appearance. However, to Jennifer the fact that he was fit enough and keen enough to walk her demanding dogs weighed heavily in his favor. Together with the fact that being an ordained minister who could one day perhaps fulfill her destiny regarding David and eternity, it convinced her that they were ideally matched. A marriage in heaven at last within her grasp.

Again and again Jennifer scrutinized her efforts to outwit Nature and make her the most irresistible puffer out of candles of any fifty-three-year-old's birthday cake! That is how Giselle would see her and Jennifer would take her at her word! Did she not say that she was a "honeypot whenever men were buzzing around"? So she felt confident that she was the flame that would set that confirmed bachelor's heart on fire and make him propose for the first time in his life.

Shaggy Robert Bearded Collie and sleek David Greyhound sat together and watched the proceedings before the mirror, but kept their thoughts to themselves until Robert gave voice in a bark that even he did not know the reason for!

"What's that for, Robert? Don't tell me you disapprove," she inquired in kind tones. "Would you have me do more to make myself beautiful for Bernard?"

The response was deafening!

"Okay, okay, you win! Stop! Stop! Shush! Uncle Bernard will be here any minute!" And when there was peace again she went back to her mirror and both dogs now lay down together, fully prepared to be bored.

Soon the loud grandfather clock in the hallway sounded seven slow booming gongs – just time enough now to make a few more grimaces into the mirror and put on the finishing touches to its tinted, rejuvenating, reflected portrait of a lady fit for proposing to.

Uncle Bernard had earlier walked the dogs and Jennifer had fed them. He would be returning at a quarter to eight in his imposing new Mercedes. She was all keyed up and determined not to keep him waiting.

She felt confident that David could be relied upon not to disgrace her at this most important celebration of her birthday at the rectory. She held such high hopes that Bernard was going to propose – was setting up the romantic backdrop for the momentous event in a bachelor's life.

She saw through the made-up story he had told her – only too transparently, in order to find out the size of her finger, so as to be able to surprise her with an engagement ring. Thus she had listened unquestioningly to his far-fetched rigmarole about a parishioner who had lost her engagement ring and accused another of wearing it! Bernard said that he had told the loser that the ring was similar but not identical, because he could tell that the accuser's finger size was L while that of the accused was the larger size N, and so the ring could not possibly fit onto her finger! "You see," he had said to Jennifer, "I can tell that your own size is L also!" And of course, she had laughed and told him that he was wrong, that in fact it was M as he had figured she would do! What a donkey of a story with its golden carrot to swallow! But from it she had gathered that it was obvious that he was meaning to propose.

The thought put a smile into her mirror.

"What do you think, David – is Uncle Bernard about to pop the question?" she swiveled round on her chair to ask of the adoring greyhound.

Thereupon Robert replied instead – as he generally did to everything within range of his hearing – with a bark repeated till it dissolved into his infamous growl when told to be quiet.

"I was speaking to David – not you, Robert – let him answer for himself, if you please."

David meanwhile had come over to lean against Jennifer's bare thigh and to stare at her out of his soulful, exotic, pharaoh's eyes set in their soft fawn-like face. How he reminded her of graceful boyish Tutankhamen!

"We think alike, don't we, David, you and I, my pet? You know you are about to have a new father – one I know you both love."

She bent down to fondle both dogs, first of all Robert, so as not to make him jealous. Then, with her lips close to David's ear she whispered, "I'm sure you've got a tingling feeling deep inside you saying that Uncle Bernard's going to propose? It's his great surprise for my birthday present, isn't it? Not just a silly cake with too many candles. How romantic to keep it a secret and find out my ring size in that funny way he did! We mustn't let the cat out the bag and spoil his little fantasy now, must we? So we'll act terribly mystified!"

Robert, never one for fading silently out of the limelight, again submitted Jennifer to a cacophonous barking recital. How he appeared to love the sound of his own loud, deep voice!

But Jennifer being in an exceptionally good mood in view of her euphoric anticipation, let him rock the house with exuberant rejoicing about nothing he ever clearly understood.

The minutes crept past eight o'clock and still the listened-for crunching sound of snow under tires was not heard, although several times imagined.

Finally, she lost patience. "Shut up! Shut up, do you hear! How do you expect us to hear Uncle Bernard through all that racket?"

Robert sank – nose to the soft pink pile of carpet and muffled a low protesting growl.

"That's better! Now let's listen with all our ears. We've got to pretend that we didn't notice that he was late. We want everything to go smoothly, don't we?"

The minutes crept even slower until poor Jennifer Trewlove's heart was fit to burst with anxiety. Then suddenly, joy of joys! Uncle Bernard suddenly arrived – twenty-seven minutes late precisely – every single one of them having been an almost unbearable burden for her to bear in case something should have gone wrong.

But quickly he was apologizing profusely, then kissing Jennifer in a way that left no doubt in her mind that all was well between them, and that destiny had not forsaken her – that Uncle Bernard had not suddenly developed cold feet!

While Maria held back a loud, boisterous Robert, the three of them, Jennifer, Bernard and David piled into the minister's big motor car – the latter passenger happily spreading himself over the luxurious leather of the back seat, but without eating it as Robert would have done until it bled yellow!

They gently slid and crunched away, with Uncle Bernard in a cheerful chatty mood and Jennifer the perfect listener. Her hand was resting uninhibitedly upon his knee as he drove carefully over the slippery roads between the dunes of the snowploughs.

Bernard explained how he had been delayed by having to interview organists, especially one who insisted on proving himself to be as good as the man he was replacing by playing the latter's difficult fugues by *Buxtehude* and *Bach*.

"I kept looking at my watch, darling, but he just wouldn't take the hint – his feet kept flitting and his hands kept twiddling and those pipes kept roaring away like a lion with earache! Oh dear, that *Buxtehude*! And even after I warned him that *Buxtehude* was definitely off the menu!"

Jennifer, recalling the hilarious incident of the mouse found in the organ pipe, thus altering the quality of the notes played, tittered.

"What happened to your other organist, Bernard? The little one I know?"

Bernard hesitated. "Was it to do with the mouse being found in his organ pipe and making him look a fool?" prompted Jennifer.

"Let's say he made more than a 'moustake'," said Bernard dryly. "We had our differences. People get tired of hearing *Buxtehude* all the time, as if it were by special request. Something had to be done or I'd be preaching to empty pews. Now I've got to convince this new guy all over again. No wonder that mouse died in the pipe – got bored to death having to listen to *Buxtehude* I suppose."

"Oh, you can be funny, Bernard," said Jennifer approvingly, and squeezing his thigh. "I love you best when you are not too serious. Comes from living all alone, I suppose. But you are your true self only when you are with me – remember yourself saying that to me in bed, Bernard? Oh it gave me such a thrill to hear you say so – I know I can make you happy as you have made me. Isn't it wonderful to be in love, Bernard? Do you know I've never really been in love before – this time it's the real thing for the very first time."

"Same with me, sweetheart," assured Bernard softly.

He took one hand off the steering wheel and while looking straight ahead, cupped his hand over hers, squeezing it more intimately into his thigh, as he murmured, "Darling, you too have made me happier than I have ever been. We must never do anything to hurt each other. Love is too precious to be trifled with. And we must be careful not to let anyone spoil our happiness together, mustn't we?" She nodded in the affirmative while seeing in the mirror above her David's breath clouding a rear window.

Suddenly they were in the rectory driveway. The trio descended onto the crisp trodden snow and with David unleashed at Jennifer's heels, began crunching up the remainder of the path leading to the impressive church-like front door with its brass roaring lion to summon shuffling Mrs. Broomworthy still untying her apron strings.

About halfway up the intersecting snowy path outlined by footprints, the sexton in a long black cassock flowing down to his ankles was seen in the moonlight like a small black ghost flitting out of the church by a side door.

Intercepting his tall rector, he stood on his toes to whisper into his ear as he handed him a bulging envelope, which Bernard hastily slipped into his overcoat pocket. Then the black ghost with a white face flitted away, bidding Jennifer a cheerful, "Happy birthday Mrs. Trewlove – happy birthday – congratulations – I'm late for my wife's dinner you understand – excuse, excuse – must rush."

Jennifer's heart fluttered. How romantic! There was the ring – arrived at the last possible moment like in some ephemeral paperback romance bought at a food store.

But now it was believable – because it was all happening to herself!

"All ready for you, sir, in the living," said Mrs. Broomworthy with a rare smile for her employer and one of vinegar mixed with molasses for Jennifer, as she voiced her congratulations. She was manifestly dreading the prospect of another woman usurping her authority. She had happily served a confirmed bachelor loyally for two decades and could not bear to part with the hard-earned status quo.

Jennifer's eye roved the empirical privacy of the rector's solitary bachelor domain as he took her woolly coat smelling richly of perfume, which she noticed him inhale before hanging it next to his own long black raglan in the closet.

Compared with the spacious open plan of Jennifer's own house, his was but a beehive of chambers – large, square, dark-paneled hall with closed dark doors in all its walls leading into more dark rooms with heavy drawn curtains.

"What a lovely house, Bernard!" enthused Jennifer, as soon as the housekeeper had ceased peeping from behind her kitchen door. "How I admire all this beautiful warm wood paneling! It must have cost a fortune."

"I don't pay the bills, Jennifer, God does – indirectly I mean, through his ministry – come, let me show you round."

As David began to sniff new interesting territory, Bernard cautiously dragged him away from an antique mellow-ticking grandfather clock, in case it was mistaken for another magic pine! But Jennifer liked its comforting pacing of rectory life to its regular, relaxing, unhurried measure.

"Now don't you get any ideas, my friend! That is definitely not a ticking pine!"

"Shall we lock him up in the kitchen, Bernard – just in case?" inquired Jennifer anxiously.

"Perhaps it might be wiser – till he gets used to the place – I'm sure God would understand if he did anything – but in the eyes of Mrs. B. it would be Sodom and Gomorrah and perhaps even worse!"

Jennifer warmed to Bernard's allusion to a future time when David would be getting "used to the place" – an admission, surely, that the rectory would become his future home?

David, as if understanding the situation and begging not to be incarcerated, went over to lean against Bernard's long legs. It effectively won him a reprieve.

It warmed Jennifer's heart to observe a soft side to the rector's nature.

"No, David, you want to be with us, don't you?"

David wagged his tail and licked his hand.

"Did you see that, Jennifer – it's uncanny how he seems to read our minds, although it can't be, of course, because only God can."

"Are you sure, Bernard?"

Bernard frowned. "Of course I'm sure!" replied the man of the cloth with sudden vehemence. "I'm surprised that you doubt."

"No, I mean sure about David not disgracing us, I meant to say," answered Jennifer hastily, to reassure him.

"All right then, we'll give him to Mrs. Broomworthy to look after. Anyway he's got to get used to her. But she's taking the evening off so that we can be alone for your birthday, so we'll have to take him back later when she leaves. Does that suit you, my darling?"

It appeared not to suit the dog who gave the unequivocal impression of having understood the conversation, for he began to whine and to lean against Bernard's legs again as if asking for a reduction of sentence.

"Okay then, David, you can stay!" said he, hoping to win favor with the dog's mistress, in hope also of a reward to follow upon the couch in the living room after the blowing out of candles. For their time together had been planned with as much precision as the ticking of the grandfather clock. An hour apportioned to the showing of his paintings and another for the champagne and buffet and yet another for indulging in his sexual fantasies before Mrs. Broomworthy returned to cast her puritanical eye on the morals of her minister, forever at the mercy of her tongue.

Jennifer was delighted, for she knew she could not bear to hear David whining, whereat the festivities for her would be ruined.

The quieted greyhound paced himself to the rector's heels as he led the way through the paneled dining room and so to the kitchen by a second door. Jennifer smiled to herself at observing the eavesdropping Mrs. Broomworthy mopping a spotless counter.

"You see, Jennifer, Mrs. Broomworthy keeps a tight ship!"

"You sound like Giselle's yachtsman husband, Bernard. Don't tell me you are a sailor too."

"Used to be, Jennifer, in my college days. I often crewed for my rich uncle. He had a fine sailing yacht. But can't afford one myself, alas, nor have I the time to go sailing with all my parish commitments, have I, Mrs. B.?"

"You can say that again, sir. You've certainly got your "ands full with this parish, that's for sure. And if you takes on a wife she'll have 'er hands full, too. Parish work, like housework, is never done."

"Not trying to put her off are you, Mrs. B.?" said Bernard smiling.

"But it's true, you must admit, isn't it, Reverend? You're not one for telling lies."

"Very true, Mrs. B. How is the living room coming along – all ship-shape, is it? Up to your usual impeccable high standard, I presume?"

"Of course, sir, do I ever let you down?"

"Never, Mrs. B., you run everything for me like clockwork. You are a model of efficiency and loyalty."

The hanging parade of shining copper pots and pans and various kitchen knives slotted into wood, plus spotless, spacious, expensively tiled working surfaces and enviable modern stove and cooking utensils, bore threatening testimony to that efficiency which Jennifer feared she would have to be contending with in the near future. How would she be able to get along with such a woman and even more important, how would Mrs. Broomworthy take to the dogs?

Chapter Ten

With Jennifer in raptures, Bernard showed her round his fine old rectory. He proudly pointed out the signatures on his prize collection of secular and holy oil paintings.

At a large Venetian scene with cracked varnish, which looked blurred at most angles of approach and made viewing difficult, Jennifer became transfixed in silent contemplation of the apparent Renaissance masterpiece.

"That's an Antonelli – a pupil of Caravaggio," said Bernard impressively.

Jennifer remained silent, as if she knew the name and the kind of work Antonelli did and so had no need to do more than nod and say, "I can see. Such fine art. You can't beat the old masters."

Bernard came over and lingeringly kissed the back of Jennifer's creamy neck beneath her specially blue-tinted ponytail flaying the plunging neckline of her black silk evening gown. The intimacy thrilled her, she found the sudden boldness in her lover promising. One thing, she felt, was unhurriedly leading up to another, more intimate, more causative to the dramatic moment when he would be springing upon her – no doubt with some original romantic flourish – that little ring in a velvet box so crucial to her future happiness. *Most likely*, she thought, *in the faint lovely light of the cake's symbolic circle of candles.*

When he slipped a well-cared-for hand over her shoulder and into her bosom's silken cleavage, Jennifer was passively aroused. It felt so right – so leading up to that engagement ring. Where was it? In the pocket of his overcoat still or surreptitiously transferred when her back was turned to a pocket of his black jacket ready for the moment of surprise?

Eventually they passed into his more intimate quarters – Bernard's bachelor bedroom – spacious, paneled, and puritan. Jennifer's heart began to pump. The curtains were cardinal-red and drawn. The huge bed was a canopied four-poster, with sumptuous velvet drapes tied back with ribbon, revealing sheets and pillows immaculately ironed by the house-keeper. The master's pale blue pajamas, like some sacrificial offering, she had laid on top of the pile. There was only one painting this time to view – of Jesus on the cross by an unknown. A beautiful mahogany chest of drawers dominated. It was large enough to contain the underwear of a convention of bishops. There was a single sagging upholstered chair beside it, where the Reverend Bernard Houndsditch sat to put on his socks. But what thrilled her most to see, like some spire or cross on the top of its mountain of mahogany, was her own photograph in a highly polished silver baroque frame, with Jennifer being buzzed by embossed flying angels with trumpets.

She felt David lean heavily against her as she stood and gazed. She knew intuitively that his very sharp greyhound eyes had recognized the likeness to his mistress. "I'm sure he recognized you, dearest – did you see him stare?"

As she turned to answer, he smothered the words she was about to say with a kiss on her open mouth.

It was a long passionate kiss and it made her gasp for breath. As soon as she had recovered, she sighed, "Oh Bernard, my love, I've been longing for this moment all day – did you miss me?"

"Not only missed you, sweetheart, but craved for you – I couldn't get you out of my mind and I had to struggle not to let it show – a rector has his responsibilities – indeed it wasn't easy."

"Oh, Bernard, it's been the same with me – I was reliving—" She broke off as she saw Bernard's arched brows knit. "No darling, not that part – I could have killed Giselle when she did that to you when you were all locked up in the bathroom – but despite everything, it's all turned out for the best, hasn't it, my sweet?"

Bernard did not answer but instead abruptly changed the subject.

"Happy birthday dear Jennifer, happy birthday to you, my darling! Come let us celebrate."

He reached for her hand and gently pulled her towards the door and the staircase beyond – past the lovely Venetian scene by the pupil of Cara-vaggio and then downstairs to the dining room, with David overtaking and descending at a gallop.

"Jennifer! Come, let us celebrate," he repeated as he held open the dining room door and shut it after her. "We are alone at last. Mrs. B. has already left."

There before their eyes stood the Moet et Chandon champagne bottle in its bucket of ice cubes on the sideboard. Mrs. Broomworthy must have been active behind the scene, for it was not there before, nor were the array of decorative plates of delicate little triangular-shaped sandwiches with their variety of fillings from smoked salmon to caviar. Nor was the crowning achievement of Mrs. Broomworthy's many talents – the birthday cake itself – fit for a queen with its cream calligraphy squiggled all over: "Happy birthday, dearest Jennifer," beautifully done, as if Mrs. Broomworthy really meant it, which Jennifer felt was most unlikely!

Her seductively coalesced bosom ravishingly contoured by her revealing haute couture black silk gown, she noted with satisfaction, constantly drew his straying eyes, the while she was resonant with expectation that the great moment must be imminent. The glorious moment of truth when the Reverend Bernard Ignatius Houndsditch would symbolize his solemn commitment to the state of holy matrimony for the first time in his life.

Surely it must happen after blowing out the single candle and cutting the cake – so reminiscent of a wedding, akin to a rehearsal for her own.

There was a gleam in her bright cougar-eyes, as Bernard leaned over her shoulder to press down on her hand to cut the cake – just like at a wedding, she thought at that moment! Her engagement ring finger was firmly clasped in Bernard's big hand – the finger he had professed to be able to tell the circumference of at a glance!

"To your forty-third birthday, Jennifer, and may our good Lord grant you many more!"

Jennifer blushed inwardly at the lie she had told as to her age. But their glasses clinked as the bubbles rose like an aerated aquarium.

From the refectory table where there was a bewildering assortment of delicacies to choose from, David, unable to resist temptation any longer, repeatedly took advantage from his great height behind their backs. Ironically, he stole most from a plate under the very nose of the Messiah in a hanging portrait with hand raised as if to bless the deed!

"He's quite an accomplished thief, that dog of yours," chuckled Bernard, picking two cherries off the centers of their respective pastries when Jennifer's attention was distracted.

The two lovers drank their celebration's wine in silence – kisses being found to be sweeter than words. Their eyes met lingeringly many times over the bubbles while her hopes soared. He kept topping up her glass and kissing her mouth when it was black with caviar. Between them they emptied the magnum bottle.

"The ring! – The ring! – The ring! Surely now is the moment! Come on Bernard – I'm waiting!" the unspoken words of her heart's desire silently echoed in her mind. And her head was spinning and light with wine.

He would repeatedly squeeze her hand, squeeze her waist, linger with his fingers in her bosom, thread them through her ponytail, but fail to accomplish what to her meant everything.

Suddenly and incredibly the shy cleric had lost all his inhibitions – he could arouse her through her erogenous zones. He impishly dropped down her cleavage when she was not looking, those two cherries he had picked off the pastries. It made her squirm as his fingers roamed to retrieve, no, not the cherries but what resembled them, the risen nipples of her breasts eased out from under her scant brassiere.

When midnight jarred loudly later in the hall, and they were huddled together on the drawing room sofa, he whispered apologetically with his housekeeper in mind, "I'd love you to spend the night here with me but you must realize it wouldn't be wise, would it? – One day but not yet. So it must be at your place. Believe me when I say I'm thinking of your own reputation as much as mine.

"To pretend to be sleeping in separate rooms may fool your gullible Maria, but not my suspicious Mrs. B. She puts everyone on a slide under her moral microscope. I've often caught her in the act of focusing through keyholes when she pretends to be dusting."

"Sounds like a nice woman!"

"Oh, she's very loyal," said her employer in mitigation, "And a good soul behind the protecting shield – devoted to me – absolutely irreplaceable."

"I feared as much."

"Don't be put off by her manner. It's a bit on the heavy side at times but you'll get on fine when she takes to you eventually."

"You really think so?"

"I do, indeed," said Bernard in a long-drawn-out tender embrace, with David looking on soulfully and Jennifer passive but thoughtful. Afterwards, he took her hand again and led her out, a trifle unsteady on her feet, to the hallway for them to put on their coats. As he held hers gallantly and guided her arms into its sleeves, she could not resist prompting him, "Are you sure you haven't forgotten anything, Bernard – the envelope your sexton gave you – isn't it important? Haven't you forgotten to do something?"

The Reverend Houndsditch momentarily looked perplexed. Then suddenly recalling the incident, replied brightly, "Oh yes! I'm glad you reminded me." Jennifer's heart leaped again and she thought hopefully – At last! At last! In anticipation of him making her in the world's eyes an honest woman.

But the euphoria was short-lived, for when he delved into his overcoat pocket and produced the bulging envelope the sexton had given him, upon it being opened Jennifer could see with bitter disappointment that its contents were a far cry from the expected. Instead of the little velvet box containing her engagement ring was a very different kind of ring containing church keys! Bernard, without realizing what was going on in her mind, reached over her head and hung them on a hook, saying, "Glad you reminded me – mustn't forget these! Our new organist will be asking Mrs. B. for them in the morning!"

What a let-down! All the magic of the occasion was over. And Bernard was to pay dearly for that fated omission. Upon taking her and David home, as he opened the car door for her in her driveway and the dog shot out, followed moments later by its mistress, he was taking for granted being invited to follow also. But he discovered to his dismay that she had developed a sudden severe headache!

Chapter Eleven

The Rev. Bernard Ignatius Houndsditch greeted his housekeeper's knock on his door that fated morning with less than his customary courtesy. He unfairly barked at her to enter with his cup of tea in bed. He had slept very badly; that sudden bad headache of Jennifer's having dealt him a punishing blow which had left him sexually roused and cruelly frustrated.

To him it had been such a wonderful evening until at the very end she went cold on him without any explanation. She had allowed the repressed bachelor to indulge in his fantasies without offering any resistance and seeming the while to have been enjoying the experience as much as he.

Then what could have gone wrong? Women were unpredictable creatures who, with his limited intimate knowledge of them, he could never quite figure out. He was a passionate man, filled with longings and fantasies about them, making him feel ashamed. He was perpetually praying for forgiveness and deliverance from his obsessive, secret, carnal thoughts. Enacting them with the uninhibitedly passionate Jennifer had surely been a game of love in which the participants had played quite happily and according to the tacit rules – like all games always fair and pleasant until one of the players is caught cheating! But he had not cheated on her, he told himself, even in thought and word as well as deed.

How ironic, therefore, that on the very night that he had planned to surprise her romantically on her birthday with an engagement ring slipped onto her finger as she blew out the candle on her cake, everything had suddenly turned sour!

The man who had been entrusted with altering the chosen ring for the jeweler had had a heart attack, preventing the ring from being delivered on time. The difficult inscription (because of its length) inside the ring was to have been UNTIL DEATH DO US PART.

Therefore, the romantic betrothal had to be postponed and kept a secret or it could not be a surprise. His altered plan had been to invite her to attend a wedding ceremony at which he would be officiating. There he would surprise her with the ring under a shower of confetti. He had visualized her face being as radiant as the bride's.

Bernard gulped down his tea and dressed hurriedly, his blood a churning maelstrom at the prospect of meeting Jennifer, and with a chance of restoring himself to favor. After all, what had he done so dreadful that it chilled her love? Was it the prankish cherries at the birthday party laid on at the rectory? He had been looking forward to it but now he regretted that excuse to savor her nipples. Yet surely there were worse things in heaven and earth! Could a mature widow like her really be acting like a virgin?

Had the erogenously conceived act of fingering her breasts so offended her inbred modesty? If so, how was he expected to know that such intimacy was joyous when practiced naked in the bedroom, but when dressed in the dining room was abhorrent? Why did she not give out some hint earlier at the time and he would have desisted immediately and remained in her esteem. For her now to be thinking of him, as she must, in terms most shameful was more than he could bear.

In truth, he never suspected that she was other than an ecstatic, willing participant until the very end. How could she so have changed, grown unaccountably cold towards him upon the journey back to her home? It never entered his head that she could have been expecting more than the titillation and the entertainment, both of which had been well received it had seemed at the time. So why the unexplainable revulsion?

When he arrived at Jennifer's Greenwich mansion in his big Mercedes to collect the dogs for walking round the Port Chester Lyon park, Maria gave no clue that he was other than welcome. But when he returned them to her an hour or so later, however, and asked if he could see her mistress, he met with an impassable barrier, "Sorry, Missis Jennifer in bed – she has catch cold. She now sleep. Not possible come Missis Jennifer. She say thank you for walk the dogs. Tonight please come for walk dogs."

And Bernard did not need a translator to know the reason why Jennifer was not waiting for him as usual, sprawling cougar-eyed on her leather sofa and dressed in her kimono – welcoming him with open arms in the halogen haze of her romantic drawing room where it all began and blossomed, till the frost bit hard under the potted palms.

So there was nothing to do but to keep walking the dogs in order to maintain his lifeline, and continue hoping that the coldness would soon wear off.

On the way back to the rectory and the bustling, overpowering Mrs. Broomworthy, his mind was a kaleidoscope of happy memories. Vividly, he saw Jennifer in bed voluptuously naked, gloriously uninhibited, thrilled and thrilling, romantically inclined; Jennifer in haute couture stylish yet girlish, an overgrown schoolgirl with her swishing ponytail tickling David Greyhound constantly as she talked to him like a person – his velvety head lying on her lap. And Jennifer doing likewise to himself as he lay in the halogen haze with his own head on her lap and looking up into the valley of her breast; Jennifer and he together doing this, doing that – always with Jennifer and, of course, her dogs. And one in particular regarded as a revered person in her life. Bernard's own world now revolved around the trio – Jennifer, his infatuation; David, silent and mysterious, and Robert the forever barking, lovable bearded collie. He had become their walking satellite. His comings and goings to deal with those dogs were as regular and predictable as the moon's pulling tide. Suddenly his introspection was cut short by his housekeeper.

Heavy Mrs. Broomworthy in an apron came waddling out into the slush when he applied the brake and the big car slid to a halt in his own driveway.

"Reverend, our new organist wants to see you; I've put him in your study and told him to wait. I said that you were visiting your parishioners but you'd be due back soon. Hope I done right, sir?"

"Excellent, Mrs. B. You always do what is right."

Mrs. Broomworthy, a woman of the world beneath her bigoted religiosity, looked maternally and sympathetically at her sad employer, as she had done so many times before when he had been seeing a woman and had barked at his housekeeper afterwards. In her mind she had always prejudged the woman and found her wanting if not actually wanton! Her employer was a man of God, was he not? If he had been sidetracked from the path of righteousness, the woman must have led him astray!

A few moments later, respectably dressed in his dark suit and wearing his dog collar slightly askew, the tall gaunt rector with daunting magisterial presence, entered his study to attend to the needs of his new, timid little organist.

Bernard was suddenly in control of his own passionate emotions, perfectly orientated in his pious line of duty. He had again become the comforting man of earth and heaven who listened sympathetically to one's own side of the story and gave wise council; a man whom one could trust wholeheartedly, a man who stood between the soul and God at the font, at the altar and finally at the graveside, while in-between made one's purpose in life crystal-clear from the pulpit every Sunday – now clothed in white like an angel.

The meek little organist got up from his chair beside the rector's huge intimidating desk littered with the letters of his parishioners, plus one or two from his bishop. Nervously fingering his tie, the chubby little man in a blue serge suit with a very shiny seat to his pants, looked up at the hawk-like face of his giant employer and did everything but kneel in homage. He was prepared to concede to every requirement. He had his own invalid wife to keep.

After waving the man back into his seat, Bernard sat down at his desk and commenced a diatribe against the composer *Buxtehude*, simply because he was not to Jennifer's taste.

The little organist became visibly alarmed. He had to appease. "*Buxtehude* is out! Not popular with the parishioners – I fully understand, Reverend. How about *Haydn*? No – well, *Bach* then? 'Where sheep may safely graze' – that kind of thing? – Nothing too heavy, I fully understand."

Bernard kept hearing in his mind Jennifer's favorite hymn and began humming it for the other to identify. He would get the man to play it often. He could picture in his mind her softening towards him – especially after hearing her favorite *Crimmond* version of the twenty-third psalm to follow, plus – ah, yes "Where sheep may safely graze" – good suggestion on his part to end in a quieter lyric mood to melt her estranged heart.

"Lovely words, those, Reverend," beamed the little man, recalling the harvest hymn Bernard had hummed at the beginning. He was most anxious to please in his new post and it showed. He cleared his throat, took a tuning fork from his pocket and tapped it on the edge of his employer's desk, while the latter raised his eyebrows.

"'And His mercies shall endure'," the little organist sang quietly in a perfectly pitched, trained tenor voice. "—so reassuring, Reverend," he broke off to say in his normal, meek little speaking voice, "and such a lovely tune."

"Have you any other suggestions?" asked Bernard, beginning to like the servile little man whose destiny he now linked with his own and Jennifer's – perhaps capable of leading him back to her through his music?

"'Jesu Lord of man's desiring.' It soothes the soul – one of old man Bach's best – I never much cared for the son's work – too twiddly in the top register for my liking – you need to be an octopus to play it properly. Unfortunately I've only got two hands and feet."

Glancing up at a framed photograph of a robed chair frozen into grinning "cheese" under a tree in strong sunlight, their new choir-master inquired, "On a scale of one to ten, what's your choir like, Rev. Houndsditch?"

"Oh, about a two," replied Bernard smiling, "But I'm sure a trained singer like yourself can soon lick them into shape."

"I'm afraid, rector, only God can turn crows into nightingales!"

"Then we must keep praying, mustn't we?" said Bernard, with his renowned beatific smile charming away all opposition.

Finally the ice had been broken. Bernard had warmed to his chubby little Vincent Bellentoni, organist and choirmaster, whom he hopefully began to see as a reconnecting link in the broken chain of his love for Jennifer. So, the smile that was a model for all smiles, charmed once more, sunning all over the chubby face of the man who professed to love Jennifer's favorite hymn.

"Yes, add 'Jesu Lord of man's desiring' to your repertoire, Vincent, and don't forget – drop *Buxtehude* entirely – too heavy. We need something light and breezy."

"Don't worry, rector – from now on light and breezy like you say."

Poor old Buxtehude! thought Vincent Bellentoni to himself, as he cheerfully took leave of his intimidating new employer on Christian-name terms. "Poor old *Buxtehude*! Nobody loves you but me!"

Chapter Twelve

David had become a person now in Jennifer's life, so it was the solemn occasion of David Greyhound's inaugural visit to the Trewlove family mausoleum where her late husband and beloved son were interred. She was thinking of what to say to the gravedigger if they encountered him and he remonstrated with them. She had a fifty-dollar-bill handy in her trendy black leather overcoat pocket, in order to meet the contingency – hoping the man would be susceptible. In her present mood, she was even prepared to raise the stakes in order to fulfill her overpowering need to be sharing a sentimental journal with a surrogate of one whom she had loved deeply and had lost in tragic circumstances. Although she had loved him dearly, it was not her late husband at this most poignant moment who was most movingly framed in her mind but their son, with whom she had had a very special and happy relationship.

He would have loved David, as he had loved all animals. If only he had been spared to live long enough to be of comfort during this breaking of her heart over Bernard, whose intentions Giselle had confirmed during a long intimate discussion, and which betrayed themselves for being less than honorable.

"But he said he loved me and hinted, at the birthday party, that David and I would soon be sharing the rectory with him," she had confided to her best friend. How Giselle's reply had filled her with shame and regret!

"All men say they love you, don't they, to get what they're really after? Don't be fooled by the dog collar, deep down there's a dirty dog underneath!"

They were cutting words, especially when applied to her Good Samaritan, but Jennifer knew that her best friend was only trying to give sound advice – to bring Jennifer back to her senses.

The devotion to dog-walking, according to one well versed in the subterfuges of men, had only been a means to an end – physically as well as literally – she had added with a smile.

"But," Jennifer had countered, "he still walks my dogs."

"Wake up! Poor naïve thing, that's only to save face, isn't it? Plus a good chance of getting you back on the same terms. Just as the pen is mightier than the sword, the smack is mightier than both! Surely you must have found that out? This isn't the first time, is it?"

The reference to past painful, evaporating romances cut even more deeply; for she had loved and lost when they had loved and left, leaving scars that were slow and painful in healing.

Yet fond memories of the Good Samaritan still lingered and she could not prolong her "cold" behavior indefinitely. And what of the dogs? Would it not be just prostitution of her body for their sake? Unthinkable! She had to be in God's good grace, she reasoned with herself, for Him "Whose mercies shall endure" to grant a very special indulgence she had yet to ask in favor of David and concerning their all-important afterlife. Hence their sentimental visit to the mausoleum to prepare him for the journey – and to seal, as it were, a sacred covenant.

God who could read her mind would surely give forth some heavenly sign if he were displeased – it would suddenly thunder or lightning would strike signifying His rage?

But the churchyard was peaceful and still and God manifested no displeasure at David being at her side. As they walked gingerly in the gritted sunny white churchyard with its new and ancient gravestones rendered equally unreadable, David was showing uncanny understanding and respect. He did not strain on his leash or disgrace himself, although the temptation must have been strong. Instead, he walked solemnly in step at her heels, carrying his burden of restraint and she her burden of woe and remembrance of the still living past. The departed were never departed from her mind.

Meanwhile she was mindful of past favors from the Lord. David had been lost and the Good Shepherd had found him and crooked him back into the fold when he had been given up for dead – all because she had had enough faith; for was it not written that faith could move mountains, make possible the walking on water?

She had set her heart upon marrying the Almighty's earthly ambassador in the shape of the Rev. Bernard Houndsditch and so be in a stronger position for communicating with God. But now she had lost his hotline with heaven (as Giselle, in her facetious fashion, put it), while desperately needing to be in touch for that one last favor – to raise David to the status of a human being that he may not be excluded from her afterlife. Was he not as much one of God's creations as any human being, and freer from sin and more dependable and loving than most? They were inseparable now and for ever. To be in heaven without her loved ones would be like waking up in a garden crowded with strangers and devoid of sunshine and flowers.

So reasoned the grieving widow as their cautious footsteps whispered into the white underground of resting bones sleeping in promise of eternal life. Inevitably her thoughts meandered towards her other faithful companion, her bearded collie, but in view of the undeniable fact that he did not possess the higher intelligence and understanding of a human being, she would leave Robert out of her unorthodox behest. Otherwise it could be akin to taking advantage of the Supreme Deity and likely to result in Him granting her no further concessions. She would give the bearded collie, therefore, a proper burial in a dog's cemetery that had headstones to put on record how sadly one's pet was being missed. He was a senior dog, thus likely to go first. She would be able to bring David openly and legally along to visit his cousin's grave at anniversaries and special remembrance days.

They passed a deep gaping hole, waiting for its future occupant. Snow-flaked earth was newly piled beside it, ready to be shoveled back whence it came. A crow or raven looked down, appearing very black against its white background of yew trees shivering in the chilly breeze.

It caused Jennifer to tighten her collar with her free hand and she smelled the acridness of chrysanthemums, as her bouquet brushed into her face. It reminded her of the acridness of death.

No gravedigger was in sight, and not being the Sabbath, visitors were few. To Jennifer's immense relief, they were also distant in the large, hilly, nonsectarian cemetery. They mainly became visible when it began to drizzle, whereupon they sprang up like walking black mushrooms. Jennifer did not have her umbrella and she felt the droplets cold upon her check, and David soon damp to the touch.

Innumerable were the graves with their headstones which the strange pair passed – the woman in black wearing a scarf over her head, the giant greyhound on a leash, as handsome as a show dog.

Nowhere did David disgrace himself, despite the countless temptations. Jennifer, greatly impressed, saw it as a favorable omen for her future plans. She thought that God watching must have been very pleased!

Otherwise, assuredly, He would have sent lightning and thunder as a reminder and to scare them away. Thus the drizzle was well received and the umbrella, consequently, not missed.

Much to Jennifer's concern, one of the moving black airborne mushrooms was suddenly heading her way. Jennifer felt uncomfortable but there was no escape. An unfortunate meeting was inevitable. That walking mushroom turned out to be poisonous and collapsed in front of them, whereupon a bulbous stalk of white mackintosh vented righteous indignation.

"No dogs! Have you no respect for the dead?"

Jennifer did not answer but hurried out of range of the angry voice and the scowling white face. "Ay! Come back – I'm speakin' to you – next time I'll call the police!"

Jennifer was jolted out of her introspection and fled as fast as the slushy conditions allowed, David adjusting his own pace faithfully at her heels. Once she almost fell but was saved halfway down by dropping her bouquet and clutching the surefooted powerful greyhound with both hands.

Eventually, she drew comfort from catching sight of the Trewlove imposing stone and marble mausoleum, protected physically by its leaning palisade of stalactite-like black ironwork and spiritually by a white angel, rendered whiter than usual by its garb of dripping snow.

Upon arrival Jennifer put down her bouquet on the slush and released David simultaneously. She wiped her wet face with her handkerchief and then, picking up her chrysanthemums and drawing a deep breath, she swung open the creaking iron gate. David followed her through to the three steps leading up to the tomb's entrance, which resembled a smaller replica of a church door. The fantasized initiation ceremony had begun – David had been introduced to his final resting place after cremation at the end of his short life. There in her own pre-made casket he would be sprinkled to await his mistress' ashes – all dependent, naturally, upon the will of God, her prayers, plus an enlightened, sympathetic clergyman. Alas! Bernard had been discarded as being that enlightened sympathetic aide. So a mist of uncertainty now veiled their distant future together.

At the door David sniffed and began to whine pathetically, as if he could read her mind and knew what lay in store for him – namely, that one day he would be compelled to wait in that dank, forbidding chamber a long time for his mistress to return. This confirmed in Jennifer's mind that her dog was not only telepathic but also clairvoyant. As she replaced the decayed flowers in the mausoleum's stone vase with her bright chrysanthemums, David leaned heavily against her and continued to whine. Jennifer now could not control her emotions. Tears joined the droplets on her cheek from the drizzle and she could taste salt in the corners of her mouth. She wiped her lips with the dry palm of her wet glove, as her delicate handkerchief was soaked. She was seeing meanwhile in her mind the inscription on the tomb unreadable through the dripping snow.

"You can't read, can you David? No, of course not – silly question. Silly Jennifer!" David jumped up upon her gently and rested his cat-like paws upon her shoulder. She recoiled but managed to retain her balance on the slippery steps while his long tongue licked the rain and tears off her smudged cheeks. When David slipped down to lean against her weightily again, Jennifer continued. She held his passive head in her gloved hands while she spoke, bending over him to look into his beautiful, elongated, pharaoh-like glowing eyes.

"But you know what the blank space is for, don't you, honey? It's for you and me. One day we shall both be inside this tomb at peace for ever and ever. Your ashes will be mingled with mine in accordance with my will left with my attorney – but I've still to add a codicil when I find the right priest for us – not easy, David – not easy, my dear one – but with God's help we shall find him. I will never give up until we do. You know that, don't you, David – you can read my mind?"

Jennifer freed the dog momentarily so that she could wipe away more tears. Then she took his face in her gloved hands for the last time and kissed the top of his head.

It was time to go home.

Chapter Thirteen

That morning when Jennifer was with David at the cemetery, Giselle received a telephone call from the Rev. Houndsditch, for whom she had lost her high regard because of the suffering he had caused to her best friend.

"Tell him I'm out," she had instructed her daily help at the mention of his name.

"But he says it's very important and urgent – are you sure, Mrs. Carboni?"

Giselle put down her violet eyeshadow and followed the woman downstairs to the telephone – there not being one nearer, for she was averse to even the presence of one by her bed. The woman had always to answer first then use her discretion.

"Yes, Rev. Houndsditch, what is so urgent and vital to us all?" she asked in acid tones.

The voice on the line hesitated then came back sounding unfamiliarly weak and lacking in its customary captivating resonance.

"You are Jennifer's best friend, that is why I am appealing to you – because she puts down the receiver as soon as she hears my voice—"

"I don't blame her!" said Giselle coldly. "Good heavens! What has she told you?" The voice seemed unnaturally reedy as if under great strain.

"All I need to know – so come to the point – what is so urgent?"

"It's about the dogs – I can't take them out this evening – she must be told," the voice said quickly as if in fear of being cut-off.

"You mean you can't take them out, period! Don't you Reverend? Be honest!"

"Please! Please! You've got to listen to me – obviously there's been a grave misunderstanding between us – but I appeal to you as the best friend of the woman I love and hope to marry—"

Giselle cut him short again. Her voice was harsh.

"Don't you dare deceive her any more!"

"I haven't deceived her—"

"Oh no? You were going to propose to her at that birthday party. It was obvious you led her on to expect a proposal."

"I really was going to – really!"

Giselle again cut him short.

"You were going to propose but you didn't!"

"It wasn't my fault – really it wasn't – it was going to be a surprise and—"

He did not get a chance to finish the sentence, for she was in a mood to give him a hard time.

"You lost your nerve?" she cut in again.

This time resonance crept back into the voice. There followed a quick flow of imploring, impassioned words as if the speaker was determined to have them all heard before he was interrupted once more.

"Giselle, we can't go on like this – cat-and-mousing over the telephone. Please! Please! Let me come over and speak with you – grant me a hearing – if not for me at least for Jennifer's sake – I can't believe that love ends at the first tiff. Let me come over and explain matters to you and you will see them in a different light. The telephone is so cold and impersonal unless there is some rapport between us and quite clearly there is not."

"Can you blame me for that?"

Finally, Bernard, with infinite relief, saw his chance of breaking through the hostile barrier Giselle was placing between them.

"I never blame anyone before listening to their side of the story. Things are not always what they seem. May I come over please, I beg of you? Even a criminal has a right to be heard."

Giselle relented. "Very well, come over if you must – but I warn you it had better be good and you've got to convince me you are not going to hurt her again. She has suffered enough."

"I'm coming right away! Thank you! Thank you! God bless you, Giselle!" quickly came the jubilant response.

"I'd rather you kept God out of it if you don't mind."

"As you wish."

She put down the receiver in order to report the proceedings to her best friend and to say that Rev. Houndsditch was coming over to do some explaining and did she want to be present? But Giselle was surprised to discover that Jennifer had left with David for a destination Maria was unable to disclose. That she should have taken the dog with her put "paid" to the immediate conclusion that she had gone to church to pray. She knew her friend would not dream of leaving him alone in the car to whine dreadfully, as he most certainly would. Giselle could think of no other explanation than that Jennifer must have taken him to the veterinarian, which sadly seemed to imply that he had been taken ill during a period of great distress in her life.

Maria could only impart that "Missis Jennifer not say where go." And in answer to Giselle's other question, "David good – eat good – eat dinner – Maria feel David good."

Giselle was puzzled. They were very close – confided in each other every day. Then why hadn't she telephoned her best friend?

She was still puzzling over the matter, together with that other mystery which Bernard was about to unravel in private, when she recognized the distinctive tapping sound of the rector's Mercedes diesel engine in her driveway.

She sped back to her bedroom whence she listened for the doorbell and her daily woman ushering the visitor into her drawing room.

Giselle purposely made him wait several minutes until she completed her colorful make-up while grimacing leisurely into her dressing table mirror, before descending regally to give him the cold shoulder. Let him stew a little in his own juice!

Upon her stagy dramatic entrance, clicking her pearls like castanets, Bernard rose from his low leather chair like a jack-in-the-box. His hands were clasped as if in prayer – but imperfectly so, for one arm was in a sling. At that moment as his tall skeletal frame bent over her, bowing with exaggerated politeness, he reminded her of some grotesque human form of praying mantis.

"What happened to your arm?" Giselle was more curious than sympathetic in asking the question and it showed.

"Unfortunately, you didn't give me a chance to explain, my dear," replied Bernard sweetly, without the slightest hint of reproach in his mellow voice, as Giselle waved him back into his chair while she sat herself down very formally opposite.

The room was large and almost as sumptuously furnished as Jennifer's, but the lighting was more natural. There was no extravaganza of halogen lighting to haze over their expressions. Hers was hard and daunting in the blunt no-nonsense daylight reflected by the outside thawing snow.

As in the layout of Jennifer's own drawing room where once the three of them had sat down together happily making conversation, there was a similar low glass table separating them again, plus the same low seating position which had elicited many an embarrassing stares from those sitting opposite.

This time Giselle pulled her slinky tight black silk dress down well over her knees with uncharacteristic modesty, as she squelched onto her leather chair's soft cushion.

As if taking the hint, Reverend Houndsditch cast his eyes innocently away to the several large framed watercolors of fine racing yachts struggling in foul weather.

With his eyes turned back to Giselle, he waited for her to stop fiddling with her pearls, but was forced to speak against their interminable clicking.

"I was pulled down over a patch of sheer ice by those powerful dogs and broke my arm when I fell over them," he began, in his most ingratiating resonant voice, while the other looked right through him and steeled herself against capitulating to his undeniable charm. "Was David hurt?" Giselle blurted out, thinking that must have been the case, for it explained why Jennifer had not been available – because she must have been taking the dog to the veterinarian.

"No, David was not hurt, but I was, as you can see," replied Bernard with his renowned disarming smile in the face of her apparent unconcern for himself while showing concern only for the dog!

"Oh, I'm sorry, I didn't mean to interrupt – give me your side of the story, then. I will hear you out but I can't promise to be sympathetic. Jennifer is my best friend. I can't bear to see her broken-hearted."

Bernard noted the violent clicking of her pearls betraying her extreme emotion and he responded by appealing to her pathetically.

Holding his arm in the sling melodramatically close to his heart, he said woefully with moist eyes, "If I have hurt her, I have done so unwittingly and believe me I've been through hell these last few days myself wondering how I'm ever going to be able to explain and put matters right between us, since I can't get her even to speak with me. By the way, you didn't let me finish – I was trying to say that although I couldn't take the dogs out—" (He waved his arm in the sling at her face to gain her sympathy.) "—I arranged for my sexton to take over till my arm gets better. So, you see I do care."

"I saw you drive up – how did you manage with one hand?" Giselle inquired suspiciously.

Once again the disarming smile ushered in the words. "With difficulty, my dear Giselle, and not without some pain also. But when so much is at stake – you know how it is. Besides, I had to drop everything to come right away. I had to give the woman I love priority over all. As for the pain in this arm, it was nothing compared with what I've had to endure emotionally these last few days."

Giselle vouchsafed a patently insincere single word "Sorry" while looking down to inspect her beautiful fingernails once more. She had heard remarkable lies or exaggerations from me in her time. It would betray vulnerability if she were caught listening to them too attentively.

Bernard hesitated till she looked up to say, "Continue."

"Well, I've got my sexton to take my place for the time being – as I said. That was the first thing I did when I returned from the hospital."

Bernard paused, daunted by the fact that even the mention of the word hospital could not distract those pretty fingers from their irritating habit of playing with the precious ropes of pearls swinging from her neck.

"Go on."

"Well, to cut a long story short, she was simply euphoric at that birthday party and I couldn't for the life of me imagine what could have gone wrong when at the very end she turned suddenly cold on me. You see, we had been so very close together – very close indeed!"

"I can well imagine!" insinuated Giselle, looking up with her theatrically painted face that reminded Bernard of a mocking, overpainted harlequin.

"Can you? I wonder! Have you ever been deeply in love, Giselle? You must have been."

The hard nut to crack suddenly split.

"Yes Bernard, I have, that's why I fear so much for my poor Jennifer."

"Then you will understand and you will help me – that is to say after you have learned all the facts – our miserable luck that turned against us and drove us apart.

"I did actually plan to surprise her with a beautiful engagement ring at the party but everything went wrong – not my fault – the engraver who was to put the inscription inside the ring had a heart attack and the ring could not be delivered to me on time. I was crestfallen but decided to postpone my little romantic surprise for another occasion soon to be – a wedding I was to be officiating at, whereupon I would slip the ring surreptitiously to my own beloved Jennifer at the very moment they started throwing confetti at the bride and groom, and with everyone smiling to the cameras flashing away. It would have been the greatest moment of my life just to have seen her face. I still wanted it to be a romantic surprise for her – something really original and romantic for her to look back upon. Very ironic, as it turned out. I had no idea she thought I was ducking my responsibilities."

"And the ring is still at the jeweler's I suppose?" said Giselle, not totally convinced that she was hearing the whole truth but only perhaps a version of it, romantically embroidered to win a lost lover back.

"No, it is not!" declared Bernard triumphantly, "It is in my pocket!" Hastily, after some fumbling because of having to reach over his arm in a sling, he leaned over the table to hand his tormentor a small blue velvet box. Giselle opened it at once and a great solitary diamond blazed most convincingly – more so than all the words he had spoken.

"Now," said the other, charming her with his radiant smile, "please read the inscription."

"I'm afraid, I can't, Bernard my dear," said a very changed Giselle, squinting through her contact lenses, "The words are too minute."

"Then try reading them through this, dear lady," said Bernard, enjoying his victory as he produced a magnifying glass from another pocket of his jacket.

Giselle snatched the glass and, visibly moved, read aloud the poignant inscription, UNTIL DEATH DO US PART.

Afterwards, genuinely overjoyed and theatrically demonstrative, she went over to fling her arms round the startled Bernard and print her lips upon his immaculate dog collar, meanwhile smudging it with her eyes and cheek and making that collar as spectacular as a sunset!

Chapter Fourteen

The long telephone conversations that awaited Jennifer upon her return from the cemetery restored her faith in human nature – turned her back into a complete, wholesome, charming person once again – no longer that bitter shadow of her former self. Giselle, in a state of great excitement, first broke the good news. She explained in detail how Bernard had been ironically misjudged – how fate had been very cruel indeed to the lovers and how things were far from what they had seemed at the time.

As the Rev. Houndsditch himself confirmed over the telephone, he was coming over that very night to put the fated ring upon her finger. This time Jennifer listened euphorically.

But first she had to wait for his sexton who was being sent over in his place to walk the dogs, as Bernard's arm was still in a sling.

Upon hearing the slushing sound of motor car tires in the driveway, the two fretting dogs began circling excitedly in the hallway. The bearded collie was loudly heralding the arrival of the car.

Jennifer warmly greeted the little sexton as the dogs, waving banners of delight, engulfed him with noise plus a volley of leaping paws of welcome.

"Down! Down!" shouted the little man warding off the onslaught with chic, black-gloved hands.

"Good evening, Mrs. Trewlove," he managed to say at last after getting his breath back that had been knocked out of him by paws of greeting to his stomach! Jennifer shouted at her pets into calm, and apologized for their unruly behavior.

"Sorry I'm late – the Reverend warned you, didn't he, that I'd be a little late this first time? I see you've put on their leashes all ready for me, so we'll be off, then? Have a nice day and a pleasure meeting you, Mrs. Trewlove. Come on, you impatient dogs! – Walkies!"

Jennifer reopened the door and in a flash they pulled the little man headlong into the white slushy night. The dapper little black-coated man cursed profusely under his hat, which was quickly gathering snow and threatening to blow away. It was not the best of nights in the inchoate blizzard for walking the dogs. But he soldiered on, trying to make a good impression with the attractive widow.

Jennifer began dreaming, as she poured herself a sherry and examined her face critically in the mirror of the cocktail cabinet. Was it a face fit to bear the scrutiny of the man who was about to put the coveted ring upon her finger when he arrived later? Unwise to omit putting the icing on the cake! Her own future and that of her beloved pets was at stake. She was only too aware of the fact that he was a much respected eligible bachelor and there would be rivals galore in the offing if he should entertain second thoughts.

The return of the boisterous ones occurred three quarters of an hour later and she could hear that the dogs were dominating. The man's shrill voice of command went unheeded.

"Do come in, won't you," said Jennifer hospitably to the breathless little sexton who was already taking off his coat and hanging it beside his Stetson, without waiting to be invited. Brusquely, he shoved off David who had protested with a friendly double paw attack upon his corpulent person, whilst Robert's voice reverberated fit to knock the plaster off the walls when the stranger stamped his wet feet on the mat.

"What lively dogs, you have, Mrs. Trewlove!" he replied to Jennifer's profound apology for their behavior.

Maria was on hand and waiting and Jennifer turned and said, "Take them in the kitchen please, Maria, and keep them quiet with their ice cream, will you? And see that our guest is not disturbed."

Maria grabbed both dogs unceremoniously by the collar and in a trice the pair had been arrested and marched off – David meekly, Robert growling.

The little man looked on approvingly as bulky Maria dragged away the offenders, mumbling as she went.

"Yes, Missis Jennifer, Maria make bad dogs good – no more disturb Mr. Reverend no more time." To her every gentleman dressed in black was assumed to be ordained!

"She's an asset to you, your Maria, Mrs. Trewlove – those dogs need a firm hand – the rector's too soft when it comes to dogs – no doubt it accounts for why he let them pull him along like a dog cart till eventually he fell down and broke his arm. I've told him time and again you've got to show 'em who's boss or you're in for real trouble."

"How badly is he hurt?" asked Jennifer, looking most concerned. "You must tell me all about it over a glass of sherry or whiskey if you prefer – you are not a teetotaler by any chance, are you?"

"No, whiskey will be fine, thank you."

"Follow me into the drawing room then if you please and make yourself comfortable," she added. His face brightened as he looked around at all the luxury and exotic, exceptionally tall potted palms.

"It's a bit like a botanical garden in the moonlight, isn't it, with all that fancy soft lighting. Very romantic I must say!" he added, as he sat down on the sofa and stared at her disconcertingly.

"According to the X-ray it's only a minor bone chip – not a serious fracture, thank God," said the sexton as he took his glass of whiskey a little too lingeringly from the hand of his hostess in haute couture, ready to receive Bernard.

He paused till he had her attention, then began feeling the soft leather with his fingers, sensuously, as if it were a woman's skin. Jennifer was repelled by the suggestive act of the unprepossessing stranger. Or was she mistaken? Surely the prudish Reverend Houndsditch would never keep in his employ a man who was depraved? Yet she felt in his presence uncomfortable – even vulnerable.

This seemed indeed a very dubious beginning to the relationship forced upon her – or was her imagination running riot? Giselle was always telling her as much.

"The name's Jeff Harding – call me Jeff and may I call you Jennifer, now that we'll be seeing each other twice a day?"

She very reluctantly assented with a nod. Intuitively, she felt that she might be letting herself in for trouble with the insensitive, overly forward and repugnant, yet indispensable, dog-walker.

"How long will it take to heal fully, do you think?"

The corpulent little man with the ugly strawberry nose made a grimace, shrugged his bottleneck shoulders and scratched his remaining sprinkling of hairs. The pink haze of halogen-diffused light failed to do much for his image.

"A few weeks I guess – I'm not a doctor – but if you're worried about the dogs there's no need – I've got plenty of spare time to take care of things for you, Jennifer. I get paid by the rector just the same. Besides, it will be a pleasure working for you, Jennifer, my dear."

She recoiled when Mr. Harding suddenly leaned forward across the low table – as if, she thought, to place a hand upon her bare arm. But if that had been his purpose he did not do so, but fiddled awkwardly with his Venetian goblet indecisively, as she withdrew the temptation as a hint.

"I know how to handle dogs because I've handled them before for Reverend Houndsditch," he continued after the veiled rebuff.

Jennifer pricked up her ears. She felt strongly that she needed to know as much as she could glean from whatever source available about the occasionally evasive Reverend with whom she had slept and whose wife she had hopes of becoming. But she would bide her time – unwise to make an employee suspicious and thereby cautious about jeopardizing his relationship with his own master. To catch the man off-guard during casual conversation at a later date would be more fruitful.

As if they had overheard the man's claim of being able to handle dogs, David Greyhound and his companion (having escaped from Maria) sailed in boldly to put the boastful claim to the test! Lashing low bric-a-brac with their tails, they sent china crashing onto the floor. Maria, hovering on the threshold, was aghast. She looked uncertain whether to intervene until Jennifer signaled her away.

"Stay! Sit!" shouted their mistress in alarm, as she and Mr. Harding rose hurriedly to pick up the fragments and throw into the brass coal scuttle. But stay they did not, and David followed Robert the leader and instigator in all mischief, as they circled clumsily round the big room, dodging its plethora of antique furniture, with Jennifer and Mr. Harding looking on helplessly. Several times the latter lunged forward in an attempt to catch a dog by the tail or collar, but in vain.

"I guess they'll calm down if we go back to our seats," said Mr. Harding.

Jennifer was impressed when the little sexton's guess proved correct.

As soon as they were seated, both dogs in turn came over to lick the face of the self-proclaimed licker-into-shape of dogs. Suddenly they were all over him in play, with Robert barking and tugging at his sleeve and at his shoelaces, much to Jennifer's embarrassment. She imagined that because the man was so small they had mistaken him for a child, for the bearded collie was renowned for playing with children. And in whatever he did David was bound to follow.

The sexton brusquely asserted his authority with great difficulty, but succeeded eventually in pushing them off as Jennifer apologized once again for their most unruly behavior.

"Sit!" he roared at them, stretching up to his puny five-feet-nothing in his shoes with oversized heels! Both dogs obeyed in their fashion on the Persian rug nearest to their mistress, Robert as dogs normally sit and David in his curious side-saddle position. In the climbing heat of the radiators and electric log fires, plus halogen lamps providing more heat than light, both dogs looked round with smiling faces and panting with tongues dripping like leaking faucets. Thereupon, tiny Mr. Harding looked very pleased with himself, imagining he had redeemed himself before Jennifer.

"You've got to let them know who's in charge," he boasted. "Keep them firmly in check and they soon catch on. No good letting them get the upper hand. It's no good treating animals as if they were higher human beings. An animal's just an animal and should be treated as such – that's what I say. Of course, I don't mean no disrespect to your two fine pets. They're truly magnificent looking animals, Jennifer – especially the greyhound – looks like you could put stag horns on his head and he'd look like a kind of forest king. Nevertheless, you must agree, my dear, they are terribly spoilt – spare the rod and spoil the child. It applies to animals as well."

Suddenly, the jealous bearded collie very loudly took exception to the stranger cozily sipping whiskey with his mistress. The shaggy dog's throaty pipes resounded as he got up on four legs to protest. It had obviously occurred to him that what they needed was a dog-walker, not a dog-talker and usurper!

"Quiet, you two! Robert, quiet, do you hear me?" Jennifer stamped her own authority with her foot.

"Quiet! Quiet! This is your new walkies till Uncle Bernard gets better. Now I want you to listen to Mr. Harding and behave yourselves this time – you should be ashamed of yourselves, putting your poor kind Uncle Bernard's arm in a sling."

"Let me handle this, Jennifer," intervened the sexton bravely, as he leaped from his chair to take over.

He looked so much shorter, it struck Jennifer, than when she had seen him that night, elongated by his drape of black cassock, flitting like a ghost in the moonlight from his church's side door.

"Sit! Robert sit!" she heard him roar savagely and the bearded collie sat, as he always did upon hearing this succinct command which universally rooted all canine posteriors to the ground.

"There you are, Jennifer – you've got to be firm with them or they'll walk all over you," declared the self-satisfied little man in command.

Both dogs heard the familiar sound "walk" and the sound was immediately confounded with "walkies"!

Thereupon pandemonium broke out. They ran around wagging their tails and leaping at their corpulent newly made friend, while a veritable avalanche of shouting falling about their ears from the besieged, humiliated sexton still failed to command obedience. He could only bring them to heel by repeating venomously, "Sit, sit, sit!"

But on this occasion they sat in their own good time and not in his – a difference of several loud barking minutes! The more he threatened them the more they got out of control until he shouted with increasing ferocity the magic word over and over again!

Jennifer looked quizzically at the insensitive little man with the strawberry nose and struggled with her feeling of contempt.

But unfortunately he was indispensable. After all, she consoled herself, he was responsible to his employer. She could always complain to him if need be.

Thus, she helped the humiliated little man save face as he went back to his chair. From her low seated position, she stamped her foot at the bearded collie, then hastily gathered her skirt modestly round her knees, in view of the man's roving eyes.

"Robert, quiet! Quiet!" she commanded, whenever the bearded collie broke silence, and she sent him down growling, nose to carpet.

A detached David who meanwhile had been observing, came over to lean against her legs, as if he felt her discomfiture and was screening his beloved mistress from those too shamefully seeking bleary eyes.

"I'm sorry Mr. Harding—"

"Call me Jeff."

"I'm afraid Jeff, they are terribly spoilt and untrained – how could you possibly know what to expect? But after you've trained them with your special masterly technique," added Jennifer with tongue in cheek, "I'm sure they'll be a lot more manageable. We're very lucky to have you and I'm very grateful. Can I get you another whiskey, Mr. Harding, I mean Jeff?"

"Call me Jeff, Jennifer, everyone calls me Jeff including the rector," said the sexton reaching for his goblet to gulp down the remains of his drink.

"Very well, Jeff," said Jennifer, inwardly wincing as she imagined trouble ahead for herself invited by over-familiarity. But she was in a Catch-22 situation.

As she pushed David gently aside and got up to go over to the cocktail cabinet, she debated the matter with herself. How she detested him taking that liberty with her Christian name! Thank heaven Bernard would soon be taking over again!

Upon returning to the table with their two red Venetian goblets refilled with her best sherry and whiskey, she opened up the conversation casually with, "I wonder if I know any of those dogs you used to walk for your rector, Jeff, when he was too tied up to walk them himself. I have so many friends with dogs," she added, fishing for information, hoping at the same time desperately not to discover immediate cause for jealousy.

"Oh, there were several ladies in need of dog-walking."

(She could not help feeling dismayed at his suddenly having revealed to her how the Reverend's Good Samaritan acts of dog-walking had been linked with ladies beside herself.)

"As I recall, at different times over the years – several Labradors, two German Shepherds, one St. Bernard – no relation to the rector" (his little sexton irreverently added with a chuckle). "But they were mostly mutts. If you know their names, Jennifer, they might ring a bell – or perhaps if you could possibly help me by naming some of your dog-owner friends it might jog my memory too."

Jennifer became flustered. Her bluff had been called and she could not think quickly of any names except Giselle's and her dog Satan.

"Was Mrs. Carboni's Doberman called Satan one of your rector's dogs that he used to walk, do you remember, Jeff?"

The sexton held his glass to his lips with one hand while he scratched his sweaty balding scalp with the other.

"No, I can't say as I've taken out a Satan." Then he chuckled and quipped while he put down his glass and caught her eye mischievously,

"Well, it wouldn't be proper for a minister of the Lord to be seen out walking with Satan, now would it, Jennifer?"

Much against her own feelings, Jennifer could not help smiling at the man's quick wit.

Suddenly, the telephone rang and she saw Mr. Harding looking perturbed, as she leaned over the table to answer it.

"It's for you, Jeff," said a relieved Jennifer, handing the instrument across to her tardy guest. "Your rector wants to have a word with you."

Chapter Fifteen

The marital engagement of the widow Jennifer Trewlove to the Rev. Bernard Ignatius Houndsditch was a euphoric lightning affair. As everyone expected, including several coveting spinsters and widows, they were married even before the snowdrops began to peep through the snow.

The wedding took place in Bernard's own Episcopal Church and the service was conducted by the Rev. Golightly from a neighboring parish, because the Rev. Houndsditch's living was too poor to be able to support a curate.

As a wedding present, Giselle had booked them into a hotel on the seafront in Brighton, England, with all good wishes for their honeymoon. David and Robert were left in the care of Mr. Harding and his wife who were installed in Jennifer's own house for that purpose, after the groom had satisfied his bride that she had been completely mistaken as to the character of his sexton, whom he vouched for in glowing terms. It made Jennifer feel most guilty and repentant of the thoughts she had entertained about a pathetic, henpecked little man always ready, apparently, to do anyone a kindness.

On the airplane going over the Atlantic, Bernard whispered into her dozing ear that poor Jeff was starved of affection by his own wife and latched onto anyone not visibly put off by his cruel physical defects. His "forwardness" that Jennifer had found so offensive and alarming was merely a "cover-up for an inferiority complex and merited pity, rather than censure."

Now she felt reassured. Able to bask in the warmth of their marital sunshine under its ephemeral cloudless sky. She fell asleep; high above the ocean the clouds, steadily banking up beneath them, invisible until they condensed into England's notorious rain at Heathrow airport.

The few boring miles on the terminal bus through the drab suburbs of London, along narrow, wet, depressing streets took an hour. The exciting fifty-mile scenic train journey south from Victoria Station to Brighton, which lived up to its name, took no longer.

Compared with Connecticut, the bordering counties of Surrey and Sussex through which they passed were so different – so very English, thought Jennifer. The difference was refreshing, charming and delightful. She passed euphorically from the New World into the old, impatient to taste the pure honey of her marital moon. She kept exclaiming to her groom, "Oh! Look, sweetheart! So British and charming! It's the best wedding present in the world. So thoughtful of Giselle." They gazed enthralled through the train window at the still faintly medieval appearance of the hedged-in countryside, its weathered stone or brick little cottages and bigger farm houses. Plus churches so old that around them time itself was gathering moss!

Heightening her euphoria was the prospect of spending two glorious weeks beside the English Channel, peering misty-eyed out to sea from the balcony of their hotel room, with Bernard's arm around her waist, and in their ears the plaintive cries of gulls to be followed by nostalgia.

Here winter had no business with the British who were born to be umbrella people, blessed by being without severe ice and snow beneath their tires and heels. But it rained all the time as if weather had a duty to keep English people wet, while the wind blew strongly from the sea, to add salt to the wound.

Beside her as they strolled through all the historic places, Bernard was always the pious, passionate lover, dignified and tall as a telegraph pole in a dog collar. Never without his arm round her waist. Every moment was filled with the magic of his very loving presence. Away from his parish and its suffocating burdens of duty, he had suddenly become transformed and she freed from the yoke of lonesome widowhood. Free as the wind from the sea.

She was thankful for his being so tall, for in the crowded streets – even out of season alive with tourists and students – he could be picked out above their heads, like a human totem pole, when they got separated in the occasional crush. She was proud also of his dignified appearance aided by his British umbrella! And the captivating charm of his dark brown voice resonated with the islanders, while his inimitable, renowned enslaving smile could send the local ladies into ecstasy!

The odd-looking couple – the one so sartorially correct and the other so casually dressed in jeans and sporting a ponytail trailing from a silk square tied round her head – passed nearly unnoticed in Brighton. On the southern shore facing France across the English Channel, the tourist Mecca was the most continental and cosmopolitan town in Britain. The anonymity seemed to attach her more closely to the one person to whom she could truly relate – fittingly, her own husband.

Like overgrown schoolmates they got sticky with candyfloss and the famous equally sticky Brighton rock, and got ice cream dripping all over their shoes as they walked by the sea.

On the merry-go-rounds, out of season and not yet swinging, they sat laughing on the wooden horses put out to pasture until the opening of the tourist season. They cannoned into each other on the miniature electric racing car track opened early for business. Exhilarating were the ozone-tanged sparks flying out from under their feet as the toy two-seaters constantly bumped into one another and shunted clear to excited cries from their occupants.

They splayed their noses against the effervescing mouths of strange fishes blowing bubbles at them through the glass of the pier's fabulous aquarium. They joggled Siamesed in a rattling, crowded, doll-sized train of open carriages along the narrow-gauge railway that ran below the high chalk cliff.

They were deafened by all the screaming children. Sadly, that reminded her that David was not sharing their enjoyment.

Thus casually glimpsed by any passing gull taking a bird's-eye view of humanity, the joyful, uninhibited newly-weds could have seemed like any other pair of tiny tots worth pursuing for what they offered or left behind to litter the esplanade!

"Let's take a peep inside the onion palace," said Bernard enthusiastically a few days later to his bride, as a special treat.

She had heard from Giselle that the famous royal palace was the local nickname for the curious multi-domed multi-styled oriental white elephant of mad King George's eldest son, Prince Regent. He built the sprawling, low, cream stucco edifice to entertain and impress his mistress, Mrs. Fitzherbert – and at the same time be a monument to his own vain everlasting glory. His paramour's famous distinction apart from her connection with the prince: she made history (reminiscent of George Washington), as the first of her sex since the ancient Egyptians to have worn a full set of false teeth.

The Pavilion – the official name given to the onion palace – was but a gull's swoop from their bedroom window near the pier. On foot she found it was but a ten-minute stroll from the Steine's peninsula of public gardens with its beaming illuminated fountain playing music by night and shooting wet rainbows at the pigeons by day.

Very soon they were purchasing tickets at the onion palace entrance. Jennifer tittered when the ticket collector said, "You're from America, aren't you, I can tell by your accent," while Bernard replied with a straight face, "That's very perceptive of you!"

In the extravagantly ornate and sometimes bizarre interior of the fabulous royal love nest with its famous domes like bulbous mushrooms sprouting into the clouds, Jennifer suddenly burst out laughing. The view from the windows was of innumerable pigeons defecating over the pink paths and onto the tourists. She had seen several visitors looking up expressing something less than joy.

The American bride and groom had been especially entertained by the pictures of His Royal Highness (who had become His Majesty at last) grown fat as a hippopotamus and being hauled out of his bathtub by a block and tackle suspended from a beam in the royal bath chamber.

The human block and tackle was still hanging for the delectation of tourists, including Bernard and Jennifer.

After viewing the humorous pictures, they examined the staircase handrail of cleverly camouflaged to look like bamboo on their way down to the kitchen, which was almost as big as the sumptuous ballroom, while its walls had more copper in pots and pans clinging to them than to a frigate of Nelson's navy.

Eyeing the innumerable huge copper pans, Bernard commented dryly, "I daresay you'd need that many to satisfy an appetite like His Majesty's!"

They went up the fake bamboo staircase again and marveled at the painter who could imitate bamboo so perfectly and endlessly on cast iron.

A notice by the great draped four-poster in the king's bedchamber warned visitors not to touch anything. "No doubt the combined sprung weight of the hippopotamus king plus Mrs. Fitzherbert over a period of time had taken its toll!" Bernard commented dryly.

Of an evening after taking dinner in their hotel, the pair would stroll by the seashore listening to the murmurings of the tide, and in the daytime wander through the famous narrow cobbled Lanes, with their quaint little shops displaying antiques.

In one of the little latticed windows Jennifer spotted a silver sprinting greyhound pin just begging for Bernard to be pinning it to her breast!

The trader said it was made of antique silver. Jennifer's eyes were begging because it reminded her of David and of course Bernard succumbed to making her happy.

How David would have loved to run along the golden sands, splash into the tide, rub noses with the crabs!

The weather was so wonderfully mild and the ground bore no evidence of snow ever having fallen – like the cold corpse of winter having peacefully passed away in its sleep.

In Connecticut, she reflected, the snow ploughs could still be ploughing the streets – so unlike Shakespeare's GREEN AND SCEPTERED ISLE.

Yes, she would like to visit Anne Hathaway's genuine Tudor cottage in Stratford-on-Avon and see the stone hearth with its witch's iron hook which held the kettle which brewed the tea that might have inspired Macbeth and Hamlet if it hadn't been supplanted by lukewarm strong British ale. Bernard said they didn't drink tea in those days and that the sonnets weren't written for Anne Hathaway but for the handsome young Earl of Southampton – a man!

Besides, Stratford-on-Avon was nowhere near the sea – that all-important factor to them both. As far as they were concerned, Neptune, and not Hamlet or Romeo, was the moment's supreme romantic. To Jennifer her own husband, in bed, caressing and gentle yet imaginative and adventurous, sometimes even a Catherine wheel between the sheets, was the definitive Romeo.

Where they were was everywhere they needed to be. No change of venue would make them happier. They only had to step from their bed to their balcony to feel the sea god's wild hair in the wind and taste the salt from his trident.

He lisped to them more romantically on the incoming tide than Romeo and Juliet and all the sonnets put together!

Looking far out to sea to the fireball sun quenching in the eternal horizon and with the gray-white gulls like a swift cloud screeching, they felt fulfilled. If only the feeling could last forever! Hopefully it could. Hopefully it must.

But when they returned and the yoke of duty fell again on those broad square shoulders, would he ever be the same man again? Would she ever be able to confide in him as she desperately needed to do, when even her best friend Giselle, hedonistic irreligious woman of the world that she was, wouldn't even listen? He was a sailor in the wind but still a clergyman under the skin.

Yet she needed his cooperation and she was prepared to risk all, marriage included, to ask the favor of which she dared not yet even speak.

Yet speak she must and would when she had earned the right by becoming the rector's perfect wife.

Meanwhile, the day must patiently bide its time. It could come tomorrow or the next, or in a month or a year or a moment. But she felt that in some mysterious way, if she kept faith, God would give her a sign. Perhaps, who knows? – Again through the medium of David himself whom Bernard had grown to love?

She was thus engaged in introspection while sponging her beauteous cupola-shaped breasts in her bubble bath, when Bernard strode in all naked and with an erection. Warm vapor filled the narrow, black-tiled room, making the apparition surreal.

"Oh, Jennifer, you are beautiful," he whispered, as he knelt on the cork bath mat and began kissing and sucking her risen nipples through the soap bubbles.

And her mind at that instant was like the released spring of a fully wound clock, spinning her thoughts wildly into making an instant decision. He was caught when he was at his most vulnerable, as a drone to the queen bee! *Now was the time or never*, she thought.

But did the groom ensnared in her bridal suds only promise the moon?

Chapter Sixteen

Whilst Jennifer had been skillfully leading up to her controversial subject, neither realized they had forgotten to hang a sign from the doorknob of their bridal suite. Upon giving a most perfunctory knock a chambermaid laden with towels breezed in and immediately gasped at the sight of the naked Bernard seen through their open bathroom door!

After her hasty departure, the spell was broken and a most embarrassed, shy rector was not being his normal self when only too readily agreeing to almost everything being put to him under duress. Caught saying "Yes" to everything as a distraction from his predicament. But perhaps unwittingly he had said "Yes" to baptizing David and Jennifer would be holding him to his promise!

The honeymoon was over only too quickly. Suddenly much too soon for Jennifer's liking, the dream was over – she would have had it go on and on, and be a child of pleasure for ever and ever! The packed suitcases plus Bernard on his knees fixing the return flight labels made it only too plain that she had now to be thinking of herself in terms of a serious rector's wife. She would have duties to perform – a matter filled with uncertainties as to whether she could fulfill them all to her demanding husband's complete satisfaction? Then again, she had the formidable Mrs. Broomworthy to deal with, and Jennifer, who had always led a peaceful life, independent and firmly in charge, with her own live-in servant, became apprehensive concerning the built-in conflict.

She was so efficient, this Mrs. Broomworthy – much too efficient by far! She was capable of showing up her new mistress' own deficiencies through the former's lack of extensive domestic experience and knowledge, not only of rectory problems, but the whims and fancies and abhorrences of her fastidious rector. Moreover, she was a lady entrenched in her own power and her own self-righteousness. So how would she take to playing second fiddle? Another negative factor in her character seemed to suggest that she was no dog-lover! How then would she react to the invasion of her premises by two big dogs with one of them being a silent giant and the other having a giant bark? The thought was too frightful to contemplate.

"You're very quiet suddenly, my angel," said Bernard instinctively through a label held between his fine white teeth.

Jennifer did not answer – her mind was far away.

Bernard took the label out of his mouth and inquired, "Dreaming about that wonderful ketch, honey? She was a real beauty, wasn't she – fifty-five feet of nautical perfection – and there's no doubt about her being capable of going round the world single-handed, in spite of her size, because she's already done it! Sir Francis Chichester proved it beyond dispute at the age of sixty-five and with cancer to cope with! Can you believe it – what a man! So you see, my love," he added, grinning, "there's still a chance for us some day perhaps?"

Seeing her husband so boyishly enthusiastic about the beautiful black, custom-built, exceptionally light wooden sailboat, which they had both drooled over and coveted at Brighton's big marina the day before, Jennifer wondered if her husband had not missed his vocation, he had seemed so enthralled.

"Just imagine it, love," he said, still on his knees by their bulging suitcases and looking up into his bride's beautiful, bright cougar-eyes, "The Gypsy Moth actually did a somersault in the South Seas somewhere during a hurricane. Can you imagine it – turned right over and up t'other side, right as rain and none the worse for wear. And the old man took it all in his stride and sailed on to Australia! He went on to finish the course – that is, round the world single-handed at six-five and with cancer. Then he sailed up the Thames with all the tugboats hooting away like mad. And of course, the queen invited him to Buckingham Palace to tap him on the shoulder with her magic wand and turn him into a knight. Sir Francis Chichester now."

"Perhaps she'll knight you one day, Bernard."

"You mean tap me on the shoulder with her umbrella more likely."

"Stay kneeling," she laughed, coming over and tapping him on the shoulder with a stick of Brighton rock, "Rise, Sir Bernard Houndsditch and do up her bra for your loving wife!"

Chapter Seventeen

David Greyhound bounded up from the carpet with the acceleration of a soaring lark and became a second in flight, before landing in front of the double inner doors. With his cat's paws and badger-like claws, he prized them open.

From his waiting place in the dining room with its commanding view across the hallway tiles to the front door (a position which he took up and could not be made to leave, between walks), he had kept ears and eyes primed, keen as a tiger in ambush, for signs of the return of his beloved mistress.

At last he had heard those long-pined-for sounds and so had Robert sleeping on the doormat – the faint tapping sound of Bernard's diesel Mercedes. Mr. Harding had gone off to meet the newly-weds at the airport.

But moments before they had even pulled into the driveway, both dogs felt with uncanny awareness their longed-for approaching presence. Robert naturally was heard loud and clear this time with real meaning in his bark.

Maria, Mrs. Harding and Giselle dropped their teacups in the kitchen and flew excitedly out onto the now practically snowless driveway to greet Jennifer and her new husband. The two dogs led the chase in the bright sunlight.

As Bernard got out and began helping his sexton unload their suitcases, Giselle rushed forward to hug her best friend, while tall, angular Mrs. Harding was left struggling to hold back the two powerful dogs on leashes extended to their full length after the dogs had been recaptured by heavy Maria, who afterwards fled back to her kitchen to attend to luncheon!

"Welcome home Mrs. Houndsditch!" Giselle cried aloud. "How was it, Jen, did you like the room I booked for you facing the sea? How did it go? – The honeymoon, I mean – romantic and exciting, I bet. I can't wait to hear all the gory details. But it will have to be later – those poor dogs are just dying to get to you, especially David – Mrs. Harding says he never stopped whining and looking for you."

Suddenly David broke loose and almost knocked over Giselle to get to his mistress and lean heavily against her legs, while Bernard gave Giselle a telling honeymoon smile in passing. She could see that all had gone well between them. He lugged their two heavy suitcases to the house, leaving the light luggage for his tiny sexton.

Jennifer noticed Mrs. Harding trying to restrain Robert with two hands until Bernard, dropping his burden, gallantly came to her rescue. After rubbing his belly until he was silent he let him go to be petted by his mistress, rooted where she stood by David who refused to budge. Now that he had her again he was not going to let her out of his sight.

Meanwhile, Bernard inquired of his sexton's wife if the dogs had behaved themselves and she told him how both dogs had kept a constant watch by the door for their return and how David had whined pathetically.

Giselle, finding herself at a loose end, brushed dog hairs off her elegant pleated mauve skirt and kicked a few small stones with expensive mauve patent leather shoes, while her Tiffany pearls clicked ceaselessly. She watched the Reverend and Mrs. Harding eventually go into the house and then, as her best friend, dressed in a smart chalk-striped two piece slightly travel-creased costume was still heavily locked in with the dogs, waited for her moment of questioning.

It was a long while before they joined the others in the halogen-lit big drawing room after having left the two dogs with Maria. Bernard then drove the Hardings back to their house, leaving his wife and her best friend alone to discuss the honeymoon.

"On a scale of one to ten, what was he really like as a lover?" Giselle weighed up all her lovers on her Venus' metric scale and took great interest in the findings.

"Do I really have to answer that silly question?"

"Remember who found your romantic love nest and who paid for it – can't you give me my money's worth, you stingy old thing."

"Since you put it like that, I would say ten out of ten for me – I don't know how you would rate him yourself and I don't really care. I don't judge my husband in bed by the number of springs he breaks."

"If you give me the details I'll tell you."

"If you expect a blow-by-blow account of what went on you're barking up the wrong tree – he really was wonderful and I'm afraid you'll have to let it go at that – but your hotel room was out of this world – and the English channel – how romantic with the sun on it and gleaming in the moonlight."

"With the rain on it, you mean surely?"

"Oh yes, there was plenty of that too, but not all the time. It came and went and came back again pretty well every few hours. No wonder the Englishman Fox invented the umbrella. Whatever did they do to keep dry before that? But we got used to it and anyway Bernard always carried an umbrella as big as a tent. But the weather was so mild – not a drop of snow in sight. I even saw palms growing outside in a town nearby called Bournemouth when we went to a concert there. A gentleman staying in our hotel drove us there along the coast through the lovely New Forest where he pointed out a tree where King Rufus was killed by an arrow."

"I see you had your history lesson."

"Well, there was a lot of it about and some of it very comic – the Royal Pavilion, for instance."

"I bet that royal bed took a beating – did you see the gantry to haul the royal carcass out of his bath?"

"Yes indeed! It had Bernard and me in stitches."

"Poor Mrs. Fitzherbert, it must have squeezed the life out of her having that royal hippopotamus on top of her!"

Jennifer laughed heartily. She was surprised at how she seemed to have lost all her prudish inhibitions.

"So everything came up to your expectations?"

"Oh, yes Gizzy! Bernard's been absolutely wonderful – and so romantic! You'd never believe he was the same person."

"Not the stuffy old Reverend Houndsditch we used to know then?"

"A completely changed man on our honeymoon, Gizzy."

"Thank God!"

"No, I thank you, Gizzy – that hotel you found for us was terrific. The view from our bedroom window was breathtaking! And the sea breeze blowing in was heavenly! Gizzy, it was the kindest and loveliest wedding present. I shall never forget you for that – you really are a thoughtful, true friend. What made you think of it – memories I suppose? Did you and Peter Craven go there by any chance?"

Giselle burst out laughing. "So you cottoned on. You are right. Same room, same black bathroom tiles. By the way, how was the bed? Did it squeak?"

"Horribly."

"Thought so – same old bed. History repeating itself. And those terrible springs – just like Westminster chimes!"

"More like Big Ben with Bernard; he's a lot heavier and bigger than your Peter."

"You are right, but I didn't think he had it in him! But for your sake I'm glad I was wrong."

Both ladies burst out laughing together, as they recalled their separate experiences in the same bed.

Giselle paused meditatively and Jennifer imagined she knew she was reliving the scene with Peter Craven.

After the brief reflection, she came back with, "Did you visit Rudyard Kipling's house just outside Brighton – you know, darling one, Kipling the little bald Rule Britannia sort of guy who wrote *If* and *Barrack Room Ballads* and *Jungle Book*. Peter took me all those years ago."

"Yes, we did pay a visit as a matter of fact, it was a gloomy old Victorian house with a stone wall all round it."

"Probably to keep out the working class, he was a great snob you know. Any more interesting places you visited?"

"Only the bathroom."

"I should hope so, you were gone two weeks!"

"Very droll! Listen, Giselle, there's a funny story attached. I was in the bath all decently covered in suds but with the door open and saw it all."

"Saw what for heaven's sake? Don't lie."

"Well we obviously had forgotten to put the DO NOT DISTURB sign outside the lovely suite you booked for us and the girl with the towels came bursting in and caught poor Bernard in the buff. And you know how shy he is?"

"I do indeed. I find it hilarious."

"And guess what?"

"You are getting mysterious, enlighten me O wise one."

"Poor Bernard, he didn't know where to put himself, because the girl got an eyeful of you-know-what? Well, you can imagine the rest. You know I don't like crude terms."

"He was caught a little larger than life you mean?"

"Well larger than normal, at least at that unfortunate moment, because he was about to join me in the tub, you see," laughed Jennifer with a girlish giggle and a swish of her ponytail.

Chapter Eighteen

People started to arrive for the garden party on the spacious rectory lawn. The momentous occasion was to celebrate the marriage of the rector of All Souls Episcopal Church and to introduce his attractive wife to his parishioners.

The gossipy event had been well promulgated from the pulpit, and by furtive whispers in the pews, and in the parish magazine, plus the local press. The latter treated the affair as front page news, worthy of a picture of the newly-weds, flashed posing radiantly at the refreshment table piled with cakes and buns for the notables to nibble at and pass down to the begging dogs.

The dignitaries included the corpulent Mayor Favioli and doyens of the village administration, plus a glamorous, powerful soprano of generous proportions, enveloped by a costume of stars and stripes and hired to sing *God Bless America* under an awning, rain or shine.

The dogs had spent several weeks at the rectory adapting themselves to their new habitat. There they found themselves being constantly harassed by the formidable Mrs. Broomworthy who could scream louder than thunder and who would, if she could, sweep bearded collies and greyhounds right out of her life! But now they were members of the garden party and there was nothing she could do about it.

The dogs were having a wonderful time – cakes galore piled high on the tables well within reach of the paws of big dogs. And the smell of jaundiced grass turning green and fragrant after the snow was like a canine aperitif. Robert had just eaten some delicious grass, which tasted all the better for a dog having passed by within living memory, as he could tell by his exceptionally fine nose for such delights. But David knew that eventually Robert would be regurgitating the delicacy in the form of a sticky ball on the tiles, or on the precious carpet – setting the housekeeper's fiery temper alight.

However, the weather for the garden party was in answer to their prayers. At noon, it was spring masquerading as summer. The several rectory willows had given birth to their buds, proud of being the first trees to do so, while the barren dogwood trees not yet in their glorious bloom, enviously looked on and frowned at David and Robert, as if to say "dogwood trees are definitely not for dogs"!

But the air was exhilarating and the ground was earthy between the fresh green grass; while the sun was warming up its oven ready to melt the icing on the cakes and buns on the tables. White-coated lady volunteers were busy behind them, serving continually to the rain of coins dropping into the parish poor box.

Mistakenly perhaps, it occurred to Robert that they did not serve dogs, neither did they permit dogs to serve themselves as they did humans. Both dogs were greatly put out by the unfair discrimination. But nature steps in to redress such anomalies and equips dogs with special begging skills in the guise of their hypnotic eyes. Thus a good dog can achieve more by begging than a bad dog can by stealing. It is one of the furry facts of life. Unfortunately Robert, perhaps aiming for double indemnity, used eyes and mouth together to shatter the delicate ears of the ladies, eventually to his own bitter cost.

David, on the other hand, patiently waited and selected the legs of promising philanthropists sporting delicacies in their hands. They were the richly rewarding legs to lean against, and it didn't produce adverse reactions from the voluntary serving ladies in white. Whereas Robert soon discovered that barking was definitely the wrong way to proceed.

It was not long before, and in view of all, three wise crows on the blossomless boughs of a dogwood tree were sitting judgment upon the sins of Mrs. Broomworthy being visited upon innocent David, whom she had mistaken for the culprit Robert! However, she had wielded her broom wildly and had just chastised the cake on the table with the clawprint of the criminal visibly imbedded.

Undoubtedly Robert, classified by Westminster's "Mr. Dog of America" show as a "working dog" was therefore working class and a trifle short of refinement. He possessed too loud a voice to suit the delicate ears of elderly ladies at a rectory garden party and he lacked begging survival technique. What hope had he against the officers regulating the event comprising, among others, the diminutive sexton Mr. Harding in charge of the bar, Mr. Bellentoni the organist to accompany and charm the black soprano, and the dreaded Mrs. Broomworthy acting as judge and jury of canine crimes. Under her rigorous supervision the bearded collie was doomed.

He was soon reported by Mr. Harding, ever on the alert for suspicious or terrorist acts such as barking threateningly at timorous guests at the confectionery tables near his bar.

After the cake fiasco, while the ladies were still engaged in wiping cake off their clothes, Mrs. Broomworthy quickly stopped apologizing and made off to arrest the correct canine delinquent.

Jennifer, from her own table selling pious pamphlets and the Reverend Houndsditch's self-published book entitled *The Painless Path To Jesus*, witnessed the sad arrest of her poor misguided bearded collie, who was being hauled away in disgrace to be incarcerated in her kitchen.

Jennifer's eyes searched apprehensively for the absconding David and eventually found him safely shadowing her husband and being given the show-dog treatment synonymous with "class." He was obviously behaving himself before everyone from garbage man to mayor. He looked and was truly – every slender, lofty, delicately strutting inch of him – an aristocrat. And he behaved like one of long breeding – proud, slightly aloof but gracious. To a few who knew him better, he was also fascinatingly mysterious.

Jennifer was locked into her duty at her stall while visitors browsed and made her throat dry in vain promoting *The Painless Path To Jesus*. If only it had been a good mystery or a fine romance like *Gone With The Wind*, she would not have felt so useless and of little credit to her husband as a rector's wife. But she was stuck with her unpopular pamphlets and that literary treasure of her husband's, the alleged painless path that nobody could be made to pay to tread at six dollars a throw into the poor box. They compared miserably with the cold iced buns selling like hot cakes. So for Jennifer, stuck fruitlessly to duty at her station, time drifted into dreaming under the sun's capricious wandering in and out of wispy clouds.

Her glance fell upon the resident crows which had been sitting in judgment on the stark dogwood trees. They had dismissed their case against Mrs. Broomworthy, and were darkly flitting from bough to bough and possibly considering paying a flying visit to a refreshment stall. Should this be the concern of a rector's perfect wife?

Better keep an eye open, she thought. Why couldn't they be content like the smaller birds happily picking up crumbs from the lawn? If they swooped was it her duty to leave her stall and take over? Capable Mrs. B. was away acting as jailer to the bearded collie. Whose duty was it? Those clever crows were flitting cunningly from bough to bough, ever getting nearer those precious cakes and none of those silly white-coated ladies seemed to be noticing. Should she leave her stall unattended? But supposing the crows were innocent of any criminal intention. Would she be made to look a fool in front of all those people? But those unguarded vulnerable delicacies were the means of filling the poor box, not the stomachs of the crows. On the other hand, if the worst came to the worst, how many buns could those suspiciously lurking crows eat? Perhaps not worth the risk of leaving her stall?

Nothing must be allowed to go wrong during the trial run of her first day in office as a rector's perfect wife.

Most of the strollers passing her stall were her husband's parishioners and she was exceedingly conscious of the need to be appearing before them as their rector's perfectly supportive spouse.

But was she really being so, and seen to be, which was equally important? Her husband's book was not a best-seller. Sales of her husband's pamphlets were equally depressing. Could it be her fault? Were her sales techniques not sufficiently persuasive? Should she and not Mrs. Broomworthy have intervened in the fiasco involving Robert and the cake? But again, it would have meant leaving her post. Still, surely no one would have stained his conscience by stealing that questionable masterpiece, *The Painless Path To Jesus*? Too heavy-going – not painless at all! Bernard was so much better in the pulpit! So perhaps she could and should have deserted her post? Many disturbing questions to peck her conscience while keeping an eye on those crows.

Her mind drifted to her appearance – was she dressed for the part? Bernard had said so – but it was the parishioners who judged and gossiped. Was he afraid to say that she was too haute couture to be demure? Was she perhaps a trifle overwhelmingly stylish, like Giselle whom she could see flaunting her charms before the yacht club members at the bar, a long way off across almost an acre of lawn?

In her mind's eye Jennifer reverted fleetingly to Bernard in the pulpit, more eloquent than ever and down-to-earth because of their wonderful honeymoon bringing forth a new richness in his life, and making him realize that God was not all pain and misery and penance and remorse. God was happy to see His children happy and all His creatures, too – yes, even the crows. Perhaps they had a right to share in the buns, as well! Perhaps in mind if not in deed, she was overreacting like Mrs. B?

She recalled Bernard in the pulpit saying as much, mellifluously, in the dark brown voice of his. Saying how William Blake the English poet who left us "Little lamb who made thee – gave thee such a tender voice making all the vales rejoice" – said on his deathbed that he felt happy because it was just like "passing from one sunny room into another."

When Bernard had put that cameo into his sermon upon that particular Sunday, she had been sitting under his pulpit, wearing the same outfit as now – dark gray with a chalk stripe, little suspecting that so soon after, she would be wearing it on her honeymoon.

Perhaps she had failed him as a model rector's wife? Surely he must have counted on her enthusiasm to be able to sell his precious books and here they were still piled high enough to reach heaven itself if stood on end! But it proved to herself that to be so concerned about them she must really be in love with their author.

And as she dreamed on the sun was again baking the cakes and buns and the backs of the coveting crows. And away in the distance she could see Giselle having a whale of a time chatting up the yachtsmen at the bar. Dear wayward Giselle who had provided for her dream honeymoon by the sea on a distant shore remote from the cares of the world. How she liked chatting up those jolly yachtsmen! Life would be "dull without them! Jen darling, it would be about as exciting as trying to play polo riding on the back of a donkey!"

Suddenly she caught sight of the tall figure of her husband threading his way towards her through the strolling, browsing crowd visiting the stalls.

As she glanced at the obviously undiminished pile of unsaleable works, Jennifer felt uneasy about the comment he would be sure to make and wondered how she could reply delicately.

The moment came and she tried impossibly to match his greeting smile, which was indeed attempting the impossible. However hers lasted longer, because she was waiting for him to speak first. Meanwhile, David at his heels nearly knocked the table over in trying to reach his beloved mistress. He almost tipped her off her chair!

The flimsy table spilled the pile of his books onto the grass, whereupon a scared dog in getting away ravaged more than a few precious books with his great greyhound's claws!

Jennifer gasped but the author took the desecration of his masterwork stoically.

Getting onto his knees to pick them up and eyeing them sadly, he said, much to her astonishment and relief, "You know Jennifer, this may be a blessing in disguise and make them sell like hot cakes!"

"Why my darling?"

"Because they are probably the only books on record to have been actually autographed by a greyhound!"

So the catastrophe was glossed over and Jennifer was reaffirmed in her love for the husband who could take the matter so lightly.

With uncanny intuition, as if he felt sorry for his misdeed and wished to be at Bernard's side to console and make amends, David suddenly left Jennifer and leaped along after him as he wended his way back to the bar to joke with the jolly members of the yacht club.

Man and dog intercepted Giselle leaving her male yachtsman acquaintances with whom she had been flirting. She was on her way to be with Jennifer at her stall.

"Good timing, Giselle, I think she could do with a little help on her stall," said Bernard in passing.

"Okay, Bernard, I'll try my best with your best-seller," breezed a slinky Giselle, skipping to a halt in a fabulous seafaring outfit no yachtsman would be seen wearing. She bent down to pet David with fingers shackled to diamonds and neck clicking to parrels of Tiffany pearls.

"Well, I'll be off then, to boost your masterpiece. You're a sort of evangelist in print, aren't you Bernard?"

She looked up with a grin not easily decipherable through her bright cosmetics, while those costly pearls clicked constantly through her fingers.

"Same firm, but different department – mine is the genuine antiques, a difficult sell – evangelism is the easy bargain basement. I wish you luck," replied the grand mellifluous voice.

"I'll hurry then and try and launch a few sales. Send the barflies over will you, and I bet I'll hoist a few sales out of those naughty nautical lads!"

"I'm grateful to you and tell Jennifer I'm very proud to have her as my wife. She is making a great impression with the parishioners," said Bernard catching a whiff of Giselle's erogenous perfume.

"Okay, I will, and don't forget the lads. Tell them the new commodore's wife wants to see them urgently, and no messing about. It's a command. Bye, David, beautiful dog – bye Bernie!"

After she had precariously tottered away on her ridiculous heels for a sailor, the somberly dressed Rev. Houndsditch continued on his way. Approaching the bar, he heard them laughing and joking with glasses in their hands. Their contents were liquid gold destined to pour into church funds. For Bernard, it was one hundred per cent profit, because the bar had been stocked from Jennifer's colossal cocktail cabinet, plus reserves from her enviable wine cellar. The more they drank the more went into his empty pocket, so he was in no rush to send the hard-drinking yachtsmen over to his wife's stall for the bar to compete with *The Painless Path To Jesus*.

So, stopping short of the bar, he made a detour to circulate among his guests, making himself popular by showing off his wonder dog at other tables – intending to come back and have a drink with the jolly yachtsmen later. David, of course, favored the maneuver, being a strict teetotaler and more partial to foodstuffs! Against the legs of a possible donor he would lean heavily and beg with his eyes, as if communing with the person's soul, when he was really communing with his cake or sandwich!

"Oh how cute and so handsome!" he had heard said of himself so many times as he leaned against prospective philanthropists. They imagined the handsome hound was enthralled by mere physical contact with the human race.

Bernard proudly introduced his wonderful hound to the corpulent mayor who shared with him all manner of delicacies. The mayor being very short in stature, David found himself leaning against the mayoral big belly spilling over his trousers – like a soft pillow. Thereupon the lady with whom the mayor had been talking uttered the familiar sound, "Oh, how cute – so affectionate!"

"I think it's more like confectionery than affection!" commented Bernard dryly.

The lady who had paid the tribute was a lady of considerable girth herself and was able to conceal, for several minutes of congratulatory chatter, a minuscule dog carried under her armpit.

It was a tiny, fluffy, something or other, quite extraordinary, and it struck Bernard as resembling a pop-eyed hairy canine caterpillar, while it probably cost a king's ransom. David approached and sniffed cautiously as if undecided if it were vegetable, animal or mineral.

"That's a very beautiful puppy you have there, Mrs. Timmins, great courage I presume," said her rector, smiling graciously. "He doesn't seem to be afraid of taking on David," added Bernard tongue in cheek, as the fluffy canine caterpillar began to squeak ferociously at an aloof, indifferent, giant greyhound.

"Oh, she's got lots of spunk, my little Fee-Fee," said Mrs. Timmins proudly, "I think she doesn't realize she's so small. But some big dogs can get quite nasty, can't they Reverend? They are not all like your big David. He's so gentle – so like a fawn. Yet he must be very strong with all those rippling muscles – how much does he weigh?"

It was Bernard's turn to be proud.

"Now he weighs over ninety pounds. And he's still gaining weight because he eats like a horse. He'll eat all day if you let him. Not too good for him, I suppose. That's what happens after starving him at the racing kennels. And he guards his bones as if fighting for survival. You should know, Mrs. Timmins, that he weighed only forty-nine pounds when my wife rescued him with the help of that wonderful Greyhound Rescue Society in Florida. I'm sure there's a special place for them in heaven. Can you imagine such cruelty being perpetrated by so-called human beings? David had been caged up like a battery hen, hardly room enough to move, and there he was left to starve slowly to death with his muzzle strapped on tightly and with no food or water left in his cage! Absolutely unspeakable! After only two years, you see, their racing career is over and they are sacrificed to the worst Gomorrah of the dollar imaginable!

"He was only two years old when we stepped in and saved him. As I said, with the help of that humane society. And when we telephoned them they sped hundreds of miles to help us rescue David from his abominable kennels. There were other worthy rescue societies nearer, of course, but my wife was a friend of one of the officials."

"It pays to know people, doesn't it?" commented Mrs. Timmins. "That's how I got Fee-Fee. I knew someone at the pound and she picked me out something special. That's why we spoil her," said Mrs. Timmins struggling to extract a peppermint from her pocket with her free hand.

"So you understand why we spoil David also, Mrs. Timmins. Why we go out of our way to give him a happy life."

"Dreadful! Dreadful!" said Mrs. Timmins. "They should be shot, those wicked devils doing that to poor David. Still, we got to look on the bright side – keep smiling as they say."

"And while we look on the bright side and keep smiling, Mrs. Timmins, on the dark side, thirty thousand innocent greyhounds continue to get slaughtered every year."

"I didn't know there were as many as that," said Mrs. Timmins, popping a second peppermint into her mouth, "It must have been said on the TV after I switched it off. Those awful pictures were too gruesome to watch. It put me off my dinner – those pictures – too dreadful to watch!"

"That's part of the problem, isn't it, Mrs. Timmins? Too dreadful to talk about, too dreadful to watch and we switch off the television and it's out of our minds. So the cruelty goes unchecked and nothing gets done about it. Our wonderful politicians are too busy chasing votes—"

"You rescued David, Reverend – your conscience is clear – isn't that so Fee-Fee?"

Fee-Fee switched the question out of her mind.

"There you are, Mrs. Timmins, even Fee-Fee doesn't give a damn! One out of thirty thousand, Mrs. Timmins does not clear my conscience. But if you care to read about what does clear my conscience you'll find it in my book on sale here at my wife's stall. It deals with the problem of dogs like Fee-Fee and how we should treat them. The title is *The Painless Path To Jesus*. If you bring it to me, I will autograph it for you if you like."

"Reverend Houndsditch, I'm not a great reader myself, but I'll buy it for my husband. Oh, that reminds me, I must tell you, sir," said the garrulous lady, chewing incessantly, "George – that's my husband – reads the newspaper to Fee-Fee, he does – and would you believe it? Fee-Fee listens, actually listens to my husband reading out loud. But sometimes she gets too close to him and he says it's impossible to continue, because he says Fee-Fee suffers from halitosis."

Mrs. Timmins turned in deference to a VIP.

"But I don't think Fee-Fee's breath is all that bad, do you Mayor Favioli?"

The very corpulent mayor thus addressed eased himself sideways from David's heavy leaning body and to oblige the lady, sniffed gingerly close to the dog as it flicked out its tiny tongue. Mayor Favioli could find nothing wrong with the dog's breath and said that it smelt all right to him – perhaps in view of his reelection campaign coming up!

Mrs. Timmins looked happy with the stout man's confirmation.

"There you are, Reverend, that proves there's nothing wrong with Fee-Fee's breath, but my husband makes faces all the time. So I tried dissolving a couple of peppermints – extra power ones – the big ones to dissolve in Fee-Fee's milk. But still my husband complains and won't read to Fee-Fee any more – but perhaps your book about the pain and Jesus will make him think again."

"*The Painless Path To Jesus*, Mrs. Timmins," corrected the author.

"Sorry, Reverend 'painless' of course – just a slip of the tongue. Anyway to continue what I was saying, I like my George to have a good read. It keeps him in a good humor! You can't win sometimes, can you? Not with my George at least. Still," she wound up with a whale of a sigh as she wedged her dog more securely under her voluminous armpit, "you've got to look at the bright side – otherwise life wouldn't be worth living."

Mayor Favioli, having distanced himself from Fee-Fee's breath, agreed. With a quick glance at his watch and after excusing himself graciously and patting David on the head as if he were a child, he withdrew to mingle with those who could keep him in office and were now at the garden party, conveniently gathered for his purposes.

The exceptionally tall rector watched the exceptionally short, exceptionally broad-shouldered, most corpulent mayor, waddle away like a lame, overfed duck waddling off to quack with the inhabitants of its human pond. Meanwhile Bernard was struggling to keep a straight face. David, mesmerized by the sight of the sticky half-eaten napoleon still clutched in the mayor's chubby hand, saw him as a kind, generous philanthropist. Definitely one worth leaning against!

Afterwards, Bernard became conscious of the powerful greyhound's ribcage buttressing the clerical long legs. The lucky dog still had a bit of sticky napoleon in his mouth.

The babbling brook of Mrs. Timmins kept trickling on relentlessly. All her platitudes seemed to terminate in "Still, we have to look on the bright side."

Fee-Fee started squeaking in earnest again and spitting from a safe distance at David's peaceful fawn-like face.

Mrs. Timmins drew back in alarm with the spitting, squeaking, minuscule creature struggling to get out from under the rolling mills of fat that threatened to flatten its tiny body!

"Fee-Fee, that's not nice! You mustn't hurt the poor little big doggie – he's had a bad time – we've got to be nice to him after all he's been through. Come along, Fee-Fee, shake a paw and make friends. Let's look at the bright side, shall we?"

Bernard felt that if he heard any more about the bright side he would scream! He saw a way to escape. Suddenly, frowning intently at Fee-Fee, he assumed the pose of someone having observed a very embarrassing situation for her mistress.

"Excuse me interrupting you, Mrs. Timmins, but Fee-Fee has just wet her pants! What bad luck!"

An alarmed Mrs. Timmins felt Fee-Fee all over and said, with a puzzled look on her many-chinned face, "I can't feel anything – she seems as dry as a bone."

"Ah!" said Bernard with his beatific smile, "That's because she did a little trickle in that half-open purse of yours hooked on to your elbow! It's no joking matter – but, as you say, we should be looking at the bright side – could have been worse – could have poured into your shoe!"

Mrs. Timmins was too agitated to be listening and Bernard, with a sailor-like quick reaction, just caught her hand in time.

"Wouldn't be wise," said Bernard restraining the woman gently from putting her hand into her purse. He disarmed her with a smile again – the smile that could disarm any creature upon earth except Fee-Fee.

"Thank you, Reverend, for stopping me in time. I wasn't thinking straight. Wouldn't be wise like you say and you're dead right – we've got to look on the bright side – it could have been a lot worse like you said."

He towered over her, paternally counseling, with his ravishing smile still lingering, his hand still lingering on her free arm and David still lingering at his side.

"Go along now to my wife's stall and she'll help you – I don't know what else to suggest. What bad luck! What bad luck! But you will find comfort I'm sure reading my little book – there is only one title so you can't go wrong. I should hurry along if I were you. They tell me they are selling like hot cakes." And, chuckling to himself, he pointed out his wife's stall.

With mingled guilt and relief, he watched the poor woman's departure on her way to mystify Giselle and Jennifer with the baffling case of the phantom urination!

Chapter Nineteen

At last Jennifer had a customer actually asking to buy her husband's book and when Giselle arrived followed by the barflies she suddenly had many more. She felt gratified. Perhaps she wasn't such a bad salesperson, after all?

Bernard, now freed from the garrulous Mrs. Timmins, led David away. The giant greyhound with the strange glowing eyes followed him through the strolling crowd, to the sound of admiring voices, "Oh, Reverend isn't he cute! Such a handsome dog and so friendly and such lovely bright eyes, how old was he when you rescued him? Only two was he, did you say? Only a puppy then, still growing, is he? He'll probably end up bigger than a Great Dane. Give my regards to your lovely wife." After many such passing eulogies to slow down their progress, they finally made it back to the bar. The dapper, breezy little Admiral Jack had just arrived but was already firmly in command of his dozen or more bar crew of yacht club members returning with their copies of Bernard's book in their hands. They were quickly put down and exchanged for glasses of whiskey, beer or rum.

"Hi there, Reverend Houndsditch! That's a fine sea hound you've got there, what's the weather like in heaven?"

Bernard suddenly felt uncomfortable as though he was being placed in the stocks and verbal tomatoes and cabbages were going to be thrown at him! Instinctively the frustrated sailor under Bernard's collar took to Admiral Jack, who was intervening to get the men to stop teasing. Clearly the well-respected little rear admiral was the professional sailor among his fellow amateur sea folk. Yet Bernard wished he himself could stop bristling at the amiable, irreverent banter.

But he was dyed in the cloth and Admiral Jack was indifferent and overwhelming.

However, the former was thankful he could look down on them from his dignified imposing height, which forced them to have to look up to him, at least physically. He was indeed a fine figure of an athletic man and Admiral Jack was insignificant by comparison, except for his uniform with its galaxy of gold braid and eye-catching decorations glinting in the sunlight. But with his Olympian height and slim, square, athletic build, Bernard could dwarf them all with sheer innate dignity in the manner of Abraham Lincoln, who depended neither on uniform and medals nor handsome features.

As man and dog drew near, the three resident crows had moved over to an adjacent dogwood tree and were now like the power of darkness sitting in judgment upon the bawdy yachtsmen. The fluttering heralds eyed David with considerable concern and loudly to all and sundry gave warning of his approach.

"Shoot the buggers!" shouted one drunken voice, "one of them shitty birds just missed pissin' in my beer!"

"Serves you right Bill," said Admiral Jack, "for being wrong side of the wind! You don't piss to wind'ard if you don't want it back in your face!"

The jolly yachtsmen made grimaces at each other.

"Put a sock in it Bill, crow piss improves the flavor, you jerk!"

"Cut the crap, you men," warned the little admiral. "Shame on you in front of Reverend Houndsditch! Sorry, rector," said he, turning suddenly and latching fearlessly upon Bernard's eye.

David went over to lean against the seafarer's sharp blue serge trousers. "My apologies on behalf of all of us here for rudely stranding your good rector like a jellyfish." He then cast a sly wink at the men. "Especially when he's gone to all this trouble to provide us with these wonderful liquid necessities of life, even if we have to pay for them."

Bernard felt apprehensive about what might be coming next from the glib seafaring mouth for him to be stranded like a jellyfish and have to bear. He felt trapped; the badly needed bar trade he could not risk being scuttled by the yacht club! He had a rich wife but he guarded his independence, towards which sales from *The Painless Path To Jesus* could only be a drop in the ocean. He needed the bar trade at the various functions to supplement the tag sales and donations, which mainly went to charities. So he decided to hang on and be their guest; bracing himself for their stories and banter while trying to be as broad-minded as he could. He recalled the famous anecdote about the preacher Wellesley coming upon the sailor who was addressing his chickens in four-letter words, one of them beginning with the letter "f". "Excuse me, my good man, why don't you try saying Shoo! Shoo! Shoo! And they'll fuck off by themselves!"

The admiral turned to command his quarterdeck with the succinct, "Aye lads?" for them to jump to.

"Aye-aye! Admiral Jack, the Reverend did us proud!" they chorused, some of them slurring in their speech, with one among them slurring more than the rest. He came forward less than steadily and forced a glass of rum into Bernard's hand.

Bernard sportingly raised the glass on high.

"To the yacht club!"

"To the yacht club!" they echoed in return.

The admiral turned to face Bernard again to toast him with, "Up noggins lads! To the Reverend Houndsditch and his beautiful bride – and to David their magnificent rescued greyhound. Look at him, isn't he a fine specimen of sea hound? I don't need to repeat the unspeakable things that were done to him where he came from. Thank God, he's now among decent human beings, thanks to Reverend Houndsditch."

The toast quickly over, they could now get on with the main business in hand represented by their tankards, which seemed to require endless refilling! But it cheered Bernard tremendously, as the liquid gold poured fruitfully also into the poor box.

Miraculously they remained sober enough to tell and to share their salty seafaring anecdotes. Sober enough to tell them without losing their audience entirely to the bar or horizontally to the grass floor! Bernard listened apprehensively like a fish out of water while one of their jovial members staggered to his feet from his bar stool and slurred into speech. "When we're three sheets in the wind we're all abandoning ship by taxi, I promise you," he announced and immediately sank to the grass!

"I'm not surprised," commented Bernard in his loud, distinct, pulpit voice, "either that or by ambulance!"

"I like you, Bernard," said Admiral Jack, leaning suddenly dangerously over David's high back to clutch the rector's arm in a vice-like grip. "You're one of us under all that battleship-dressed-overall-for-President's-Day kind of manner! I like you Bernard, you've got a sense of humor like one of us. Relax and listen to old Barnacle Bill here. He can tell a good yarn."

"You think so, Admiral Jack? He seems a little incapacitated to me, don't you think?"

"I'm not incompatipated," objected Barnacle Bill, rising to his feet slowly in defiance of the laws of gravity! "Well," said the rising fat man in a navy blue blazer (like all the rest of them) and with more braid on his cap than gingerbread on a brig's bow, "Are you listening, lads?"

"Sure, take the bung out the barrel, Barnacle."

"Well," the fat man in the blazer continued. "My little Blossom – that's my wife's dog – well—" Barnacle Bill staggered and leaned on the bar table to collect his thoughts.

"Come on, Barnacle," commanded Admiral Jack severely, "Let go fore and aft, we haven't got all day. The good Reverend Houndsditch has got to get back to his flock. So what about Blossom? Did he do anything worth listening to or not?"

Barnacle Bill hazed into recollection. "Well…" (long pause), "Well…" (pause) "Well – let me take a sip first."

"Come on, man! Well what?"

"Well, little Blossom is always driving my cleaner woman crazy because Blossom keeps chewing off the old gal's coat buttons – makes her furious! I imagine Blossom thinks she's taking aspirins because she always tries to take a couple after meals! Well, well—"

"Well, what? Do you expect us to swallow that garbage?"

"Well – I don't remember any more. I think I need another drink, Admiral Jack, so you finish up for me, will you please."

And to a round of ironic, slow clapping, Barnacle staggered to the bar to refresh his memory.

"Yes, Admiral Jack, you tell us one," they all chorused.

"Okay, I'll oblige, but first I want you to know that we should be saluting the hero in our midst, a man who saved the life of this lovely creature leaning against my topsides.

"Take a good look at him. What a gentle creature! What power in his stern muscles – they could propel an aircraft carrier, yet he's as innocent and gentle as a lamb. And those eyes – glowing like phosphorous waves in the moonlight!"

"Give us a break, Admiral Jack – you're an admiral not Lord Byron!"

"Don't tell me, Jock, you're too drunk to see straight through bloody Scotch mist!" He turned to address his amateur quarterdeck.

"What kind of eyes has David, you men still capable of speech?"

"Glowing, Admiral Jack, glowing definitely, and brighter than any dog's eyes we've ever seen!"

"Fuckin' unnatural and mysterious, Admiral Jack," confirmed another.

"Mind your language, Jim, you jerk! Don't get too rawhide under the parson's nose!" chuckled yet another yachtsman of the shallow sea.

"In one word then, what are they, you thoroughbred brothers of the brine," said the admiral ingratiatingly and tongue in cheek. "Glowing or not? They look glowing like a phosphorous wave to me and I think Neptune would say 'Aye'!"

Bernard was listening intently and didn't understand why, but he felt greatly disturbed when there was a general loud chorus of "glowing" from these very down-to-earth men. He had always, for religious reasons, pooh-poohed his wife's claim that David was anything more than just an ordinary naturally handsome dog with bright eyes. Bernard was even more disturbed when a fairly sober young man mixing raffle tickets in his nautical cap suddenly exclaimed, "Holy cow! The admiral's right! I thought at first it must be the rum – but it's not – just look at that dog's eyes! Like Admiral Jack says it is just like phosphorous. I can't believe it's actually coming from a dog's eyes!" Bernard stared hard and was quite shocked to see that out of the shadow which enveloped him David's eyes seemed quite definitely to be getting suddenly brighter as if illuminated from within. No, he had not had too much to drink. He actually wished he had, so that he could explain the phenomenon away to the satisfaction of his religious conscience.

"Okay, lads. So we've seen a miracle," said an obviously inebriated voice in matter-of-fact tone. "Now let's listen to Hans Christian Admiral Jack tellin' us his fairy story."

"Holy cow! Jesus! Look lads, the sea hound's anchor light's gone out!" exclaimed someone as David turned his magnificent head away and out of sight of the men.

Admiral Jack had enjoyed some breathing space to refresh his throat and had taken full advantage of it. He put down his glass hurriedly when he saw he had their undivided attention again.

He stopped playing with David's velvety ears and leaned towards the bar to take up his drink, after putting it down for the sexton to refresh. Then quickly downing the hatch and assuming the oratory stance – hands in uniform pocket, medals jingling, blue eyes twinkling with perfect timing – the nautical yarn spinner was now ready to deliver to a hushed audience. David, for the moment, was forgotten – then suddenly remembered as he felt extra pressure against his legs.

"You're a teetotaler aren't you, shipmate? So I'm afraid you have to put up with someone else to lean against – how about your own master for a change?" He was astonished to see the graceful animal obey the suggestion immediately.

"Holy smoke! The dog understands American. How many other languages does he know?"

"Probably ancient Egyptian and a little Greek," said Bernard, tongue in cheek. "Greyhounds were mascots of the pharaohs, you know."

The admiral did not bother to puzzle this one out; his thirst had got the better of him and so it was time to refresh the awaited oratory.

"What about the story you promised us, Admiral?" said a red-faced man impatiently to his former commodore as he returned to his oratory stance near Bernard, while the dog returned to leaning against the sharp nautical trousers.

"A true sea dog, I see, can't bear to be parted from a shipmate. He's one hell of a dog, aye lads?"

"Aye aye Admiral Jack, but we're waiting for that story."

"Well, I can tell by all your faces that you are all dying to know what our little Horatio did – I called him Nelson for short – you know that British Admiral stuck in the sky in Trafalgar Square to act as a 'heads' for the pigeons!" He paused for dramatic effect, took another sip of Scotch by leaning over the dog's back for his glass parked on the table.

"Go on Jack, let's hear the rest before you get three sheets in the wind!"

"I never get three sheets in the wind, an admiral stops at two!"

"Rings the Lutine by the Turk's head, eh?"

"Don't show off to us, Jim – you know you've never sailed further than Long Island Sound on the ferry!" The whale of a big man, harpooned with humiliation, dived into silence.

"Well," said Admiral Jack, hands in pocket again and speaking to the tune of his medals as he moved, "Nelson struts in bold as brass and salutes my housekeeper's leg from abaft while she's with her stern turned head to wind by the sink, peeling potatoes. I saw her stockings oozing urine with my own eyes, but I daren't repeat what she let fly into little Nelson's ear. Not even in front of you bold thoroughbreds of the brine. And specially in front of our good rector here with his ears as pure as a virgin's you-know-where!"

Bernard winced but wisely held his tongue. He knew he was no match for Admiral Jack.

A bald Doubting Thomas, quarrelsome when inebriated, mockingly slow-clapped in applause and tottering onto his feet, slurred into speech, "Here it comes straight from the gallery newsreel!"

"Shut up Big John – park your ass – belt up!" and other picturesque words of advice from shipmates eventually allowed the admiral seaway.

He began with a broadside at the bald, tottering interrupter being held down onto his chair by several pairs of hands.

"I swear it's goddamn true I tell you, Big John – true as that nice new Danforth you fouled in our yacht basin!" the seasoned seaman slipped in pointedly.

"Well, to continue, Horatio being a very shallow draft type of dog, it nearly all siphoned into her shoes and she takes them off and her stockings as well right in front of my very eyeful, not caring a seagull's fart whose eyes they be. And she straightaway yanks the sopping things all dripping over the carpet up to my late wife in bed for a showdown!

"Horatio was Pam's own private pet, you see – mine is a German Shepherd as you know, but a plucky little Tom Thumb of a terrier was that dog of my wife's – a Jack Russell. We've got him buried in the Hartsdale Dog Cemetery, with a little flagpole of marble with an angel at the truck, plus those little stones like cat's litter sprinkled over the deck. Pam's last wishes carried out to the bo's'n's whistle! Not Westminster Abbey – we couldn't quite manage that."

The admiral paused for refreshment and one of the men snatched the bottle from the barman and ran round to fill the storyteller's glass. "Thank you. Ah! That's better! Let me see, where was I?" His words faded into a hiccup and he looked around.

"Westminster Abbey, Jack, like Lord Nelson?"

"No, not quite, but nevertheless all very shipshape and Bristol fashion – lying fore and aft between a Labrador and a Saluki, as sacred mooring buoys. And the whole caboodle cost me as much as berthing a corvette in a foreign port.

"Yep! But well worth it, if it gets him to wherever he's going, poor little thing!"

"Just a bloody nuisance when he was running around, but I sure do miss him now! I hope old Charon takes dogs on board his ferry – you never know with these Greek skippers!"

Taking refuge in the applause which followed the relating of this apparently true incident in his life, Admiral Jack fleetingly passed the back of his hand over his watering eyes and then, producing an immaculate white handkerchief as large as a flat, blew his nose into a gale.

While folding the material neatly and putting it back in his pocket, he said emotively, "Horatio was so like my dear Pam. Funny it may sound to you but it's true, every bit of that story is true. And Pam worshipped the little dog. Pity she couldn't take him to heaven with her – what harm could it do?"

He looked up at Bernard who was touched but remained silent, vouchsafing no more than a smile because he knew he could not bend the rules, as he interpreted them inflexibly, to comfort Admiral Jack.

"Perhaps you should have a chat with the Franciscans – they are particularly sympathetic towards animals and could answer your question better than I, Admiral Jack. I think you should consult them. They allow animals into their churches on the feast of St. Francis of Assisi on October the fourth for THE BLESSING OF THE ANIMALS. Your Pam could have had Horatio sprinkled with holy water by them and perhaps – I don't really know – why don't you find out from the Franciscans? It may well be of comfort to you to pay them a visit. I think their church in New York is called the Sacred Heart; you could look up their number in the telephone directory."

Upon this advice given to him by an ordained clergyman, Admiral Jack's face brightened and he leaned forward again over David's tall body to clutch Bernard's arm once more in a vice-like grip, no doubt acquired by pulling hard on warps at sea in his younger days.

"I like you, Bernard," he confided again, "you're like one of us – like one of our naval chaplains – you should be at sea, you'd make a fine chaplain. Thanks for the helpful advice – I'll have a chat with those kind Franciscans."

Bernard had not failed to glimpse the jolly yachtsmen straining their ears and looking serious and remaining silent throughout the conversation. The little admiral had obviously gone down well with them.

"Three cheers for Admiral Jack! A couple more for Reverend Houndsditch for rescuing our bright-eyed sea hound!"

And Bernard didn't care if it was just another excuse for putting liquid gold into the poor box.

Bernard couldn't help being greatly moved by the resounding cheers of the club members and the toast to his name in club barroom. Meanwhile David, with exceedingly uncanny intuition, leaned more heavily against the legs of Admiral Jack, as if showing solidarity and gratitude on behalf of innocent sacrificial greyhounds everywhere.

Bernard was elated and was left with a sudden nostalgia for those happy sailing days of his youth.

With the strolling crowd focusing upon the cheering, and no doubt curious as to its cause, Bernard looked across the vast lawn and saw the dignitaries on the platform standing behind the glamorous black soprano in her costume of stars and stripes already before the microphone, ready to shatter the approaching sundown with GOD BLESS AMERICA to the accompaniment of tiny Mr. Harding looking like a goblin sitting on a mushroom, as he dexterously twiddled on the keyboard of his portable harmonium.

Chapter Twenty

After the introduction to the parishioners at the garden party, Jennifer could rejoice in looking forward to becoming the rector's perfect wife that she had set her heart on becoming.

Bernard was delighted to see how responsibly and devotedly she took on her parochial commitments, such as visiting the sick in the hospital and at home and giving her own money to the poor. And so May and June passed, if not completely as idylls, then at least as homage to love and charity and compassion and the honoring of marriage vows under a rector's roof.

Also, importantly, Jennifer and the two dogs had served their apprenticeship in the difficult art of living peaceably with Mrs. Broomworthy. Each in their different ways had succeeded beyond even their own expectations. Jennifer had resisted throwing a brick at the housekeeper and the two dogs had peed rarely on her carpets and had learned that it was an unpardonable crime, even though she had not always let them out when first warned by their barking! Perhaps upon consecrated ground she had been expecting miracles!

It was time to celebrate. The weather was fine, too fine perhaps for comfort indoors. The air conditioners were blowing hurricanes and gusting the moths out of hiding in the curtains. It was a time for the happy family to blow their own cobwebs away by the seaside.

Bernard came rushing excitedly to his wife's side on the rectory doorstep. She was busy brushing her bearded collie into shape as a show dog and hair was flying everywhere. He did not have fur like short-coated dogs; it was strongly rooted to his skin with a strong tendency to become matted. It came out on the brush with a bark upon each stroke.

"Darling, put down that brush and listen. Do you remember our honeymoon by the seaside in Brighton?"

Jennifer stopped brushing and looked up at her suddenly rejuvenated husband in surprise.

"Bernard, what a funny question – do I remember indeed! I'll never forget how happy we were with the tide coming in whispers almost to our very feet, as we looked down from our bedroom with its funny bed. Do you often think back on it? No, of course you don't. You are too busy with your work. That comes before everything including your own wife! No, don't interrupt – you are not in the pulpit – hear me out for a change."

Bernard was stoned into silence by her vehemence. He had come all excited to suggest dropping everything and just taking off to the seaside with the two dogs! But she went on relentlessly, not giving him a chance to speak until she had had her say.

"Don't you remember that bed – how its horrid springs were acting like Westminster chimes? Every night it was and the hotel staff hovering in the corridors could have set their watches by them! You had such energy! Have you forgotten? Where's it all gone? Into your wonderful sermons I guess! Do you realize you have hardly touched me these last few weeks? A woman needs loving, you know, not just piling on charm when you need her for something else. It's not as if you were not good at you-know-what. It's a wonder they didn't put it on our hotel bill – for wear and tear on those dreadful springs! In England on our honeymoon you were simply wonderful – so exciting! Why can't you be like that now? You led me on to believe you would be – with all those pretty words and fantastic promises – so impossibly romantic – but heavenly to hear just the same."

Whereupon, without even looking at her husband who had turned quite pale, Jennifer resumed her show-dog grooming of long-haired, wispy Robert.

"You see," she continued, unheard words simply gobbled up by the dog protesting in his fortissimo canine solo.

"How can I hear you, sugarplum, through all that racket? Stop brushing and he'll be quiet."

"Want to bet?"

"Very droll! You are leading up to saying I'm not my brother's keeper, aren't you? Well, the Good Book says that I am."

"You are, dear heart – that's the good in you and I admire you for it – but aren't you my keeper also?"

Now the beautiful blue cougar-eyes swept up and beamed their unspoken reminder of a time that had been and could still be again.

Mrs. Broomworthy, eavesdropping, was expecting a showdown with her rector putting his rebellious wife firmly in her place; but she was disappointed. Instead, she suddenly heard laughter and spying on them from behind a screen in the hallway, she saw her tall employer drop to his knees to kiss his sitting wife's neck, then whisper into her ear.

Most mortifying to Mrs. B., she was made to prepare a picnic basket. No sooner was it ready, then off went the family in Bernard's big Mercedes to the seaside and out of range of the housekeeper's eagle eyes and beagle ears and broom of chastisement.

The rear window was let down on one side to allow giant David in the back seat a chance to drool into the exhilarating current of air, while Robert sat in state between master and mistress, looking forward through the windshield and loudly hailing every dog in sight.

The mutually agreed destination was a romantic little cove about thirty miles distant. There both dogs could be their true selves like their wolf ancestors – born free, not shackled to the whims of human society.

The dogs could run along the golden sand to their heart's content, while man and wife sat and watched the tide rolling in suds over the smooth whispering pebbles. The humans could be their own true selves also, released from an endless stream of conscionable commitments.

Indeed, there had not been an opportunity since their ecstatic honeymoon in England for Jennifer to look forward to such pleasure. She was longing to see David streaking along beside the waves and to share the experience with her new husband, and immortalize it in snapshots for their family album.

Eventually they left the highway and continued down winding rural lanes till they suddenly smelled the tangy sea breeze blowing off the incoming tide. Soon was heard the cries of gulls hovering somewhere out of sight. Both dogs were now panting with expectation and Robert was exceedingly anxious to get out and explore the landscape. David, leaning out of the back window, was whining his impatience.

"All out!" cried Bernard, applying the brake when they ran out of the lane onto the dunny foreshore. The Atlantic stretched in shimmering rolling blue fathomlessness out onto the blinding far horizon. A few wisps of altostratus drifted lazily across the hot blue sky, screening the screeching hunger of sea birds swooping in hope of feeding on the wing.

A fine large close-hauled sloop was slowly making way against impossible odds. It seemed to be just wallowing dangerously awash, bobbing up and down and making scant progress.

"That's the life for me!" declared the cleric passionately. "I should have been a sailor!"

"Why weren't you then, Bernard?"

Her husband had not a ready answer. He was reflecting wistfully. His dog collar gleamed in the sunlight like a restraining yoke. He put down the picnic basket with the dogs sniffing eagerly through its wicker lid. He still remained silent.

"Was it because of your parents, Bernard – didn't they let you go to sea?" persisted Jennifer, spreading a rug onto the sandy weed and pebbles.

"I really don't know, Jennifer, but it wasn't because of my parents. The sea and the ministry are two strong callings and I felt them both so keenly I couldn't make up my mind and I suppose I just drifted into the ministry."

"Did you have any regrets afterwards?"

Her husband hesitated. "I suppose at times I did – but then if I had chosen the sea I would have also had regrets perhaps. So you see I could not win. It was a Catch-22 situation."

The yacht went about and Bernard seemed fascinated with the commonplace maneuver. Jennifer watched him and wondered if he had spoken the whole truth – was there still a sailor in irons inside her wistful husband, struggling at times to break free?

"Where's that sausage I saw Mrs. Broomworthy hide in that hamper?" loudly barked the frustrated Scottish sheepdog, as he eyed David Grey-hound trying to prize the lid open with his long forepaw's badger-like claws.

"Wait your turn, you two boys," reprimanded Jennifer, lowering herself slowly onto the rug in her tight jeans. "We've got to feed your sailor father first."

"No, feed the dogs," said Bernard, focusing with his binoculars. "I want to see what that sloop's doing – oh, what a beautiful sheer she's got! – Just like a slice of melon. Here, take my binoculars and have a look-see. The focus is spot on for my eyes but you shouldn't need to adjust much."

Jennifer took the binoculars and as she viewed the undulating yacht, asked, "What's a sheer, Bernard? Is it the type of sail or what?"

"No, darling," laughed her husband, "It's her fore and aft lines when viewed across your vision. She's curved up slightly at both ends like a slice of melon on a plate. Some boats are straight and ugly or broken like a motor cruiser with wheelhouse – this one is beautiful. She has a flush deck – that is to say no top hamper, just low teak hatches and an aft cockpit. Very seaworthy. And romantic as the new moon on its back, which her sheer resembles. And look at that towering masthead rig – that's some spread of canvas! But it must be a devil for one man to handle. She needs a crew for safety. You remember Sir Francis Chichester's *Gypsy Moth* I showed you in Brighton Marina, remember?"

"Oh yes! I remember how you told me the whole story – how he made it single-handed round the world and with cancer into the bargain. What an achievement. No wonder he was knighted by the British queen. Yes, I remember everything. You got me excited too."

"Okay. How many masts did she have, do you remember?"

"Two."

"That's right. So what was she, a schooner or a ketch?"

"A ketch I think, you said."

"Why, sugarplum? You are doing fine so far, I'm impressed."

"Because the taller mast is in front of the mizzen."

Robert barked as if to say, "Congratulations, I couldn't do better myself!"

"I bet you can't tell me why that sloop out there may be in difficulty? She's wallowing like a turtle, isn't she?"

Jennifer screwed up her pretty face. "Because she hasn't got a crew, I suppose?"

"Partly so, but the main reason is that she must have a screw worked loose in her mast track and it means climbing up that Eiffel Tower of a tall mast to get the sail down any further! Just try to imagine it in a storm!"

"Oh, I see what you mean," said Jennifer showing some real interest now, and wrinkling her face to see clearly through the powerful lenses. "And I can see the man sitting beside that handle on the rudder."

"That's the tiller."

"What do you think he's going to do?"

"Pray, I suspect, or wet his pants."

"Don't you think we should do something about it – call the coast-guard station or something?"

"The station is less than half a mile away. I'm sure they are keeping an eye on him."

Robert barked as if to say, "And what about me!"

"Oh, you sailors with your fancy names! Topping lift, top hamper, you name it – what about a bit of lunch? Aren't you hungry? I know *you* are, both of you, aren't you my pets?"

Both dogs wagged their tails like windmills while Robert put several loud woofs into the wind, quite unable to comprehend the man who preferred viewing boats to sausages.

When finally tossed into the wind, there was a scramble with the screeching, swooping gulls beating the dogs without the loss of a single feather. The next time the delicacies were fed straight into the loser's teeth and all was forgiven.

Jennifer, now lying on the rug, was enjoying immensely playing hostess to her large luncheon party. She kept throwing bits of Mrs. B.'s sandwiches into the wind and then watching the gulls swoop to catch them before they hit the shore. The sound they made was bedlam! She kept throwing and felt like a young girl on an outing. For a couple of decades she had not felt so young at heart.

Bernard eventually put his binoculars in their leather case and deigned to join the youthful luncheon party. The sun still played upon the yoke of his stiff dog collar. His black, formal, clerical suit seemed so incongruous for picnicking with his wife dressed in jeans, plus her two dogs upon the beach, together with the gulls screaming madly round their ears. *Why in heaven's name*, she thought, *had he not changed into something more in keeping with the holiday spirit?*

But after he had eaten and taken his coat off, rolled up his trouser legs, and begun running to the scudding breakers with the two dogs chasing after him, Jennifer divined beneath the staid façade the adventurous, frustrated sailor.

David, finding himself completely free for the first time since his adoption by Jennifer, suddenly and without warning, put his head down and raced along the edge of the white horses till he was almost out of sight.

Jennifer, who had started off by being thrilled at his phenomenal acceleration, became alarmed as he turned into a tiny dot and threatened to disappear completely. A few sunbathers sprawled here and there along the beach, sat up and watched the spectacle. Bernard, in the meanwhile, kept shouting like a madman but in vain. Both he and Jennifer became hysterical and Bernard sprinted hopelessly in pursuit until he ran out of breath. Several young men joined in the chase, echoing the name they heard being shouted.

Suddenly the dot was increasing in size, indicating that the greyhound was returning. Bernard, now less hysterical, watched with the profoundest relief as the greyhound, easily dodging his several pursuers, slowed down to a sprightly canter and came to lean heavily against Jennifer's shoulder where she sat, legs outstretched. He was not even panting or showing any signs of physical exertion. Robert, by comparison, who had chased nothing faster than scuttling crabs, was breathing heavily.

Bernard and his wife became aware of a number of people clapping in the distance, but their applause was soon drowned by a resounding outburst from the bearded collie, seeing that all the attention was being diverted from himself.

"Phew!" aspirated the winded Bernard, "I thought he'd never stop till he reached Cape Cod! But at least he's proved to us that we have nothing to fear about his coming back. He's your dog, Jennifer – he'll always come back to you. But I'll go and fetch the leash if you like?"

While he was gone, both dogs suddenly spotted a small child at the breaker's edge busy emptying the sea with its gaudy little pail.

A very interesting performance, thought both dogs. We must investigate. So off they trotted together as Jennifer watched, not at all anxious, knowing they were both wonderful with children.

The foaming surf was about fifty yards distant and in between upon the golden sand littered with pebbles were scattered small rocks bearded with weed, the inviolable fortresses of a secretive army of assorted crabs.

One of these heavily armored low crusaders challenged the two trotting dogs in its path. They halted cautiously, never having seen a live gray plate with legs before, especially one brandishing great sugar tongs!

David, being the more courageous, gave the weird crusader a lightning tap on its all-enveloping shield. The humiliated crusader fought back ferociously but was not quick enough to make contact with its incredible swift long-legged tormentor, and went sparring and retreating hopelessly out of enemy range.

Boastful Robert looked on pretending to be absolutely unimpressed. He decided to take on the crusader himself and show David what a better dog could do! He approached the enemy boldly, seeing that it was a great deal smaller than himself. He put his nose down to the creature's level and sniffed cautiously. The crab emitted a most unfamiliar stink and to a Scottish sheepdog unfamiliar stinks should be approached gingerly. So he wisely drew back in order to give his slow mind sufficient time to plan the next move. He had to impress David yet preserve his own skin at the same time! The fierce great pincers nipping the air looked extremely dangerous.

He had seen David Greyhound with his delicate cat-like paws give the crab a swift light pat on the back. With his own massive sheepdog's paws, Robert was convinced he could do better in front of David who had withdrawn to a safe spectator-viewing point.

Approaching the enemy again, the intrepid bearded collie took a massive aim with paw well aloft. The impact slayed the crab and sent it writhing against the sand. But it recovered quickly and closed in with a counter-attack with its colossal pincer on clinching Robert's paw, whereupon the valiant crab held on whilst it was being whirled about like a pinwheel through the air.

The beardie screamed like a pig with its foot caught in a trap and it brought Jennifer, despite her arthritic hip, rushing to the scene, profoundly alarmed. By the time she arrived the crusader had retreated to its rocky castle, while the battle-scarred and battle-scared beardie was licking a bleeding paw, with David beside him sniffing the light wound sympathetically, licking it better.

Somewhere Jennifer had read that sea water was mildly antiseptic and so she hurried the wounded hero to the rolling surf and swilled his paw in it, drowning her own wristwatch and shoes at the same time. David looked on after testing the tide with a furtive, long, exploratory claw and then retreated upon discovering that the sea was actually wet! It was only too painfully remindful of those sadistic kennel men with their cruel punishing hosepipes.

"Come on, David! Why don't you take a paddle – look at brave Robert splashing around – see how he's enjoying himself? Look," she encouraged, while rolling up the bottoms of her jeans and removing her sopping shoes and socks – and forgetting that she was fifty-three years old!

She joined Robert and the child in the frolicsome splashing about in the foaming tongues of tide, which she scooped up in her shoes and flung in the air with careless abandon.

"Hey, you children!" shouted a barefooted clergyman in a dog collar, haring towards them in a manner that would have astonished his parishioners. "Wait for me!"

Chapter Twenty-one

Upon returning from that most exciting excursion to the seaside, David found himself beset with those annoying, still unsolved problems. For example, there were certain natural functions of the dog's body which he must discharge in a manner so as not to upset that most hysterical authority on dog behavior in the formidable shape of Mrs. Broomworthy.

With her arms akimbo, broom in hand and the voice of a foghorn, she could be a most challenging deterrent.

But what was he supposed to do when nature got the better of him and sometimes, depending on her mood, a bark warning of the emergency produced only a scream for them to be silent?

Danger, David reflected, fairly bristled from that broom of hers, which she wielded like a scourge of chastity to punish the foul and discourage the unclean upon her spotless domain? To whom could he turn for advice in these delicate matters? Certainly not to Robert who was not only color-blind, like all dogs, but dumb as well; though David had to admit that what that affectionate dog lacked in brainpower he more than made up for by the possession of the most vibrant vocal chords!

David slewed back his velvety tan and white rose ears till their tattooed numerals showed blue on delicate pink skin, and began to think profoundly for himself. He recalled having observed his kind, pretty, Jennifer rushing out of bed to the bathroom in the mornings and looking more relieved when she came out than when she went in. Could there be a connection somewhere which he had missed? He had investigated to see if there were a tree there, like the magic pine at Christmas. But in the bathroom he had found no beckoning fairly lights to guide dogs in need of a toilet tree. But he had noticed how the gray grass of carpet had been wet after she came out with a towel wrapped round her head! Obviously humans could dispense with a tree! Perhaps dogs could as well! It was worth a try!

There was something magical about the place which made all nature's wet calls as fragrant as flowers.

Unfortunately, the magic did not work for dogs. Such had been made clear when he had put it to the test! Mrs. B. confirmed the deduction beyond all reasonable doubt. And he had been given no marks for initiative.

Here in the rector's lair he was a learner all over again under the scrutiny of the foul weather eye of the lady with the bristly rod. But learning was an unnerving experience under guidance – more invective than instructive. The housekeeper had made it plain to the dogs at the very outset how they could only please her by their absence! She had an irritating way of speaking with a not overly pleasant expression on her heavy, ever-watchful face, conveying unequivocally that no matter what they did it was bound to be wrong.

Kind Uncle Bernard, Jennifer's new mating underdog leader, could occasionally be a problem also. He would become unapproachable at times, locking himself in his gloomy paneled private chamber, which smelled deceptively of trees and strangely scented beeswax – an outside kind of smell that prevailed indoors, contrary to dog expectations. The sole exception being the kitchen which could quite often smell delicious. What a mystery the human race was!

Even though Uncle Bernard wore a dog collar – which a dog would imagine should make him think more like a dog – he behaved like a normal human, which was a pity from a dog's point of view. He seemed most ungracious when Robert cheerfully hailed him outside that woody den of his smelling of beeswax and he would come out shouting with a pen in his hand. David had thought at the time that the angry man was going to stab Robert with it!

It was a scene which stuck in his mind, like a fish bone in his throat.

The dog-hating Mrs. Broomworthy was too often hovering around sniffing for trouble. What a miserable creature she was! Truly it was a dog's life under her watchful eye. If only she could think like a dog she would be a better human. When she got down on her knees, as if to be like him on all fours, David would come up wagging his tail, trusting that she had relented and come to her senses. But it would be only to find her threatening as always – this time with scrubbing brush in place of broom!

Suddenly one day, when he was innocently chewing a piece of meat she had obviously dropped on the floor for him and Robert, the tone of her voice as usual sounded most unpleasant. On another occasion he heard poor Robert in trouble.

"Is that bearded collie disturbing you again, sir? Leave him to me, Reverend, I'll deal with him!"

David, with his tail between his legs, had been cautiously observing. He could accurately recall sounds, but it was a pity he did not always know precisely what they meant. Yet he was smart enough to gather that his friend could be in very deep trouble indeed, when she chased him from the scene of the crime.

So a very close friendship between the two fellow sufferers consequently developed. It was, however, a mixed blessing when the dumb Robert, with a voice which few appreciated, got himself into hot water. To Mrs. Broomworthy they became a dual displeasure when fire engines went by and David had to show solidarity with Robert pointing his muzzle aloft like a wolf, and howling most convincingly. It was no longer a lone wolf calling but an earsplitting dog duet which sent Bernard into peals of laughter but Mrs. B., true to her nature, behaved less encouragingly.

If Jennifer was around he would squeeze her hand and they would laugh together.

For Robert was the loudest and deepest canine basso profundo in the quiet neighborhood, while David joining in with his muzzle also pointed at the ceiling, had a high top "C" which echoed from the pots and pans on the walls of Mrs. B's kitchen.

These were the hilarious shared moments of Houndsditch marital harmony. So the dogs looked forward to fire engines screaming by. They could then in the presence of understanding humans rejoice in flouting the tyranny of Mrs. Broomworthy with impunity.

Suddenly they would become saints. Their sins were forgiven and Bernard would say to his delighted wife, "Darling, come and listen – aren't they just the funniest, cutest pair of creatures you ever heard!"

Chapter Twenty-two

Whilst Jennifer was inside her husband's Episcopal Church arranging the flowers, she suddenly paused in her work, preparing herself for asking a favor. She began in her most seductive voice, with a flutter of eyelids imitative of Giselle who nearly always got what she wanted out of males.

Like soft butterflies, the fluttering lashes of her cougar-like brilliant eyes were caught in the dusty shaft of morning light filtering through the rich robes of one of the apostles stained in one of the heavenly windows.

She felt self-consciously uncharacteristic in borrowing a trick from Giselle. But she was about to demand the granting of a very exceptional favor from a man who trod the very righteous path, the very straight and narrow path, but who was, nevertheless, susceptible to seduction. For no human is infallible. Accordingly, she was dressed for the past in her best, with her beauteous bosom uplifted to the adoring husbandly glance in a very special brassiere chosen for her by her experienced best friend. It was all very genuine as well, for she needed no extra padding. But the brilliant designer had given it that suggestive faintly protruding facsimile of a nipple. As for the timing, she deemed it just right, with the honeymoon but days behind them and the marriage still as glorious as the strong sunlight through the stained glass windows.

How beautiful she looked, caught in that violet light, thought Bernard, armed with an armful of hymn books to place in the pews. He had no curate and did his own chores. At that moment of seduction, she could easily have got him to dump the books – books which he gladly would have dumped and gone to bed with her then and there.

She swished her platinum ponytail girlishly, and squeezed his arm as he drew near.

"Promise you won't laugh at me, Bernard, because I'm dead serious – I hope you'll understand – I desperately need a favor and you promised me, you remember? It was in the bathroom in our hotel during our honeymoon."

"Of course I won't laugh, dearest, what favor do you mean, I honestly don't recall. Refresh my memory – what do you want from me?" His irrepressible charismatic smile banished the doubt in her mind. Those wondrous teeth flashed so beguilingly!

She hesitated and the Reverend Bernard, dressed in dark suit and dog collar, put down in the foremost pew the hymn books he was carrying. He returned to put an arm affectionately round his wife who was ostensibly resuming her artistic floral arrangement in the boat-shaped vase on its pedestal near the lectern.

"Come dearest, surely you are not afraid to tell your own husband – what sort of favor? I don't recall making that promise."

"One which means a lot to me, sugar," she whispered, "A very great deal. Promise me again you won't laugh. It's not a big thing – it's easily done – it won't take up much of your valuable time – but it's most unusual and that's why I ask you not to laugh and say it's just too silly for you to do!"

"Oh nothing is too silly for me to do for you, my sweet angel – if it makes you happy, of course, I'll do it – what can it possibly be?"

Jennifer again hesitated. Her fingers bit nervously into his forearm.

The cadaverous face of the clergyman now expressed anxiety as well as extreme curiosity. His hand passed nervously from forearm to the high dome of his forehead, as he bent down and began to scratch its few, carefully sprinkled, pepper and salt hairs. Knowing his wife, he divined the signs of her being about to ask something questionable of him disguised as a laughing matter. He was not far wrong.

"Come along, my darling – out with it – let's hope it's not something to make the roof cave in as you say it – you know the church repair fund is a bit low!"

"You're laughing at me, Bernard – you promised not to."

"Now I'm listening seriously – all ears!" He cupped a hand to one ear facetiously.

"It's about David—" she whispered, leaning towards her husband, a chrysanthemum still between finger and thumb, and her engagement diamond blazing in the strong shafting sunlight with its dust particles dancing.

"What about David, dearest?"

"Let me finish – I want him – don't laugh – I want him baptized! He's now nearly three years old and I want him baptized soon. You are ordained and you can do it if you want to – surely it's not too much to do for your own loving wife? Now I'm not asking – I'm begging and demanding that you keep your promise!"

The Reverend Bernard Ignatius Houndsditch was for a moment speechless. What reply could he give which would not cause a rift between himself and the woman he dearly loved? What madness had possessed her to ask for such a favor she must know he could not possibly grant. He decided he would try a little levity to see if she could be brought to her senses.

"David's too big for our font, dearest – I don't think it was designed with full-grown greyhounds in mind. Probably you were thinking of Westminster Abbey in England when we were there on our honeymoon? I'm afraid our font is too small to be practical! But I'll put a good word in for you with the British bishop if you think it might do any good."

He was relieved to see how the levity turned the corners of her luscious mouth into a smile.

The butterflies fluttered again in the shaft of intense light. "I don't mean in our font, silly! I mean just baptized – anywhere – the river – a lake – like John the Baptist. Surely that's not too much to ask for? You could go at night and do it without anybody seeing!"

"For human beings yes, of course, I would – but for a dog it's impossible! Just think about it – people will imagine we have gone mad – we have our congregation to think of. If I were to be seen making fun of their religion, it could undermine not only their confidence in their rector whom they look up to for guidance, but it could even undermine their very faith. Surely, my sweetheart, you could not expect me to go that far?"

"No one need ever know – we could do it somewhere very private – somewhere miles away – even by the sea."

"My darling, it is out of the question – it's a sacrilege you are asking me to commit. You should be ashamed of even thinking of anything so preposterous! I have my own faith to think about too. Haven't you even considered that?"

"Is your faith so shaky then, Bernard, that it can't stand doing something against your own will to please your beloved wife?"

"Be reasonable, my love. You must know I would do anything to please you if at the same time it didn't displease Almighty God. I am supposed to be His rector, you know. I am expected to set an example. This is what I was ordained for – not for baptizing animals."

Jennifer stiffened, as if conjugal rigor mortis was setting in. The butterflies fluttered no more in the shaft piercing the high window, spotlighting a myriad minuscule particles of dancing dust. The Rev. Bernard felt the submerged cold iceberg of defiance drifting between them, threatening to break up their idyllic partnership.

The church's main door softly opened and closed a million miles away and clicking feet up the aisle echoed the hollowness which Bernard suddenly felt inside his whole being. A knee-rest dropped and it sounded like a cannon.

He whispered in Jennifer's ear, "We must continue this discussion when we are in private – I'm sure you understand it cannot be here. We must be seen to be a loving couple – so please help your loving husband by continuing to arrange the flowers as if nothing has occurred between us, sweetheart. I'm sure we can reach some compromise later in my study," he added as a parting shot.

Jennifer did not answer, but she continued to arrange the flowers while giving no clue as to her true feelings at that moment towards her dejected husband, beyond manifest defiance.

The beatific smile, as ever, rose to the occasion, but this time was put on painfully for the benefit of any witnessing worshipers.

Thereupon the Reverend Bernard Houndsditch, as stately as a cardinal, picked up his pile of hymnals and, inwardly like a hound with tail between his legs, made his way sadly and contemplatively to lick his wounds in the vestry.

Jennifer knew with a woman's intuition that by the mention of his word "compromise," she had won the first round of the fight. In the bedroom if she made herself particularly seductive she could win all the other rounds in the darkness punctuated by the comforting sound of her bearded collie snoring like a carpenter sawing wood.

For she was not like Salome's mother demanding the head of John the Baptist, only for a mere dipping in the Jordan!

Chapter Twenty-three

Robert Bearded Collie vociferously bid goodbye to his cousin David Greyhound, seen with his smiling head and long pink tongue, cooling in the breeze out of the window of Bernard's new Mercedes.

His rival in Jennifer's affections was off to goodness knows where, and Robert didn't really care all that much now that he had Jennifer all to himself. She was holding on to the shaggy dog's collar with her fingers nibbling into the inexhaustible knottiness of matted fur next to his skin. He was due for more brushing. She was trying to hold on while waving to her husband waving back to her, as he slipped away.

The engine's familiar diesel tapping noise dying away in her ears gave her a profound feeling of contentment, for he was at last going to keep his promise. In the first struggle to secure David's future in heaven it was mission accomplished. It was a pity, of course, her husband had refused the font, yet Jesus was happy enough to be baptized in the Jordan by his cousin John – so what was good enough for Jesus must be good enough for David!

Jennifer began singing her signature tune from her favorite hymn, *Fight the good fight* with its telling verses so applicable to her beloved David Greyhound: "Run the straight race through God's good grace."

Dressed in a ravishing negligée in bed the night before, she had won her fight to get David baptized in a woodland lake, and she would pray for God's good grace!

She had said to her husband, whilst her naked legs were still wrapped round his bony hips, "Oh Bernard, you were wonderful – we came absolutely together!" And then, while his beady eyes were as bright as the star on David's magic pine which Bernard had bought, she had timed that very special favor to be granted!

If by her unorthodox demands she had displeased the "Creator of all creatures great and small," she had done so only on behalf of one of them. So, she could throw herself upon His infinite mercy.

In this respect she was not reassured by another poignant, beautiful hymn, *And His mercies shall endure ever faithful ever sure.*

In the evening Bernard would return with her beloved David Greyhound properly baptized by an ordained minister. His chances now stood slightly better than before of following her into heaven to be reunited with her other two Davids – father and son. She had wanted to accompany her husband to witness the destined ceremony, but she had to concede something to him also. It was not easy for him, a man with his inflexible, narrow beliefs concerning right and wrong. But he had given his solemn word that David would receive the full treatment prescribed for a human being as the first step for entering the divine kingdom. Others still remained to be fulfilled. But he being a healthy dog, they were not running out of time to complete the other requirements.

Her impatience was now great for their return, as if she half expected to see some great change in the baptized animal. Meanwhile she went about the house and the garden singing, idly occupying the time by talking to the bearded collie, as if he understood and his barking meant more than just barking.

He would sit beside her on the garden seat, with his big head like a lion's cocked to one side between responses, which by far exceeded his listening!

"You see, Robert, your cousin, when he comes back will be truly blessed and well on his way to qualifying for joining me in heaven when the time comes. That is, if God grants me my prayers to raise him to the status of a human being. But that's only possible, you see, Robert, if one has first been baptized."

They were sitting on the garden seat, the shaggy beardie half on the seat and half on her lap and peering soulfully up at her through the straggling hair over his eyes. From time to time he raised his head to lick the lipstick and powder off her face, while she made no protest.

"Well, your uncle – I mean your father now – is taking care of this most important event in David's life for me at last, and I trust God will grant us the rest in the fullness of time. Uncle Bernard, your father, says anything and everything is possible if you have enough faith – even walking on water and moving mountains. Not only did your father say so, Robert, my pet, but Jesus said so too. As far as authority goes, you can't go higher than that.

"You believe I have enough faith, don't you my pet? Wag your tail or something – I only wish you could understand me like David does. I don't know how I managed all these lonely years with nobody I could really talk to like I can with your new cousin. I'm so glad you two get along so well – it's a pity about Mrs. Broomworthy. But I'm always there to protect you – am I not, my pet, when she oversteps the mark? Wag your tail or something to say you know you can always count on your Jenny to turn to."

Robert merely barked until Mrs. Broomworthy's face appeared behind the curtains of her spying post. Jennifer saw her and waved mischievously. The face disappeared and another replaced it, nearer at hand.

"Good morning, Mrs. Houndsditch. I expect you are getting used to your new name. I heard you talking to somebody and thought it must be the Reverend!"

Jennifer blushed scarlet and hoped against hope that the foxy little sexton had not heard her monologue. It could be most embarrassing if it leaked out among the parish gossips. Bernard would be furious. Fortunately, the little man had apparently heard nothing because when she took a chance and said she was rehearsing a speech for the parish meeting, he said in reply, "Well, I'll let you get on with it then, though I don't know how you can hear yourself speak through all that barking? I only heard one word when I came up a minute ago."

"What was that?" inquired an anxious Jennifer.

"'Faith' was the word I think I overheard."

"Do you think it's a good subject for the parish meeting?" asked Jennifer innocently.

The foxy little man's eyes twinkled as he hitched up his black cassock, jingling his great jailer's bunch of church keys hanging at his belt before replying, "I think 'Gossip' would be a more appropriate subject, Mrs. Houndsditch!"

Jennifer was startled by the innocuous reply on the face of it. Could there be an innuendo beneath? Was the man lying when he admitted to hearing only one word?

He smiled and said something as he took his leave, but Robert, wagging his tail and barking, jumped up high and slid off the man's cassock, taking the words shamelessly out of his mouth.

Chapter Twenty-four

"No you don't!" said Tony, the tubby young gardener, scaring David Greyhound away from the fountain with his long rake. "Get away from that fish pool, both of you!"

David had never before seen a cut-down thin tree with a set of upper teeth without a jaw or a head. It was a terrifying first experience, especially when it was being wielded as a weapon by a not too friendly seeming person. Robert, with far greater experience under his collar, took the matter in his stride. He merely removed his paw from the fountain wherein he had been teasing the fish. He stood well clear of the rake.

David got into top gear and was at the bottom of the garden within seconds! But there trouble still pursued him, as he hid behind Tony's sacred rose bush which had been cultivated to great proliferation with loving care.

Poor David Greyhound was immediately reminded of the sadistic men at his former racing establishment which was infamous for its cruelty towards animals. The unsuspecting Tony went after him with his hosepipe!

With minimal wetting of fur by Tony, the hosepipe was very effective and removing unwanted animals innocuously from rose beds, yet it struck terror in cowering David Greyhound. He went berserk, racing round the entire garden in a spectacular fashion.

Tony just stood in wonder, enjoying the entertainment. He had never been to a greyhound racing stadium in his life and now he had all its thrills brought home to him at his place of work. It was new and very exciting. He saw how easily people could become addicted, not sadistically but merely as an entertainment.

So, as soon as David had calmed down, Tony was at him again with the hosepipe, promoting further thrills for the gardener's own delectation.

Meanwhile, the curtains were stirring in the kitchen as Robert could see upon resuming his fishing expedition in the fountain, now that Tony's back was turned. But the stirring of curtains with Mrs. Broomworthy severely behind them was being carefully monitored by the cautious bearded collie.

He had never seen David race before and was quite astonished, though not thrilled, at the incredible speed of his slender, graceful companion. He felt a trifle sheepish, realizing how he had made a fool of himself that day in showing off his comparatively lackluster performance to a virtual canine hurricane.

Mrs. Broomworthy had seen the culprit's paws dip into forbidden water. The violation merited her broom of chastisement and she was soon upon the scene of the crime by an indirect route. Being a pragmatic lady, she hastened as inconspicuously as possible via the front door and out of sight, with the element of surprise in her favor. This allowed her to reach the minister's garden chalet undetected, behind which she waited until the shaggy collie's eyes were averted, mesmerized by the fish he was ticking with his paws. Then would she pounce before the culprit could abscond. At least that was the intention behind the maneuver which, unfortunately for her, like the best laid plans of mice and men, went badly awry.

She heeded not David Greyhound running around in circles. She knew her chances of catching him were slim. The spectacle did not even impress her. It left her cold and able to apply undistracted concentration upon the beardie with one felonious paw caught red-handed in the fountain.

Tony was a few yards away, now himself hiding behind the rose bush, and waiting to aim at David with the hosepipe as he flashed by.

For an exhilarating diversion, the young gardener lassoed the pipe round in the air exuberantly like a schoolboy enjoying a prank. Mrs. Broomworthy's cold cod-eye, meanwhile, was so fixed upon her grim single purpose that she noticed little but the view immediately proximate to the fish pool and the felonious paw inside.

Suddenly the throbbing second of the kill had come. The huntress took careful aim with her broom, then ran shockingly straight into the full deluge from the powerful hosepipe!

Chapter Twenty-five

Mrs. Broomworthy's beagle ears were pressed against the door panel of her master's den wherein that little fox, her mistress, had gone to ground. She could just catch some of the words raised in anger, though not many of Jennifer's because her voice was naturally gentle. Gratifyingly, the housekeeper had also caught the sound of her mistress sobbing. The Rev. Houndsditch's resonant voice sounded harsh, by which the housekeeper gathered, with undeniable satisfaction, the drift of a matrimonial tiff. *Indeed it was high time*, she thought, *that the rector put his foot down and turned the rectory back into a place more to Mrs. Broomworthy's liking*. She resented the fact she was no longer in supreme command, and although her new mistress left her generally with a free hand, the long-serving housekeeper's imperious nature could brook no interference.

She tried hard to bridge the gaps in the conversation created by her repeatedly having to creep away from the door in case it was about to be opened. However, one thing was clear to her – that Jennifer had asked the rector's permission for a greyhound to be admitted into his church – How preposterous! For what reason she was unable to guess, not having eavesdropped upon the whole conversation.

Of course he had to put his foot down firmly – how could the silly wife have even dreamed of asking such a thing! As a pious churchgoer herself, she considered the request for a dog to be allowed on hallowed ground a sacrilege.

If she had heard Jennifer completely the housekeeper might have had a stroke! Jennifer had been subtly paving the way to having her husband conduct a funeral service for her beloved David in his Episcopal Church when it was time for the Lord to call him hopefully many, many happy years ahead.

But she had not, of course, asked him outright, because she was astute enough to realize that such a disclosure could defeat its own end. She was merely sounding the ground on the principle of "Softly softly catchee monkey!" Pretend she had heard of such a case where a mistress had died and her beloved dog's ashes had been placed inside her coffin. Did he not think it was a very touching little story? Say that she thought it was a beautiful and compassionate concession on the part of the minister involved. It would test her husband's reaction before committing herself further!

She merely wanted to have peace of mind knowing that David's future, temporal and eternal, would be befittingly taken care of. No use leaving it to the last moment and then finding it was too late to make the necessary arrangements!

Bernard, recalling the baptism, became suspicious and reacted angrily.

"I don't know what devilish conspiracy you are leading up to, Jennifer, but I'll be no party to it. An animal is an animal and not a human being with a soul – nothing will alter that in the eyes of Almighty God, and I, as His humble and faithful minister cannot allow this sacrilegious conversation to continue. Put all such thoughts, whatever they may be, out of your head, Jennifer, and pray tonight for forgiveness and I will pray for you also. I am terribly, terribly shocked to hear this kind of thing from my own beloved wife. I thought I knew her better."

This is when Jennifer subtly introduced her trump card. "That's because an animal isn't human, isn't it? Only a human being can be on hallowed ground without profaning it?"

"Precisely. So you know, don't you, in your heart of hearts that all this is very wrong – very sinful? God made the laws, I didn't."

"But supposing – just supposing God said it was okay?"

"But He wouldn't, Jennifer, trust me – He just wouldn't."

"How do you know, Bernard – have you actually asked Him specifically?"

"I don't need to. He makes everything clear enough in the scriptures."

It was at this crucial juncture that the Reverend Bernard Ignatius Houndsditch lost patience with his obsessive wife and the housekeeper heard him say, "This stupid discussion has gone on far enough! No animal has any right to be on hallowed ground and that's final! If you have any plans for David – put them out of your head – I won't be drawn into it – there's a perfectly good animal cemetery at Elmsford – that's where he should be buried when the time comes. But why ruin a perfect summer's day thinking about it now? I'm sure David will live at least another ten years. Sufficient unto the day is the evil thereof – it's in your Bible."

But the housekeeper did not hear the concluding speech, because, when she heard the irate "That's final!" she hastened to be seen dusting the picture frames.

The door remained closed and Mrs. Broomworthy returned with her beagle ears to her pots and pans. But she had heard her master say, "And while we are on the subject of burial grounds, Jennifer, I don't like you to be seen talking to the rector of St. Andrew's – it doesn't do our image any good. I know the reason why you transferred your worship to his church before we were married – to prevent gossip. That was very thoughtful of you and I appreciate it – but there is no reason to be seen talking to him anymore, is there?"

"Why not Bernard? You are not jealous, are you? I only meet him once in a while when I visit the family grave to renew the flowers."

"No, of course I'm not jealous. It's more serious than that – It has come to my notice that he's been accused of embezzlement of church funds – he'll have to stand trial and then it will be in all the papers and no doubt on television as well."

"I can't believe it! He seems such a mild, harmless, innocent little man!"

"So do they all till they are found out."

"Where did you get your information? It could be malicious gossip."

"I don't listen to gossip, Jennifer – my information comes from reliable sources, but I am afraid I can't disclose them, even to my wife. A minister has responsibilities – like the Catholic confessional. I'm sure you understand."

"But he hasn't been proven guilty and supposing he is proven innocent? I feel sure there must be some explanation other than embezzlement. I just can't believe he could do such a thing."

"I hope for his sake the jury will think the same way, but until then I must insist that you give him a wide berth if you care anything about your husband's future, as I am sure you do."

Robert suddenly appeared behind Mrs. Broomworthy and loudly vented his feelings against her presence there. The housekeeper ran for her life, but her employer was just in time to catch the flying tails of her starched apron receding round the corner, and it set him uneasily wondering how much that indispensable, formidable lady had heard.

Chapter Twenty-six

Jennifer, profiting from experience gained in her previous marriage, did not allow her disappointment and lovers' quarrel to linger on to develop into a cold war of attrition.

She knew her husband had only been acting under the influence of his unshakable belief in the righteousness and unimpugnable canons of his chosen vocation. So, despite her failure to wheedle what she wanted out of the unyielding, conventional cleric, she could still find cause to celebrate. For she had convinced herself that she detected God's helping hand working mysteriously behind the scenes.

Bernard had slammed one door in her face but God, to whom she prayed most fervently, had come to her rescue and opened another. She recalled a religious teacher saying to her that God answered your prayers, not by performing spectacular miracles, but by influencing the course of events in our favor so naturally that only the believer can see the supernatural behind the commonplace. Like in W W Jacob's story *The Monkey's Paw*.

Ironically, God had made Bernard himself, as the Almighty's earthly ambassador, unwittingly open this other door. By revealing to her that a minister was in trouble and needed help. She realized how she could become his Good Samaritan and afterwards he in return could become hers!

She would not compromise him in any way – he would be about to keep the whole affair secret. How could it be possible?

Suddenly she saw cloudily in her mind's eye, as if into a crystal ball. But she knew she was not gifted with clairvoyance. So, she reasoned, not entirely illogically, it had to be mysterious forces working behind the visionary process heralding the rector of St. Andrew's as being that very person she needed for her seemingly impossible cause. God at last was communicating! Her Reverend husband was always reminding her of the "power of prayer"!

Her cause could not be sacrilegious, as Bernard and others maintained. In fact, she had just received the go-ahead – the divine signal to reassure her that God was on her side even if man was not! Was He not all-merciful, all-understanding, all love and the Good Shepherd? His "mercies shall endure ever faithful ever sure."

David, as if the beautiful hymn had been composed with a greyhound in mind, had won "the straight race through God's good grace"!

How then could the Good Shepherd deny her David the right to follow his mistress into paradise?

What could be sacrilegious about a dog, one of God's own created creatures, entering a man-made church or tomb? After all, the Franciscans allowed animals into their churches – on October fourth, the Feast of St. Francis of Assisi. They even blessed them at the altar rail – sprinkled them with holy water. Was that tantamount to baptism? Bernard himself admitted as much. Therefore animals were baptizable, were they not? They only needed a soul (if they possessed not one already), in addition to qualify and be able to follow their masters and mistresses into heaven, as they well deserved. What a pity she was unable to argue the case with her own husband, and even her best friend Giselle, without whistling up a storm!

However, God was on her side. Of this she felt convinced because He had put into her mind the master plan in answer to her prayers! No doubt when the time was right some very natural sequence of events would give her the opportunity of testing the divine plan upon the rector of St. Andrew's! It would also provide for his own salvation into the bargain – God's fitting reward for a Good Samaritan!

What had sprung into her mind so spontaneously was programmed to overcome those man-made obstacles; because it was a divine plan and therefore perfect! Faith could move mountains and by comparison her own behest was but an anthill.

Bernard was recalled saying (during their honeymoon), how he had been sent by God in her hour of need to walk her dogs, in view of her arthritis. Similarly, Jennifer reasoned, she had been chosen to rescue the rector of St. Andrew's from a terrible miscarriage of justice and her reward would be that she should find him sympathetic to her cause when she needed him. Her old teacher was right. God worked very naturally, though in mysterious ways His wonders to perform. He simply put the solution into her naïve mind! How otherwise could she think all this out by herself so quickly? And the rest of the plan came spontaneously from start to finish – a kind of automatic writing, such as she had read about; but instead of being of the hand, in her own case, it was of the mind!

The poet William Butler Yeats had said his hand had often moved in this way, automatically, when he wrote his poems. *No wonder*, she thought, *Yeats, with God inspiring him was such a great poet and won the Nobel Prize*!

She had a vision of her beloved David lying peacefully in his casket, beautifully laid out by the parlor – just like her late son had been after the fatal car accident. He had suffered terrible disfigurement, yet the wonderful parlor somehow had sewn him together again and he had looked even better in death, if it really could have been possible, than in his sleep! Her Reverend son had been so handsome! Just like David who had taken his place in her heart, in her life, in her hopes for reunion in afterlife. Therein would be for her unending joy – united with her son and David plus her two husbands when the time inevitably came for them to be called. Whereupon, trustingly, when everybody in heaven saw how David sadly missed Robert, the grieving departed animal lovers among them might fold their wings, plus the glorious angels put down their harps or whatever, and all kneel down and pray together to have Robert also join them but with a quieter voice so as not to disturb the angels! Meanwhile, she had much praying and good works to do. She must earn the right to that very special favor, not take God selfishly for granted.

First things first! She had yet to deal with Reverend Golightly. The opportunity soon presented itself one morning when Bernard had mellowed into his usual good humor, aided and abetted by considerable rewards (ecstatic behavior in the bed chamber)!

They were on terms of endearment again and Jennifer was brushing Robert on the doorstep as usual when Bernard came striding over on his long legs from his church and stepped over the dog to retrieve his car keys from the hall table.

"Sweetheart, I won't be in for dinner tonight, I'm taking my organist with me to New York to a repair shop he knows of there for a spare part for our Sunday thunder. We'll probably be back around nine thirty, because I shall be taking him to dinner at a diner somewhere. So don't wait for me and you can give my meal to the dogs."

Then he lifted up her ponytail, as he often did, and, after tenderly kissing her neck, hopped over the dog again and hurriedly joined Mr. Bellentoni waiting by the garage door.

As she watched the car drive away she realized that here at last was the golden opportunity she had been waiting for!

Shortly after, she found the housekeeper in the garden hanging out clothes on the washing line strung between two cypress trees regularly kept irrigated by the dogs! Thus the housekeeper was a little concerned at hearing of Jennifer's suggestion for her pets!

"I'm going to tea with a friend, Mrs. B. I am just checking if you are aware my husband will not be in for dinner. You are quite welcome to take yours in the dining room with me. I could do with the company. Never mind the dogs. Leave them in the garden and they'll fend for themselves! I'll be back in time to feed them."

"No thanks, Mrs. Houndsditch, I'll take mine in the kitchen as usual if you don't mind. As for the dogs," added an unyielding Mrs. B., busy pegging her rector's underpants onto the line, "What about if they knock over my prop? Can't you take them with you?"

"I am going to tea with Mrs. Carboni, Mrs. Broomworthy – you know, the lady with the ferocious black Doberman called Satan. So I can't risk taking our poor dogs."

The heavily built housekeeper listened to her mistress with the expression on her cynical face of a regimental sergeant major being regaled with the watertight excuse of a raw recruit. She could only see difficulties in whatever Jennifer mentioned.

"What about the washing on the line? What am I supposed to do if they knock down the prop? I've only just hung everything out because I thought you would be keeping an eye on those two mischievous dogs. Nobody told me you would be leaving."

"I'm sure they won't knock down your prop, Mrs. B., but if they do I'll take full responsibility."

"And what about the rector's shirts? There won't be time to wash and dry them again for tomorrow's service. You know how the Reverend likes his shirts spotless. Cleanliness is next to godliness, isn't it, Mrs. Houndsditch?"

"Let's try to be a little less pessimistic, Mrs. Broomworthy. It's a nice sunny day, isn't it? I'm sure everything will turn out all right. We have to have faith in God's watchful eye. I'm sure His is even better than mine.

I am sure God wouldn't let anything happen to His minister's shirts and underpants. He wouldn't expect him to have to climb naked into the pulpit," she added tongue in cheek.

"And I'm sure God has more important things on His mind than minding shirts and underpants!" scoffed the difficult housekeeper, with a clothes peg trembling in her mouth.

"I'm sure you're right, Mrs. B., but let's look at matters a little more positively, can't we? I'm sure everything will be all right. Trust me. I dare say you could do with some time off," suggested Jennifer, anxious to get away. "You must have things to do – letter writing or whatever? You needn't bother to cook for me. I'll eat out."

"I suppose for once I'll have time to do my own room," conceded the housekeeper.

Relieved, Jennifer said, "Fine Mrs. B., have a good day," and quickly withdrew.

She thereupon hummed her way up to her bedroom to paint away a few more years from her most carefully preserved face, in readiness for her visit to St. Andrew's Episcopal Church.

Should she call at the church and try and find the sexton or call directly at the rectory? Should she telephone first? Not from within range of the housekeeper's beagle ears! No, better from an outside telephone. She would also telephone Gizzy to cover for her and have Bernard's favorite home-made cake ready to return with, in order to establish an air of credibility.

But supposing Mrs. Carboni was not at home? She might well return and call Bernard's rectory while Jennifer was upon her covert mission. That would be disastrous! Jennifer could imagine the longtime house-keeper gleefully reporting the matter to her master!

The divine plan stopped short of a few minor details left for her to think out for herself! But she remembered her husband saying how God only helped those who helped themselves. Therefore the rest was left to her.

She must think of everything possible which could go wrong before sticking out her own neck. On no account must her husband discover that she had disobeyed him and visited the disgraced rector of St. Andrew's.

Jennifer, still humming to herself, at last drove off in her own little car and stopped at a telephone booth along the way. After a reassuring chat with Giselle, she enlisted the help of the operator to get through to St. Andrew's rectory.

The rector's wife who answered the telephone seemed very suspicious of the woman seeking an audience with her husband! However, Jennifer was able to satisfy the suspicious wife that the caller was not one of the many infatuated women offering their services ostensibly for flower arranging!

She decided she would take a chance and call at the church to avoid meeting with that suspicious off-putting wife.

St. Andrew's church was situated ten miles away and just over the Connecticut state border. It was therefore within the boundary of New York. *So much the better gossip-wise*, she thought.

The sun shone brightly when she arrived and packed her little car near the stone main entrance steps strewn with petals spilled from a coffin carried up earlier that morning.

The air was vibrating to the sounds of an organist practicing special hymns chosen by the mourners for the next funeral. The atmosphere seemed conducive to her solemn purpose. She felt her pulse quicken as she took the plunge and entered through the heavy creaking door. The organ playing rendered everything profoundly sacrosanct, even more awe-inspiring than she had ever noticed before. Its slender pillars were graceful, its clerestory high and exquisitely vaulted, its altar screen magnificently carved, its aisle impressively long, its windows a glorious Biblical translucency of pageantry. Its timbered roof, beautifully constructed, amplified the throbbing organ, as if to add more power to uplift the worshipers and exorcise the deathwatch beetles desecrating the rafters.

A few kneeling worshipers glanced back as Jennifer began to skip forward to intercept the sexton ghosting in black from one unseen door to another, where she presumed the vestry must lie. She caught up with him at the altar steps and signaled her intention to speak with him.

He smiled immediately, put down his pile of hymn books and waited for her to approach. He was a tall, distinguished looking, youngish man – most unlike her husband's own foxy little sexton.

She found him to be most gracious, ushering her into the vestry and sitting her down on its bench seat among the choirboys' hanging Babylon of surplices, plus the rector's own, distinguishable by its ornate chasuble.

On the way she had caught a glimpse of the invisible organist suddenly revealed and putting Jennifer in mind of a lanky, bespectacled cricket, suspended aloft and making sound with his long thin legs as well as his fingers.

The sexton quickly brought back his rector who must have been very near at hand. The latter was also very gracious and certainly belied her husband's image of him as a criminal. She instantly formed the impression that there must have been a grave miscarriage of justice – as in the famous case of the French Captain Dreyfus, later vindicated by Emile Zola and proven to be innocent, and retrieved with a pardon from prison on Devil's Island. So her cause was a worthy one in the light of the vindication to be offered – comparable, she considered, with that of the French author of *Nana*!

"A pleasure to be of service to you Mrs. Trewlove – oh it's not Trewlove anymore is it? Forgive me forgetting for a moment – congratulations on your marriage to a most highly respected colleague! I trust it's not a matrimonial difficulty already?"

He smiled – not the charismatic beatific smile of the Reverend Bernard Houndsditch but one of homely sincerity. *He resembled*, she thought, *a genial Mr. Pickwick in badly fitting clerical clothes.*

The sheer patent honesty of the cherubic, plump little man unnerved her. How could she insult such a person by even hinting that he had got himself somehow entangled as her husband maintained, even if by some misinterpretation on someone's part it could be the case. So how could she broach the delicate subject without causing offence? Face to face, with his pale blue eyes looking fearlessly into hers, words faded from her mouth for want of an inoffensive opening gambit.

Her seconds of hesitation caused a chasm of embarrassment. How could she leap across it safely?

The rosy-cheeked, rotund little rector looked down at her when she was seated and smiled repeatedly, then he finally took her hand in his and examined her diamond closely.

"What a beautiful ring! A poor minister who lavishes his dough on such a magnificent ring must love deeply – but unfortunately no one is perfect – we all make mistakes, don't we? Nowhere more so than in holy matrimony."

He waved her inchoate protest away, like a school-master might do to a pupil protesting about his phantom homework.

"You don't have to make excuses, my dear. It's the old, old story – half a dozen of one, six of the other! But these little misunderstandings can all be straightened out if there is willingness to forgive on both sides. So please don't be shy my dear, I have heard it all countless times before and we have found a solution together – that is what we ministers are here for."

He patted her hand and held on to it. "Now, my dear, tell me from the beginning – don't be shy."

Suddenly she found the courage to blurt out, "I've not come about my husband, I've come to be a Good Samaritan."

"We could do with a few more of those around my dear, what makes you come to me? Does it concern a member of my parish?"

"Yes it does."

"Might I ask who you intend to be a Good Samaritan to?"

"You, Reverend Golightly!"

"I see. I think I have guessed. Are you offering your services for flower arranging? We have already too many, my dear, and my wife is becoming highly suspicious."

Jennifer suddenly became inspired for her opening gambit.

"Can I be frank with you?" She had to repeat the question because of the thundering organ.

"Of course, I hate subterfuge. Excuse me a moment – I think we have a little too much background music!"

Thereupon he hurried away and when he returned moments later, the organ was silent.

He again took hold of her hand and said, "Please continue. Sorry for the interruption."

"Well, I presume you have heard of the famous Dreyfus case in France a long time ago?"

"I have indeed! I see you know your history. The poor man was convicted of a crime he did not commit, wasn't he? Sent to Devil's Island, poor fellow."

"Yes, terrible, wasn't it, Reverend?"

He placed his hand momentarily on her shoulder and taking a deep sigh, shook his bald white head sadly.

"Indeed! A dreadful miscarriage of justice, like so many innocent people wrongly accused and made to suffer terribly," replied Golightly, now averting his pale bloodshot eyes. "But happily in his case," he resumed a more cheerful tone of voice and with his eyes no longer averted, "He was completely vindicated by Emile Zola as you mention. But what has this got to do with me and your wanting to be my Good Samaritan?"

"Well, I cannot stand by and see the same thing happen to you, Reverend – I have heard—"

"What have you heard?" His voice betrayed alarm, but he quickly recovered and tried to laugh the matter off. "I'm only a humble priest, my dear, not another Captain Dreyfus! I don't think I'm in any danger of being sent away to Devil's Island. So what have you heard?"

"Please don't be offended – I know you are innocent. I know it's all a dreadful mistake, that's why I'm here – to save you. My husband says you are being falsely accused – well he didn't actually say 'falsely' but I know that's what he meant – accused of embezzlement – a wicked lie of course that has to be put right. I'm ashamed Bernard is too scared to come forward himself to do something to help, and so, as his wife, now it falls to me. He had made me feel guilty. I cannot just stand by and let an innocent man be condemned."

She saw him grow pale and speechless, leaving her to do the talking – too much in shock to interrupt.

"For me, Reverend Golightly, it's a matter of conscience. Fortunately my aunt left me a great deal of money. She was a very religious woman and I know it would be her wish for it to be used serving God's holy ministry – saving it from being disgraced."

Jennifer felt the podgy hand which had become limp over hers suddenly tighten into a quick squeeze. She saw signs of him recovering from the initial shock and he was now seen to be listening intently.

"I have heard that it's a matter of thirty-odd thousand dollars. Reverend please hear me out."

"Of course, my dear, it's my duty to hear everyone out – especially a true Christian acting out the teachings of our beloved Savior. I shall pray for you. But let me quickly explain the whole fiasco."

"No need to explain. I've heard it all and don't believe what is said about you. Of course, you are innocent. Miscarriage of justice, and I'm your Good Samaritan sent in answer to your prayers like Bernard was sent in answer to mine when I desperately needed someone to walk my dogs. Well, I could transfer some of my own shares over to you without anyone knowing, so that you can save face. Like Zola I'll deliver you from your wicked enemies. How could they be so cruel to an innocent man – a man of God? That's why I'm here, I repeat – to put the matter right. I feel it's my Christian duty, because my minister husband has not done what he should."

"Say no more, Jennifer. Your husband is a good man – no doubt he has his reasons, however mistaken – we don't know what calumny he has heard to cloud his judgment."

She felt the podgy hand squeeze again. Her words had put life back into his veins and he was able to speak again with a new lease of life. He hung on to the Samaritan's hand which could pull out of danger a priest no longer inevitably doomed to be defrocked.

"But how do you suppose a poor minister like me could pay back a sum like the one you are offering – plus interest, naturally? I am deeply moved but I must refuse. Better to lose face than faith."

"Now you must listen to me. Hear my side of the sordid story."

Jennifer smiled encouragingly and did not try to take back her hand. She was dying to hear the other side.

"Well, as you intuitively surmised there was no question of embezzlement on my part."

"Of course not, Reverend Golightly, you were framed, of course."

"Well, to be quite honest, I was not actually framed but my actions were certainly misconstrued, to put it as euphemistically as I can. To put you in the picture, our fine old organ which you heard thundering away needed a very expensive overhaul—"

"I know what you mean," interposed Jennifer. "Bernard and his organist at this very moment are in New York arranging repairs for our own organ. A mouse fell down one of its pipes. My husband got it out but his new organist still isn't satisfied. A squeak or two now and again comes out instead of the proper notes! He says there must be a nest left behind."

"How embarrassing! I must tell that story to my own organist!" said Golightly, trying not to appear amused.

"Bernard said to him it must be the pedals – they probably needed oiling or something, but the organist insisted it was not the pedals but actually mice."

"How very droll!"

Jennifer, with her hand in slavery, smiled. She could not help warming to the plump little minister with the cherubic face and the oversized dog collar and ill-fitting clerical suit which, she thought, made him appear a trifle like a little boy in his big brother's handed-down clothes.

He suddenly let go of her hand and inquired with his hands upraised, as if he were blessing her, "Are you comfortable on that hard bench to hear me out? I don't think it wise to invite you into my study. My wife, you see – she's so suspicious – reads too many of those sexy pulp novels from her food store – thinks all my volunteer flower arrangers are out to seduce me! Here, why not let me bundle up some of these garments for you to use as a cushion? The hard bench you are sitting on was only intended for our young choirboys to change their shoes."

"No, I am comfortable enough, thank you. Please carry on giving me your side of the story."

He came to sit beside her on the narrow bench against the wall, and took her hand again after extricating himself from one of the surplices hanging down from a hook.

She noticed that she sat the taller and it gave her the impression of sitting beside an aged schoolboy from a poor family. He certainly looked as if he could not possibly have committed the crime.

"Well, my bishop wouldn't release the money for our purpose. Said he couldn't hear any cracked notes playing – probably the battery was low in his hearing aid. Then this con-artist came along smooth as they come and dressed like the president of a bank. He convinced me that a certain block of shares was an undiscovered gold mine. I may have been naïve but not criminal. I only invested church funds in these phenomenal shares, intending to put the money back and spend the huge quick profit on the organ. There was a quick profit to start with, and I spent it all on the organ – every single cent. I invested more money and got another quick return, which I also spent on the organ."

"Poor Reverend Golightly! What a swine!"

"More of a shark, my dear! I see you have guessed. Well, I don't need to tell you when it comes to selling the shares to payback—"

"They were worthless?"

"Practically. So you see I couldn't put back the money, and to pile insult upon injury the man is even suing me for a brokerage fee!"

"That's simply outrageous – you most definitely need a Good Samaritan. You need rescuing just as much as Dreyfus did or David, my poor beloved, gentle dog."

He squeezed her hand once more.

"Do you know, Jennifer, Lord Byron said a dog is the only friend you'll ever know who loves you more than himself."

"How true! Reverend – don't I just know that myself!"

This time it was Jennifer who patted the Reverend's hand.

"Reverend Golightly, I insist upon putting up the money to save you from a gross miscarriage of justice. I would have it on my conscience if you refused."

The podgy hand clasped desperately at her wrist like a drowning man at a straw.

"Magnificent act of mercy. Simply munificent! I'm sure you will be rewarded in heaven."

From his mention of a reward in heaven Jennifer quickly seized upon her cue.

"I'm sure, Reverend Golightly, God would want to include David too, since he has become like my very own son. Reverend Golightly, you've no idea what that dog means to me."

"I can well imagine."

"I look upon him as if he were my own flesh and blood. Do you know, since I lost my poor David – my first husband, and our son David so tragically, my other David has completely taken their place. He is so unbelievably loving and intelligent. He leans against me all the time, especially when I am sad and I can feel that he knows what's going on in my mind. Call it telepathy, call it what you like, but I know my David understands me better than any human being. We are devoted to each other and cannot bear to be parted. Why should we have to be? He has even been baptized."

"By the Franciscans you mean, presumably, at their ceremony for the blessing of the animals?"

"No, by my own husband Bernard!"

"You asked him personally and he said he would, you mean. Isn't that the case?"

"No, I'm sure he did."

"You are telling me you were actually a witness?"

"No, but I know he did – in a lake. He wouldn't agree to baptize David in his church font."

"I'm not surprised! But I hope you do not think that baptism will somehow prolong his life. We cannot alter our prescribed span, my dear – I am afraid we have to be brave when the time comes – but from what I have gathered from my gravedigger he is a very young dog. He could well live another ten years or more."

"No I'm not thinking that at all. I didn't have it done for that reason – not for prolonging his life. It was so he can have a proper Christian burial when the Good Shepherd calls him. I want him in heaven with me you see – I don't want him turned away by Saint Peter when he comes barking at the gate! I know he will follow me – I just know!"

"How do you know, Jennifer my dear? I'm not critical, just curious. I've never heard anyone talk like this before, you see, and I'm a little bewildered by it all."

"I just know deep down like I know David knows where he is going. When I took him along to show him our family tomb, he knew. He was whining pitifully and leaning against me like he could not bear to be separated. His remains are going to be put in a coffin placed in my tomb – and I know he knew! Are you shocked, Reverend Golightly? My husband is."

He squeezed her hand and appeared surprisingly sympathetic and understanding.

"No, I am not shocked, Jennifer. Feeling as you do I think it is only natural that you should want to have David sharing your earned reward in heaven, but there is a more practical alternative – probably you have no knowledge of it, have you? Much less controversial and all quite legal."

"Do you mean in some foreign church where the rules are perhaps less strict? – If so, the answer is no – we're strict Episcopalians not Buddhists. David and I are not converting!"

"Oh no, my dear, you don't have to convert. Nothing so catastrophic. When the bell tolls as it does for everyone – and it's wise to be prepared – your ashes could be buried with David's in a pet cemetery, you know, without causing any problems. We presume he would be called first, so it would merely entail exhuming his casket and the superintendent fulfilling your wishes before reburial.

"He could have a nice little memorial with your chosen engraving upon it just like in my own churchyard – all very peaceful under the shade of a tree and with a vase for flowers too, if you wish. And you could go and visit whenever you liked and no one would be offended."

Jennifer stiffened. "Now you are talking like my husband!" She felt her hand being squeezed again and his voice softened and betrayed alarm at unintentionally causing offence.

"I would not prevent David's ashes joining yours in my cemetery, Jennifer," interposed Golightly in a profoundly conciliatory manner, "I was only suggesting a possible, more practical, alternative, my dear. You see, my dear, I'm rather older than you and may be called sooner. My successor may think differently – think more like your husband."

Jennifer now saw the moment to seize the bull by the horns. "That's why we must make preparations now before it is too late."

"I'm not sure I understand how that is possible. No doubt you have something practical in mind?"

"I do, Reverend Golightly, I do, and I have been praying hard for God to guide me in this and he has. Just like he helped Mr. William Butler Yeats win the Nobel Prize."

"Indeed, Jennifer! You astonish me more and more. I confess you must know a lot more about Mr. Yeats than I do though I do know he won the Nobel Prize. How did God do this for him, Jennifer? I am very curious. You must explain."

"Well, Yeats said that quite often when he wrote his poems his hand moved automatically. So the guided hand must have produced his best poems – the ones guided by God which helped him win the Nobel Prize."

"Interesting – most interesting! Yes I have heard of so-called automatic writing but not in connection with Yeats. You read it in his autobiography presumably?"

"Yes."

"How interesting! I must remember that. Did you experience automatic writing yourself then, Jennifer? Tell me about it."

"No, mine was different, Reverend, not writing in my case but thoughts put into my mind – same thing – after I had been praying very hard. I certainly could not have thought them all out by myself. I'm only a simple woman – not a genius."

"Not a genius perhaps, but an intelligent woman nevertheless. How can you be sure these thoughts put into your mind were from God – absolutely sure – one hundred per cent sure?"

There was a long pause and Jennifer's heart began to thump.

"How are you sure there is a God?"

"Faith, my dear, faith – without it we are but straws in the wind."

"It's the same with me, Reverend, that's how I know God was communicating – I felt like I feel His presence when I pray."

With her free hand she squeezed his hand still holding her own and transfixed him with her beautiful bright cougar-eyes.

"Reverend, you believe, don't you, that with enough faith all things are possible – even moving mountains and walking on water?"

The cherubic face lit up with an amused but discreet fleeting smile.

"I can't say I have actually put either to the test, my dear, but the Bible tells us so. Therefore I suppose I should believe it, but whether I can as a fallible human being is quite another matter."

The cougar-eyes blazed bewitchingly and she retained their intimate pyramid of hands intact a moment longer.

"You'll probably think me crazy when I say I have put it to the test?"

"Moving mountains, or walking on water?"

Jennifer struggled to free her hands and the well known (to her friends) ice began to freeze her tone of voice.

"You don't believe me, do you? You think I am making it all up?"

"No, I don't, my dear," said Golightly, retrieving her hand and patting it gently. "I believe you. I know you are sincere. Please continue, I'm listening. Really!"

"Well, let me tell you about two separate events which should convince you about the power of prayer."

She then related in dramatic detail how David had been lost in a new neighborhood with no road sense, little sense of smell, and in a wilderness of snow, for two days. She had prayed and prayed for God to be merciful and return him to her unharmed against impossible odds – and He did.

On another occasion, David had fallen sick of a deadly poison and the veterinarian had given up all hope of his recovery. To show that she had infinite faith in her, Lord Jesus answering her prayers, she had gone about joyfully singing, even though David lay dying. Later, her Savior had resurrected David like Lazarus. Even the veterinarian could not believe how such a recovery was possible without divine intervention. So in the light of her tremendous faith in her Maker, why would He suddenly fail to answer her prayers to raise another creature of His own creation to human status in order to be able to join her in thereafter? To separate them would not be merciful but cruel. "God is supposed to be compassionate, isn't He, Reverend Golightly? Is separating me from David compassionate?"

There was a pause while Golightly tried, with well-chosen words, to wriggle himself out of the hole he had fallen into.

"I believe you are sincere, yes – carry on, I'm listening."

"Well, the soul is invisible, isn't it?"

"Yes."

"So it has no shape – agreed?"

"Agreed."

"It has no shape – so if souls have no shape they must be all the same and must be treated the same. No discrimination."

"I suppose so," humored Golightly, "but I don't see what you are driving at, my dear – you are now delving into what are mysteries to all of us including us priests. We don't know all the answers, we have to take much on trust."

"That's my point, Reverend Golightly. I have trust that God has granted David a soul and since they are invisible nobody can prove otherwise and therefore David should be given a Christian burial so he can follow me into heaven!"

Reverend Golightly became extremely avuncular, but most alarmed. He now took both her hands in his and looked most sympathetic smiling all the while as he spoke gently.

"You see, my dear, there are many learned Christians who would call your wise logic sophistry. You are very sincere which makes a difference, of course, and I must respect this. But try to put yourself in the minister's shoes. Let us say he believes you wholly, as I do, naturally – that goes without saying – but he has also to think of all his parishioners, not merely at the expense of all the others. If the matter shocked your own husband it would be bound to shock a great many good people besides – perhaps the whole congregation who look to the priest to set an example. It could even destroy their faith in the teachings of the Holy Bible and it could even lead to the defrocking of the minister involved if he led them astray.

"If you, my dear, were the minister, would you want to risk losing all your congregation and becoming an outcast plus losing your living to which you were ordained and have striven for all your life? You cannot truthfully swear to me that you would, now can you?"

"I fully agree," admitted Jennifer without hesitation. "But the secret of the confessional is not shared with all the congregation, is it? It is a secret held between the priest, the sinner and God. Why must any other secret shared between priest and parishioner be any different?"

"Ah! But you are not my parishioner, are you?"

"But I could become one, couldn't I, if it makes a difference?"

"You cannot be serious, Jennifer, in your fervor you have overlooked important considerations which make your highly controversial scheme impossible. For example, imagine the priest at the burial service looking down at the coffin before the altar. Imagine their faces when he begins, 'Our dearly beloved brother David Greyhound cut down like a flower etc. etc.' He also must pay tribute to the good things their dearly beloved dog has done and how he will be missed by all his fellow racing dogs, plus of course, his mistress. And would you have his greyhound relatives all sitting in the pews among my parishioners who happened to turn up?"

"Now you are making fun of me – I trusted you were different from all the others who mock me as well."

"I'm not mocking you, my dear, how could I be so cruel – forgive me if I did not make myself clear. I was only trying to make you see how impossible it is to give a Christian burial to a dog in public – in full view of all attending which would most likely include many diehard bigots."

"Of course not, Reverend, not in public – in private! No relatives – no mourners except myself. I would not even bring Robert."

"Robert's another greyhound, presumably?"

"No, a bearded collie."

"But my dear Jennifer! Think of what the media would make of it? It would be the kind of sensationalism which could find its way onto world television. Would you care to be the priest in the middle of all the scandal? Imagine the headlines PRIEST HOLDS CHRISTIAN BURIAL SERVICE FOR A GREYHOUND!

"Surely you can see the whole thing is impossible – purely from a pragmatic point of view, I mean. I'm not sitting in judgment on the issue – only doing my best to make you see reason, my dear."

But Jennifer was not daunted. She had come prepared for this line of argument and provided the man listened, unlike her own husband who would not without condemning outright, she felt she could still "Fight the good fight with all thy might" on behalf of David and win.

Looked at another way, in view of thirty-odd thousand dollars worth of her shares offered to be transferred to save him from ruin, she had him over a barrel!

So she outlined her master plan. It would be a secret kept strictly between the priest, herself and God, not unlike the Roman Catholic confessional. Any parishioners present at the funeral service would never know that David Trewlove was anyone but her human relative. Golightly astutely realized that the "divine" plan, God-given or not, could actually be made to work!

He only needed the cooperation of the funeral parlor and this was easy, because their involvement was purely secular and mercenary. Her favorite hymn could be sung in church over the casket which they had prepared. The chosen hymn would be accompanied on the restored organ without anyone being the wiser! At the tomb the gravedigger would unlock the door with his key and Jennifer would be fulfilled, including the Reverend Golightly! Ironically, the tribute to the deceased's virtues could be carefully worded to refer to David and yet be synonymous with the fictional David Trewlove. A very bold plan indeed for Reverend Golightly, but it was a Catch-22 situation if anything should go wrong. If only he had Jennifer's faith!

However, the director of the Sunningdale Memorial Parlor was a personal friend of his and was certainly no bigot. They did a lot of business together and the renowned establishment did a superb presentation of the body, which must meet all of Jennifer's exacting demands, and be reliably (at a price) secretive and discreet.

Yet the bewildered little man could not help but recall the bard of Auld Lang Syne's immortal lines, "The best laid plans of mice and men go oft awry!"

Chapter Twenty-seven

"What shall I do with all these yachting magazines on the floor in the Reverend's study, Mrs. Houndsditch?" asked the housekeeper triumphantly. She was seen carrying a pile of dog-eared copies in her big arms, as though carrying the head of John the Baptist to Herod.

She was hoping her mistress would give her consent to dump them, thereby igniting another domestic fuse between husband and wife! But Jennifer did not fall into the trap. She had seen how even the non-practicing, wishful, frustrated sailors who could not afford even a rowboat, let alone a yacht, poured over and held onto their beloved magazines.

They thumbed them, devoured them, dreamed through them and voyaged in phantom yachts which were beyond hope for them to possess, except through these pictures in magazines. She would often peep in at her husband while he was dreaming, and smile like a mother looking on at a little boy pouring over his comics.

But there was also a better side to unpredictable Mrs. Broomworthy, depending on whether she felt particularly holier-than-thou that day! On a good day Jennifer could become used to a hymn-singing duet in the kitchen.

This was one of those days and they were happily singing to an audience of persistent, not very tuneful dogs determined to make it a quartet in barbershop close harmony!

The two singing ladies were busy sharing the chore of polishing the brass collection plates while dreaming as well as singing and rubbing away the powdery white clouds to a sunny shine.

"They are just thrown down on the floor," went on Mrs. Broomworthy, wedging the spoken word into their hymn duet.

At last the housekeeper had her mistress' full attention, while David came over to lean heavily against her as she listened.

"And they are mostly very out of date," persisted the rector's devoted and meticulous housekeeper. "Do you think the Reverend would want to keep them for ever? It makes the room so untidy. He used to be so particular – never anything out of place. I can't see what has suddenly gotten into him. It's ever since I packed that hamper for you and you all went off to the seaside. Now he does nothing but buries his nose in those magazines – you must have noticed?"

"Yes, Mrs. B. I've noticed – but I should leave them if I were you – you know what happens when you take away little boys' toys!"

Lily Broomworthy, the church's highly moral flying buttress of propriety, remained immovably supportive of the status quo under her gray skies of duty. Like the church itself, the rectory had to be kept always immaculate, and she resented it becoming a joking matter.

"I'll put them out of sight in a cupboard, if that's okay with you?" said Mrs. Broomworthy, very seriously.

"Good idea, Mrs. B., but don't forget to leave the cupboard door open a little, so that he can see you haven't thrown them out."

"Do you think the Reverend is thinking of buying a boat then, Mrs. Houndsditch – I hope not – he could get himself drowned. You hear about it on TV all the time – the sea's no place for amateurs."

"I had a cousin once," went on the heavy woman in an apron, adjusting the long black pin in her bun, "He bought himself a little boat and a smart cap to go with it, then called himself a captain. Well, he went out fishing one blustery day and he hasn't been seen since! And the only thing that got washed ashore was that captain's cap and a gasoline can. They said the fish kept nibbling at him till they gradually gobbled him up. It just goes to show you can't fool around with the sea. Don't let him buy a boat, Mrs. Houndsditch – put your foot down. He will listen to you. He's a born preacher but he's no born Captain Bligh, he is the Rector."

"I agree with you," said Jennifer, studying her reflection in her well-polished collection plate. "But I shouldn't worry too much – I don't think my husband sees himself as another Captain Bligh, although, to give him his due, he's quite knowledgeable about boats and the sea. He told me he nearly became a sailor when he was young."

Mrs. Broomworthy's brittle genial manner snapped, and she resumed her naturally fearsome mien.

"Nearly is not enough, Mrs. Houndsditch," she warned severely. "Nearly is not enough! You've got to be a real sailor before you put to sea – not nearly one! A captain's cap won't turn you into one either when the sea starts to get rough!"

Suddenly they were interrupted.

"Jennifer! Can you spare a minute?'

It was Bernard calling from his study. A moment later when she entered, she promptly gaped in astonishment, for he was wearing a fisherman's cable-stitch pullover and gold-laurel captain's cap, while he obviously thought he was cutting a dash before his romantically inclined newly-wedded wife.

"How do I look, hon? – Quite the Francis Chichester, eh? And cast your eye on this flush-decked little yawl? Isn't she a dream? Say yes – because she's ours, dearest. Would you believe it – we now own a yacht! Isn't it wonderful?"

With a sagging heart Jennifer glanced from the yachtsman to the yacht depicted in a picture cut out of a yachting magazine and held under her nose by her suddenly boyishly exuberant husband. Mrs. B.'s warning at that instant loomed in Jennifer's mind like a buoy clanging over rocks.

"Bernard! Have you gone quite nuts! When did you – why did you—" Words failed her. She had difficulty grasping the reality taken in by her eyes and ears. How could this be the selfsame sane, dependable, conventional minister she had married for love, coupled with security? Here he was, acting like an idiot. Or would he somehow manage to commit her into paying for it without even consulting her?

The clerical yachtsman appeared visibly taken aback by his wife's reaction. Apparently he had expected his wife to be thrilled at his daring surprise package, and Jennifer felt that it was mean of her to be pouring cold water on the startling revelation. If it had not been for the housekeeper's warning, she realized she might have considered it fun to be able to go out romantically sailing the high seas in this undoubtedly very pretty sailboat he called a yawl. She was curious to know what a yawl was in the category of yachts – she could only think of a schooner, ketch and a sloop. Now there was evidently such a thing as a yawl for her to learn about. But how could it be theirs? He had no money. Nobody had consulted her about payment.

Such a yawl, she imagined, could well be capable of sailing to the South Seas and be the fulfillment of a childhood dream. She smiled inwardly at the mental picture of herself at the helm – infinitely in command, her tinted ponytail flying like a banderole from her flamboyant captain's cap! To hell with Mrs. B. and her cousin gobbled up by fishes. Bernard had sailed his uncle's yacht so he must be a real sailor, not like Mrs. B.'s cousin. Wondrous to be wrecked on some palmy lagoon with her head in Bernard's lap and dreaming to the lilt of Hawaiian guitars, as hula-hula girls, brown as nutmegs, danced on the sand by the light of the moon! To hell with Mrs. Broomworthy and her lugubrious warnings! Was her water wisdom really worth the pea in a bo's'n's whistle! Bernard in his fancy getup and enthusing in the unmistakable language of the sea – how could he be other than what he seemed – a true frustrated sea dog?

What did he lack but a telescope, a wooden leg and a parrot on his shoulder! She recalled in support of that impression the picnic on the beach during which he had pointed out to her so many technicalities about a sloop, close-hauled and wallowing like a turtle in troubled water. All that weird talk about flush decks, topping lifts etc., surely had to come out of the mouth of a real sailor?

How he had laughed that day at all her landlubber's names for things and had shown off his knowledge by correcting them as she frowned, focusing his binoculars upon that struggling ketch. Some of their conversation sprang into her mind.

"Why is he pulling on that rope attached to that swinging pole?"

"That's not a pole it's a spar – the boom to be precise, and that's not a rope it's a sheet and he's trying to go about – that is, bringing the boom to t'other side without getting his head knocked off at the same time! Do it badly and you could easily become the headless yachtsman!"

"What's he pulling on that nutcracker-looking thing on the deck for?"

"That's the Highfield lever to release the backstay so that he can get support for the mast on the opposite tack." Etc., etc. With all that language of the sea at his command he had to be, in her estimation, a true sailor.

And this was going on in the back of her mind as she listened to how his uncle had had a stroke and could no longer sail, so had given his nephew the yawl as a belated wedding present.

She saw how the yachtsman husband in his casual gear took ten years off the sedate cleric she had married. The boyish smile returned at each question she put and his answers were so reassuring.

"Did you learn at a sailing school?"

"No darling – Uncle Monty of course – the yachtsman, remember? You know – the man who taught me to sail in my college days. We used to sail from Cape Cod to Martha's Vineyard in all weathers – once in fact in a force nine – and we weren't rescued by the local lifeboat, we made it alone.

"She is maid of all weathers, is our restored *Sea Witch* – pitch pine on oak frames and the flush hatches all oiled teak."

"She must have been lovely – I wish I had known you then."

"Yes indeed, you would have drooled over her like poor old Uncle Mont did – in fact, we all did down at the yard where she was moored and maintained with no expense spared. Now poor old Uncle Mont's had a stroke and of course, he's had to give up sailing."

"Poor man! It must be a terrible blow to have to give up such a joy," said Jennifer compassionately. "Is he now in a home or anything? Should we go up and visit him?"

"That of course is a must, but not yet. I know my dashing Uncle Mont – always the swashbuckler and conscious of his image. He would not like us to see him with all those dreadful plastic tubes attached to him. Let him keep his image intact. It is kinder not to take pity. But we'll visit as soon as we hear he's up and about again and showing off to us younger folk and kidding himself that he's as young as he feels."

"Poor man!" said Jennifer again.

"Cheer up, hon, pity is the last thing old Uncle Mont would want from us. I'm sure we make him happy just being able to dream about us taking over where he left off. I know he couldn't bear to have his precious *Sea Witch* falling into any hands other than family. So you see, my sweet, it's an ill wind that blows nobody any good. I was flabbergasted when he sent me this magazine picture and said she was now mine if I wanted her. Can you imagine? If I wanted her indeed! No need for me to say my poor dear old Uncle Montague got my acceptance over the phone within seconds of my reading his pathetic letter! He enclosed that magazine photo of a yacht like *Sea Witch*, as if I could ever forget those glorious times we had sailing her down to Montauk and back to Cape Cod – and of course, calling at Martha's Vineyard for a lobster dinner under the stars."

"Must have been great fun – when did you get that letter?"

"Yesterday."

"Why didn't you tell me?"

"I wanted it to be a wonderful surprise when I brought her down, but I just couldn't hold it from you any longer. Aren't you thrilled, hon? Just think, we own a boat better than your friend Giselle's rich husband's? That should take the wind out of his sails and stop him looking down his nose at us! He may be commodore of the yacht club, but there isn't a boat there a patch on *Sea Witch* – bigger perhaps, but not with such lovely lines. And pitch pine, my dear – very seaworthy and very rare – heavy as lead – not that light knotty rubbish they make furniture out of that in rain water rots like a pear. Pitch pine on the other hand is as strong as mahogany and as rot-proof as teak."

"Oh how marvelous!" exclaimed Jennifer. "And now it's really ours – I'm so happy for you and for myself as well. I suspected, since that day at the seaside, there was a hidden sailor in you."

"Do you know, love – why don't you sit down and listen, there's much to tell."

They both sat down and faced each other across his desk littered with magazines.

"Uncle Mont spent a fortune importing pitch pine to maintain her and paying shipwrights over the years to replace every suspect plank – mostly above the waterline – between wind and water as they say – it's rain water you see, hon, that rots. Salt water is a preservative – except to metal, which rots away by electrolysis when dissimilar metals are in contact with sea water – like the iron skeg and the bronze propeller and shaft for instance."

"But isn't *Sea Witch* a sailboat?" inquired Jennifer, perplexed and trying to show intelligent interest.

"Of course, sweetheart, but a sailboat of any size these days has a motor to get to and from her mooring in a crowded marina."

Jennifer endeavored to fake kindred interest in the nautical technicalities, which were way above her ponytail! She looked up adoringly at her husband's pale, hollow face and saw that it was quite flushed with the boyish excitement of talking about his beloved new possession, while his small black eyes seemed to glow almost as much as those strange eyes of David.

"Oh, darling! Of course I'm thrilled! We must be the luckiest couple in the whole wide world!"

This having been said, Jennifer disengaged herself from the unlikely looking clergyman's embrace, as he suddenly leaned over the desk. She retreated stiffly a yard or so distant.

"Aye aye, Cap'n Bernard! Reporting to the quarterdeck, sir!" exclaimed Jennifer, smartly saluting. "Shall we set sail for Honolulu or the Marquesas?"

"The Marquesas this time, Ms. Jennifer, cast off fore and aft if you please."

"Aye aye, sir," replied Jennifer brightly, making another exaggerated mock salute.

Shortly afterwards Mrs. Broomworthy, eavesdropping as usual, was amazed to behold her pious, staid employers joining hands to do a jubilant hornpipe round the desk and chairs of Bernard's study!

Meanwhile the housekeeper of long standing, who had never seen her Rector put a staid foot wrong before, stood aghast at the baffling spectacle of this most dignified man and his wife suddenly cavorting like prankish teenagers!

Their bizarre cries of, "The *Sea Witch*! The *Sea Witch*! We're off to the Marquesas in the *Sea Witch*!" sang loud and mad in her unbelieving ears.

Tiptoeing safely back to her kitchen, Lily Broomworthy was experiencing a geography problem – the Marquesas – yes, they sounded familiar. Now where could they be?

Off Cape Cod? She wondered, fiddling with the long black pin harpooning her bun. She looked down at a leaning, questioning David, whom she brusquely brushed from her side. No, not Cape Cod, she eventually decided – the Marquesas were more likely to be somewhere near Martha's Vineyard, it being one of the rector's favorite haunts!

Those elusive Marquesas had to be somewhere not too far away – or how could he get back in time to take the Sunday service, she reasoned profoundly!

Chapter Twenty-eight

The following day was not a day for Bernard, the frustrated sailor to be climbing up dizzy ratlines to the crow's nest of his imagination, or to be dreaming of endless horizons under sail. On the contrary, it was the Sabbath and time for the rector to climb to the pulpit unimpeded by vertigo, and be the shepherd of his flock.

The sheep may safely graze the pastures of his ordained wisdom but the shepherd himself must not be seen by the flock to be ruminating!

Yet Bernard could not chase away from his mind those images of a more exciting way of life made possible by the surprising gift of his uncle's lovely yawl, *Sea Witch*. They kept wedging themselves into his prepared sermon. If he had heeded the historic preachers of the horseback-and-Bible-under-armpit era, he would have known that fire and brimstone paid off. Because it kept the listeners enthralled, whereas homely homilies allowed them to drop off and lose the thread. If they woke up yawning they had probably missed the message.

Yet Bernard was rash enough on this single occasion, when he wished to relax and put away his spellbinding oratory which required his full attention plus well-rehearsed histrionics, during which he fluttered heavenward and came swooping down on the sails of his wide white sleeves. He gave the congregation what they looked for – the magisterial performance at its theatrical, dramatic, unbeatable best. But he was unable to forget *Sea Witch*. It had cast upon him its nautical spell. His arms went up in the wrong places and the words of his brilliantly prepared sermon were not always those from his mouth because he had lost his place on the script hidden below his lectern.

He habitually simulated never to be reading from a script, but this time he had forgotten to take advantage of the wisdom of surreptitiously glancing down and had gotten himself into difficulties.

At first he floundered like a fish out of water. He rambled on about his wild youth when he had won a few dimes and quarters in a gambling machine and indulged in that sink of iniquity until he found Jesus and never put a dime in a slot machine again! Needless to say the listeners were not riveted!

No chance here for the diverting swoops and ascending angel's flutterings to get him back on course! He was on his own and descended into abysmal bathos more and more miserably in front of the uneasy, equally embarrassed congregation, some of whom imagined he must have suffered a minor stroke!

At one point he nearly said "sail" machines instead of slot machines.

He realized that *Sea Witch* had brewed some strange witchcraft in its cauldron of the sea, which made him feel more tolerant towards all God's creatures great and small, desperately in need of love and being understood – just like himself at this very moment, having to preach and not being able to get *Sea Witch* out of his mind.

It occurred to him that Jesus did not raise himself high on a pulpit but was quite happy to be with his feet in the dust of the wayside, preaching the greatest of all inspired sermons whilst sitting on a stone.

So Bernard digressed to be in communion with the common man until the common man was suddenly heard snoring!

The fiery brimstone which kept the congregation on the edges of their hard seats and stifled the coughing and the creaking of pews and the clatter of falling walking sticks and umbrellas, had petered out into a smoking small fire under heavy rain. The people had come to witness a blazing forest, a new one which he lit every Sunday. But not on this one. However, Bernard was not yet done. With a beatific smile which he used to rehearse for hours before a mirror until he got it right, he faded like a candle guttering out of wax. Something was missing from the dignity of his fine presence and exceptional stature. He looked down dismayed at the tittering faces, as a snorer in their midst continued to snore like Jennifer's bearded collie or a carpenter sawing wood. The rector pulled himself together and in a most magisterial voice entreated, "I call upon thee Almighty God to forgive them that snoreth in Thy Presence, for they know not what they do in their sleep. Here endeth the lesson, amen!"

An embarrassed congregation found itself stranded without its rector when he suddenly climbed down from the pulpit and disappeared into the vestry.

Thereupon the organist took his cue to relieve the situation with wall-trembling zest and he selected *Buxtehude*, who now came into his own, for blasting out a cover-up for his employer's unorthodox departure.

To a thundering organ finale and wall-shaking of dust on reserve prayer books piled up in the vestry, the liberated Bernard entered, bright as a midshipman on his first day upon deck.

What was that the little organist was playing with his tiny feet tap-dancing on the pedals among the spiders and cobwebs? Could it be the banished, unpopular *Buxtehude* brazenly returning to challenge his enemies?

With a change of heart now and feeling goodwill towards all mankind including *Buxtehude*, whom the little organist loved, he would let him be. Let the poor little trampled-on dog have his day and tap-dance on the pedals and thunder away to his ear's content!

With a feeling akin to Atlas having just taken the world off his shoulders, he hung up his immaculate surplice on its wire coat-hanger and kissing his gorgeous chasuble, hung that up carefully also.

The organ was still thundering – God bless the little fellow! Let thunder roll and lightning strike – but please, congregation, try and listen to this little man playing *Buxtehude* divinely, and not complain! Let there be rejoicing among you and compassion. God will not have you in heaven until you have Him in your hearts.

Sea Witch had cast on him a liberating spell. At the thought of owning her he could dance with joy. He skipped across the church lawn, and with his giant legs leaped the low fence encircling his rectory to enter the kitchen buoyantly by its back door. Naturally, the phenomenon astonished the two ladies within who also were taken by surprise; one being his own loving wife who giggled and the other the embittered housekeeper, with her false teeth like millstones grinding grain. Taking the former by both hands and laughing he cried, "Come on, Cap'n Jennifer. Let's teach Mrs. B. how to dance the hornpipe!"

Chapter Twenty-nine

"Surprise! Surprise! Congratulations yachtswoman of the year!" greeted Giselle Carboni, as she opened the door of her lovely house shaded by its splendiferous maple trees, which spread their combined splendor over practically every meter of spacious, cropped green lawn.

The September equinox had passed over a week ago but the sun continued to burn down scorchingly through gaps in the maples' shade, regardless of the Gregorian calendar.

"Holy smoke, Gizzy, this is a time for switching off personalities! – First Bernard, like a swashbuckling pirate – and now you masquerading as the civilized Vassar girl – instead of the noble savage complete with beads and war paint? How come?"

"Eyes, Jen," explained the new-look Giselle, taking her best friend's arm and leading her into the garden under its cool faintly oranging tent of maples.

"The squint doc says I can't wear contact lenses any more, so I've had to change my image – spectacles look ridiculous on the noble savage, and the bright war paint doesn't go with the Vassar girl look either. But enough about me – come on, tell me more about *Sea Witch* – you too must be terribly excited – you sounded cock-a-hoop over the telephone. When's Bernard doing the Francis Chichester act and bringing her down from Cape Cod?"

"He's waiting for the right weather – he's been in touch with the Coast Guard station at Cape Cod and all the local weather people. Bernard, as you know, is very thorough."

Giselle regarded her friend pityingly through her salmon-pink spectacles embellished with marcasite, and Jennifer thought to herself that she preferred the noble savage look to which she had become acclimatized.

Ironically, the mask had become more real over the years than what was underneath the layers of cosmetics. It had become her distinctive persona, like David's glowing pharaoh's eyes and his habit of leaning against people who mattered and his looking up with a gaze which seemed to penetrate into their very thoughts – into their very souls.

"The weather!" repeated Giselle, with a smirk on her less bright lips. "What can be wrong with the weather? Surely you can't be serious? What's he playing at—?"

"You know how fussy and thorough Bernard is – wouldn't risk our wonderful *Sea Witch* at any price."

Giselle looked at her naïve friend pityingly under the pink, scintillating spectacles that made her look as garish, Jennifer thought, as the painted mask had done.

"And you are seriously contemplating a voyage to the – let me see – ah, the South Seas, wasn't it? – With a man at the helm who's frightened to venture out on a mill pond!"

"Not frightened, Gizzy, just cautious – the sea's not to be trifled with – my Mrs. Broomworthy lost a cousin that way."

"Peter knows the boat," said Gizzy derisively. "She's well known round Martha's Vineyard where Peter often sails – and Pete says he could take her round the world himself any time in any weather. She's a marvelously tight ship, he says – a fortune spent on maintenance – you husband's Uncle Monty was very, very rich and absolutely fanatical about *Sea Witch*. You're very lucky to have her, Jen. We wish she were ours. She's so wonderfully well found, Peter says. Your yawl in the right hands could laugh at the weather on this coast right now. My naïve little thing, your imaginary deep water sailor is not as good as he pretends – he hasn't the experience under that dog collar and he knows it. That's the trouble, not the weather. It's the same with our yachtsmen at our club. Peter says – and he should know being our new commodore – they tend to overplay their skills – except our Admiral Jack. Why don't you ask him to fetch her down? I bet he'd leap at the chance. Don't tell me your rector husband is as good as sailor as Admiral Jack!"

"You know I can't do that, it would break my dear husband's heart to shatter his illusions about his wife being so proud of his sailing skills – especially after locking himself up in his study and dreaming himself into Chichester's shoes and singing sea shanties!"

"If you want my opinion, I think he should stick to singing hymns – I can't somehow imagine him in clerical gray and dog collar with a knife between his sparkling teeth and singing sea shanties!"

Jennifer giggled. "Neither could I till he burst in upon us and nearly gave Mrs. B. a stroke. But perhaps we should be patient, sweetheart – after all, I would rather he was overcautious—" She broke off, catching sight of an astral phenomenon.

"Oh, look, Gizzy darling," exclaimed Jennifer excitedly, pointing at the cloudless sky visible through a break in the leaves of the maple trees. "No, not there – more to your right – look at that star in broad daylight!"

"Are you kidding!" said Giselle, still searching in vain. "Don't tell me you're one of the three wise women foretelling the Second Coming!"

Jennifer frowned as she always did at the slightest levity impugning her religion.

"Don't be facetious," she admonished. "Take off those silly glasses and perhaps you can see better!"

"Don't be silly yourself! I wouldn't see anything then, would I? You know I've been short-sighted right from our college days."

"Well, keep looking then – it's there I tell you. I'm not mad – I just want you to confirm that it's there. Please! Please, Gizzy do it for your best friend. I want it confirmed that I actually saw it – in case it fades away. Keep looking – I know you'll see it eventually. You've got to, it's bright enough. I can't imagine what's taking you so long. Here, run your eye down my finger and you can't miss it. It's really bright."

Giselle tried everything, including following all instructions faithfully, determined to see for herself the elusive star which was making her friend so excited. It was becoming a mystery too fascinating to dismiss as mere hallucination. She had known Jennifer since childhood and she had never hallucinated before. That star had got to be there, yet it wasn't! Jennifer was so excited and certain that she could see it plainly and continuously, and bright into the bargain. But what was the use? Giselle could not see the slightest suspicion of any star but the obvious one.

"No, Jennifer, I give up – there's no star, other than the sun. Anyway, why is it so desperately important to you? Don't tell me it's the dog star and it's leaning on you!"

Jennifer frowned again, "Don't joke about such things – you know it offends me."

"Oh, you poor sacred cow! That star isn't there so don't go working yourself up into a tizzy of religiosity about it."

"Let's change the subject."

"Let's talk about Yachtsman Houndsditch then – happy as a pig in shit, is he? Is he going to join our yacht club now, do you think?"

"Don't compare your husband with poor Bernard who slaves away at his job for his parishioners working all hours of the day and night."

"So does Peter for his clients," giggled Giselle. "They seem to want his services mostly at night! He's always working late at the office, no doubt doubled up with overtime on the couch with his secretary!"

"Poor Gizzy – all marriages are not made in heaven, are they? I don't know how you put up with it."

"If it wasn't for the yacht club, which makes me a VIP now that he's been voted commodore since Admiral Jack retired, and for my darling boy Satan, I really don't think I could put up with it. It's true, isn't it, Jen, animals are more loving and lovable than humans? What say you, Jen?"

Jennifer nodded in assent.

"It's a pity," continued Gizzy. "Nature didn't program things t'other way round – let animals train us instead. The world would be a better place – at least there wouldn't be any wars and we could count on being able to sleep with our own husbands every single night for a change!"

But Giselle realized she had been talking to herself. Her friend had been stargazing again and remained silent.

"Oh, Gizzy!" sadly came the words at last. "That star that was there – it's gone!"

Giselle looked at her pityingly. The stargazer had run out of stars! But Jennifer suddenly ran out of the shade of the maples to get a wider view of the sky. She stood wondering, like a child with a balloon lost to the wind.

Giselle went over in the bright sunlight to pinch her lifelong friend's arm, saying, "Poor naïve Jen, you really do believe all that junk, don't you? You are not just paying lip service; you genuinely do believe, don't you? So perhaps you really did see that star and I'm just not capable because I'm not in tune with the cosmos or whatever there is out there which is beyond our understanding and is only reachable through faith – by a person like yourself.

"Your own David has shown me that there is something out there which he can see with his beautiful glowing eyes and you with yours. I only wish I could see for myself. I suppose signs from above in the biblical sense are like ghosts. Some can see them, but others can't. God knows why!"

"Yes, Giselle, I'm sure He does."

"Keep your faith, Jen – I really envy you in between the jokes I can't resist making."

"It makes life so much simpler when you are not afraid of death, like me, because you know there is a place out in that somewhere just waiting to make you happy – while I'm just scared of dying and waking up to find out that I was wrong all along and that there's no room in the inn for me."

"But there is, my dearest Gizzy, there really is – God will make room in the inn for everyone if each one changes his own sheets, so to speak. That is what Bernard said in his sermon this morning – before the spell of *Sea Witch* turned him into Captain Morgan, scaring the life out of poor old impossible Mrs. B.

"Can you just imagine it – the shock it must have given the poor woman I mean – seeing from her kitchen window her stuffy old hero come running out from his church and leaping over our fence. It was so comic hearing him bawling out his sea shanties at the top of his voice! Can you imagine it – Bernard, of all people, bawling sea shanties as he was sprinting along leaping over fences, Olympic style, with his long legs!

"Then I come over expecting the noble savage in all her painted glory, and what do I find instead – my best friend turned into someone I hardly recognize. An attractive, faultlessly dressed secretary with fancy glasses that every boss like your husband wants on his knee! Then the star in the sky that nobody can see but me—"

Jennifer broke off to glance at her wristwatch.

"It's time I was leaving. There must be a witch on board *Sea Witch*. Everything's changing. I hope and pray that when I get back to the rectory my David hasn't turned into a lapdog like Mrs. Timmins' Fee-Fee!"

"The one that wet her pants at your garden party right in front of Mayor Favioli, do you mean?" chuckled Giselle. "On the other hand the silly little thing didn't, did she, it was a just a joke Yachtsman Houndsditch played on the poor woman. We turned her bag upside down on your stall remember, and it didn't pour urine on *The Painless Path To Jesus*, thank God!"

"Knowing you, I bet you were hoping it did!"

"No, I didn't really. I just wasn't thinking when I emptied the contents over those precious books. Don't look like that. I wouldn't really."

"You wouldn't?"

"Well maybe! But I didn't as it happens. Please believe me – I wouldn't dare on those best-sellers. It would be like robbing the poor box, wouldn't it?"

"Yes, Gizzy and do you know what?"

"Is there more?"

Jennifer laughed. "Can you believe it? Mrs. Timmins carrying the Shitzu under her arm actually asked Mayor Favioli to smell Fee-Fee's breath!"

"What the hell for? Don't tell me – drunken lap driving?"

"No, to test for halitosis!"

"And did he survive the test?"

"I think he looked a bit groggy afterwards, but I didn't see him in the obituaries, so I presume he's still mayor," laughed Jennifer.

Chapter Thirty

Immediately upon letting herself into the rectory after staying on to dine with Giselle when the stargazing session was finally abandoned, Jennifer experienced a profound sense of foreboding. Something was definitely very wrong. For one thing, it was the very first time that David did not rush to greet her and she knew he must be missing again. She felt quite faint and had to sit down, but at the same time called out the housekeeper who came hurrying in with bad news written all over her face.

She came straight to the point. "The Reverend has gone off to Cape Cod and has taken David with him, Mrs. Houndsditch, but he said not to worry because he will look after him all right. He said the weather was suddenly just perfect for bringing home his new boat."

"Did he say when he would be back?"

"He said late tomorrow evening or the next morning if the weather holds out."

"Didn't he leave any telephone number or anything, or a note for me?" A very grave Mrs. Broomworthy shook her head. "No, I'm afraid not, Mrs. Houndsditch. Shall I send in Robert to you? He's barking his head off as you can hear. I think he misses David, because he won't eat his ice cream. That's most unusual, isn't it?"

Jennifer was too distressed to answer Mrs. B.'s question, instead she had one of her own.

"What time did they leave – by car I presume?"

"Yes, by car and I would say it was only about an hour after you left to have tea with Mrs. Carboni. So I would say they should be up there by now if the traffic isn't too bad. Maybe he'll call to say he's arrived safely."

"Did he say he would?"

"No he didn't, actually, but I expect he might. But then he's acting up a bit strange these last couple of days, isn't he? Never behaved anything like that before in all these years I've been looking after him," she ended up pointedly. But Jennifer was too distressed even to comment.

Suddenly she felt exhausted, and with her bearded collie preceding her up the stairs at a gallop, she dismissed Mrs. B. and went up to lie down on her bed. *That star*, she thought, *could it be a sign from heaven?* Giselle had jokingly said so. But then many a true word has been spoken in jest. As she lay on the bed with anxiety like a kind of soporific coldness running through her veins, she dozed off to the question in her mind, *What could that portentous star mean? Was it heralding good news or bad?*

છ

As an exceedingly excited Jennifer came rushing down to the telephone and collapsed beside it onto the pew-like wooden settle in the hallway, the majestic grandfather clock annoyingly began booming out ten resounding gongs that obliterated the voice on the other end of the line. But she recognized sufficiently, with her pulse rate accelerating, that it was her husband's. For the moment that was all that really mattered – not to be cut off.

"Wait, Bernard – how could you! Wait till the clock stops, I can't hear a bloody thing!"

As soon as there was silence, she heard her husband's voice come through as clearly as if he had been standing beside her. She even caught the faint whining of her beloved David who must have been at his feet.

"Darling, I love you, don't be angry. Mrs. Broomworthy must have explained to you in detail. I had to leave immediately – the tide wouldn't wait. The weather was perfect and I had to make that tide with *Sea Witch's* deep keel to get out of the boatyard, without getting stuck out there."

"Why did you take my David? Couldn't you spare a thought as to how you would be leaving me all alone and devastated?"

"I left you with Robert – couldn't you spare me one dog?"

"Why didn't you take Robert – you know David's scared of water. Supposing he jumps overboard?"

Now she could hear her husband laughing and it made her angry – how could he at a time like this?

"How could you do this to me? Didn't you stop to think I might be driven mad with anxiety?"

"There is no need to worry your pretty head, sweetheart. David is safe with me. He isn't in any danger, *Sea Witch* is the tightest yacht on the coast. And the weather is simply perfect now. But if I had waited I would have been a fool, the Coast Guard said, because I could have run into that hurricane creeping up from the south. I had to move quickly, I had no choice. Every hour counted if I was to dodge that hurricane moving up, my love. Try to be reasonable. I'll be home tomorrow night, God willing, and you'll have your David safe and sound. Then we'll celebrate, Cap'n Jennifer darling."

"But you could have taken me with you, you could have phoned Giselle and I would have come rushing."

"But I did phone and got the busy signal. There just was no time. I had to leave the moment I got the Coast Guard report."

"But I thought you went into the city with your organist? I don't understand."

"Unfortunately we had a slow puncture and just made it back home on the rim of the wheel. Anyway, it was a blessing in disguise because that message from the Coast Guard was waiting for me on the answering machine. That flat tire was a lucky break. Now don't you want to speak to David? Wait a second, I'll put him on the line. Don't be angry, I love you honey-bunch."

Chapter Thirty-one

Robert Bearded Collie was in a state of profound anxiety. Was Uncle Bernard in his church? But this could not be verified because dogs were never allowed inside. But more disturbing still was the fact that his pal, the wonder dog David, was nowhere to be seen.

Robert had witnessed him traveling faster than sound, for he remembered when, that day at the seaside whilst he (Robert) was keenly looking, David had sped out of sight on the water's edge before he (Robert) had finished barking!

Where had he run out of sight to this time and why had he not returned? It was a matter for grave concern. It was lonely without him. Jennifer was now always lying in bed, not asleep but listening for the telephone. Every time it rang she ran downstairs to pick it up. She never used to run downstairs before. Much of the time she spent also upon her knees talking to herself in whispers. She seemed to be asking somebody something, of somebody not there, a human mystery!

She was behaving in a way that was out of her normal routine, which was very disturbing as well to a dog, a creature of habit – something moves or is heard – a time to bark, food is put on the table, a time to beg, someone says "walkies," time to lift a leg. All essential for a dog's peace of mind.

Where was Uncle Bernard also? He too was out of routine at night, by not being in bed with Jennifer and helping to make the bedclothes move. Afterwards in the mornings, but not every time, the dogs received extra big helpings of muffin chucked to them while both humans seemed in a particularly good mood.

Robert had done a great deal of pondering upon the subject, but the results were disappointing. He could not make head nor tail of it. Jennifer was acting so strangely and was forever kissing and hugging him and he was puzzled by the extra show of affection. Even Mrs. Broomworthy was now being much nicer than usual to him and talking to him occasionally in a pleasant voice rather than her customary horrible voice.

"Poor Robert," she would say. "You miss David, don't you? You know I warned your Jennifer that the sea is not for amateurs and now he's gone and bought himself a captain's cap and taken David to sea with him in his new boat. I told her a captain's cap does not make a sailor. And now the Coast Guards are out looking for them. That's madness for you. Poor David. I hope he can swim."

Time-wise, the bearded collie was completely disorientated, for Jennifer now lay in bed by day as well as by night, always with the door open listening for the telephone and with the television on, tuned in to the news channel.

And he never did know if it was time to bark the morning reveille at her pillow or go to sleep on the floor at the foot of her bed. Or to keep quiet when she knelt down and started talking to that somebody that wasn't there, with her hands together and her eyes closed.

He had to convince himself that all was well with the world from a dog's point of view, now that David was gone and his mistress was so sad and behaving hysterically.

Robert went about sniffing those favorite haunts, including gardener Tony's wheelbarrow, where he caught, nostalgically, David's strong scent on its single wheel. At that saddest moment, he would have given up an avalanche of ice cream for the return of the sea hound.

"Robert old pal, what do you think of your old shipmate Midshipman David Greyhound sailing the high seas with Cap'n Houndsditch?"

Robert barked miserably in reply to a question he did not understand.

"That's right old fellah, bark away, I don't blame you. He should have taken you too – penalty I suppose for having the big guard-dog voice. You see, it pays to be silent sometimes. Then you don't get put to minding the premises.

"Hey there! Don't take it so serious – they'll be back soon – only sailing from Cape Cod – not Cape Horn – you must be as bad as old Ma Broomstick who thinks the Marquesas are near Martha's Vineyard – that's a laff!

"Sorry, pal, not laffing are you? Miss yer old buddy David, don't you? Hey, don't get up – roll over and we'll give the old tum another quick rub. Don't tell me you've been scratching again – the old miracle flea collar not doing its job eh? Your father when he gets back won't be too pleased – apparently he hasn't found out yet that electronic flea collars only produce electronic fleas." As Robert licked his hand as a reward for rubbing his belly, Tony exclaimed suddenly, "Robert! Robert dog! Din-dins!"

Mrs. Broomworthy was drumming with a spoon on a frying pan from the kitchen window.

And Tony said with a laugh, "Jump to it, pal, old Ma Broomstick's on the warpath."

But Tony was mistaken. Sunshine beamed from her heavy jowls as Robert was ushered in by Tony to an appetizer of ice cream, thoughtfully softened a trifle in the microwave oven to make the experience last longer.

Her manner was all sweetness and light as she said, "You will be pleased to hear, shaggy puppy, you'll be having your fast friend back soon – won't that be nice?"

Then, when Robert had made short work of the appetizer, she continued, "Here, let me give you some more, we've got something to celebrate. Your mommy had a message from the Coast Guard just now saying *Sea Witch* passed Martha's Vineyard—"

Robert looked up through his long hair over his eyes with a blank expression and wagged his tail.

"They are getting close, Robert – Martha's Vineyard is not far away. It's near the Marquesas, Robert, not far – isn't that wonderful news? You'll have your David back soon."

Chapter Thirty-two

But Mrs. Broomworthy's euphoria was short-lived. A later report threw Jennifer into inconsolable hysteria when it was reported a few hours later that a wreckage had been found, and that a plane was out searching for any signs of the two bodies alive or dead in the sea.

Very soon after hearing of the terrible tragedy from Mrs. Broomworthy over the telephone, Giselle and her husband Commodore Peter arrived at the rectory to fetch poor Jennifer and take her to their home.

They were surprised at how calm and stoical the widow seemed at the loss of her beloved husband and their dog, presumed both drowned at sea after their yacht had capsized.

But they did not know half of the story, which was Jennifer's closely kept secret.

It was a pact made between herself and her all-merciful, all-understanding God, which she of the all trusting faith would never betray.

Before the arrival of her faithful friends, and upon hearing of the horrendous news relayed by a calling policeman, she had immediately thereafter rushed up to her bedroom to become hysterical in private, with Mrs. Broomworthy trying to pacify her while having to speak through a locked door.

It was then that the housekeeper had telephoned Mrs. Carboni, her mistress' closest friend. Although Jennifer's face was swollen round the eyes and her make-up was heavily smudged, yet she appeared as calm now externally as a windless sea. The Carbonis found her door open and the widow on her knees by her bed. They caught the end of a softly spoken poignant prayer.

As he held her arm and gently helped her downstairs, and out to his waiting big motor car, Jennifer warmed to her Good Samaritan and felt a little ashamed for harboring those thoughts concerning his late office hours.

In the back seat, with Peter beside her, she felt comforted as he took her hand and held it for the journey, while Giselle drove.

Surprisingly, Jennifer suddenly found in him a true friend in her hour of need. He promised to take days off from his office, and, in his own comforting words "take care of everything."

He took charge, saying he would motor along the coast making inquiries among the fishermen and offering them Jennifer's generous five-thousand-dollar reward for each of the two bodies recovered – those of the Reverend Bernard Ignatius Houndsditch and her beloved David from late of the yawl, *Sea Witch*, that had capsized.

The greyhound's body when found, beached or fished up in the fishermen's nets, was to be handled with extreme care in order to preserve it in as good a state as possible for burial in a dog cemetery. These were the instructions for Peter to follow. Afterwards the fisherman was to deliver the body to Dr. Bigden, the veterinarian, and Peter was to contact Reverend Golightly who would see to the burial arrangements. The human body would, of course, be a matter for the police and the coroner in the first instance. But the animal would be exempt from that formality.

Peter thought it curious, as he motored north to immediately begin his investigations that Rev. Golightly should be entering into the picture at all. *Surely the veterinarian could take care of the whole thing*, he thought. But he had agreed to respect the distraught woman's behests to the letter. He would not distress her further by insensitive questioning.

However, he was surprised at how clear had been her instructions, considering the great strain she must have been under. If David had been human, as an attorney Peter N Carboni Esquire would have been suspicious.

It was as if the whole proceedings had been choreographed a long time ago in her mind. She was suddenly enunciating coherently and quietly, betraying little emotion. And it appealed to the yachtsman's seamanlike, traditionally brave front – the ship is sinking but the captain commands – cool and calm, like an iceberg with most of it hidden.

All the facts regarding the tragedy were not yet known and his call from his Cape Cod hotel to the Coast Guard stations had only revealed that a *Mayday! Mayday!* distress call from an unidentified vessel had been received and that a plane had gone out searching. Three lifeboats had been launched but had found no trace of the vessel that had broken off its distress call so quickly – after an ominous, loud cracking noise had been heard on the coast station radiotelephone. The operator said it sounded like a mast breaking up under strain.

The circumstances were mystifying. Very little flotsam from the wreckage had been seen, even by the plane whose horizon was so much wider than that of the tallest ship at sea. Moreover, during the night there had been a full moon and during the day scant mist to impede visibility. It put Peter in mind of that controversial puzzle – the Bermuda Triangle – repeating itself further north!

The sea had been choppy but not unduly rough, though there had been a treacherous onshore wind threatening any sailing vessel unwisely hugging the coast. But it would blow a fast passage for a sailboat heading south and keeping wide safe clearance from the shoreline.

Because the distress *Mayday, Mayday* radiotelephone distress message (as distinct from the Morse key SOS) had been cut short, there had been insufficient time for the coast station radio operator to take a bearing of the signal. Two coast stations had picked up the tragically curtailed signal which, if it had been completed, could have enabled the two coast stations to take a cross bearing to put the position of the yacht within a very small triangle on the chart, at the time of capsizing.

Thereupon an immediate successful rescue attempt could have been made. As it was, the searchers had nothing to go on but the fact that somewhere within the limited range of the signal a vessel had foundered. But why?

An experienced yachtsman like Bernard should have been able to handle a tight well found thirty-nine feet yawl in a sea in which any competent fisherman could have trawled his net.

It certainly seemed to Peter a trifle unwise to have set course for the narrow strait between Martha's Vineyard and the mainland in a dangerous onshore wind, when the wide Atlantic Ocean provided a safe alternative, to avoid drifting onto rocks. A more seamanlike course would have been to beat out into the Atlantic and then gain the advantage of a fast broad reach to his destination at Montauk on the entry into Long Island Sound.

On the other hand, such a course would necessarily have been considerably longer. Yet it could well have proven quicker in the long run, because any drifting south made in beating westward would have brought him nearer his destination and, what is more, upon that same favorable broad reach, the fastest point in sailing.

So Peter was perplexed as to the reasons influencing the curious chosen course. But no doubt eventually the mystery would be solved. To Commodore Peter of his yacht club it presented a fascinating puzzle to unravel.

Perhaps the Coast Guard could be mistaken – that the yacht passing Martha's Vineyard earlier was not *Sea Witch* after all?

Then why had not the plane sighted either of them if that had been the case? On the other hand, if there had been two yachts and one mistaken by the Coast Guard for the other, then two yachts must have vanished without trace – which was even more incredible!

The Coast Guards' presumptions, therefore, sounded more real. So it would be cruel to build up Jennifer's hopes on a long shot, when she seemed resigned to her fate. Instead, Peter resolved he would keep his speculations to himself, as he had done when they were driving her to his home.

He recalled during the long journey to Cape Cod, his wife Giselle, her best friend, saying as she was driving, "Leave it all to Peter, darling, I know he'll turn up trumps – he knows the coast like the back of his hand – so leave everything to Peter and your own Gizzy."

Giselle Carboni's words of comfort were no exaggeration. Peter, her attorney husband, was indeed, since Admiral Jack's retirement, commodore of his prestigious yacht club – with a knowledge of the northeast coast second only to the local fishermen and coastguards.

Chapter Thirty-three

"Jennifer! Jennifer! Hurry! Hurry! Exciting news! Peter on the phone – they've found David! I'm sorry Bernard's still missing. Maybe they'll find him later—"

Giselle broke off, seeing that she was talking to herself when her friend, despite her arthritic hip, swept downstairs and rushed past her to the telephone.

"Jennifer, Peter here," said the voice excitedly. "I'm on Long Island in a fisherman's cottage – at Sag Harbor on Block Island Sound to be precise – he's claiming the reward for David. He says he caught a dog in his net far out to sea. He's amazingly well preserved – you'd have to look twice to know he isn't just sleeping."

"Oh God! My poor David! You've seen him then?"

"Of course. And he's all in one piece, not harmed in any way visible – just drowned and looking so peaceful. Like I said you'd think he was just sleeping. Quite remarkable considering the hungry fish about, is it not?"

"Where have they put him – not outside in the yard, I hope?"

"Oh, no!" lied Peter compassionately. "He's sleeping on the sofa in the living room in front of me. Do you want me to write out a check for him now or wait and see if the man finds Bernard and make out a check for ten thousand to cover both rewards? Unfortunately Bernard hasn't been found yet, but the man says he's going out again on the next tide."

"No don't wait – pay the man now – I want to have a last look at him, you see, before they bury my poor darling."

"You really want to see him? He may not be – I don't know how to put it delicately – when Dr. Bigden hands him over to wherever?"

"You don't have to worry about that – just pay the man and have him deliver him to Doctor Bigden at once."

"What about the fisherman wanting to go out again in search of Bernard?"

"Get someone else to do it."

"You really mean that? Time is not on our side you know. Maybe you are not thinking clearly in your present state? It's understandable." He heard her sob and was touched.

"Peter! You promised me, remember? You can't let me down. You gave me your word. I'm counting on you. Do as I say, get somebody else to go. There must be plenty of other fishermen around."

"Okay then, if you insist. The man does have a son, I'm sure he'll be pleased to take over."

He heard a great sigh of relief and knew he hadn't the heart to deny her in what he regarded as a foolish demand, but which, for some quirk of womanhood, was poignantly important to her. He thought to himself that he could never understand women anyway – even his own wife! So let it be. She would hate him for the rest of her life, if he let her down. He was a successful divorce lawyer and knew how bitter thwarted women could become. In fact, "hell hath no fury like a woman scorned." Somebody had said that, he didn't know who, but it was true nevertheless.

"Will you describe your greyhound fully to me please," said the cautious attorney, "before I write out my check on your behalf?" He then waited for her to recover and patiently listened fully to her clearly detailed, long description which superfluously included some of the dog's merits.

As soon as she had finished speaking, he said without hesitation, "It's David! There can be no doubt, so I'll write out the check. The man says his son will deliver him nicely wrapped up in a blanket to Dr. Bigden first thing in the morning, as soon as his office opens. I understand that he is to deliver the dog to your veterinarian at the address you gave me – correct?"

"Yes," replied Jennifer sobbing, "but don't wait till the morning, get the man to telephone and Bigden will open up specially – he'll do it as a favor to me."

And pragmatic Peter thought to himself, *I bet that favor cost her an arm and a leg!* Women! No wonder I do such good business out of them and yet again I must be nuts myself doing all this as a true favor to my wife's friend. Although it will do wonders for my image when I tell my secretary Jane all about it on our next date. Like the famous Brit, Walpole says, "every man has his price."

After he put down the phone in the fisherman's cottage it immediately rang again. This time it was his wife. She knew the number to call because he had called her yesterday and given it to her.

"Are you going to stay over, darling, to see if you can trace her husband – or do you think it is hopeless by now?"

"Pretty hopeless, pet, unless he's been picked up by one of those Johnny-the-Greek flags of convenience ships – you know the type – well below the Plimsoll line with cargo and running on a shoestring, with their gear always breaking down, including their engines and life-saving radio."

"You know, Peter, I think you're a genius! How on earth did you find that dog so quickly? Perhaps you missed your vocation. You remind me of Sherlock Holmes!"

"I think you are exaggerating a little, sweetie," replied the yachtsman modestly, yet proudly at the same time. "I was only following a seaman's hunch – like feeling the wind on your neck and knowing which side to put the tiller over. I figured if they hadn't found any wreckage north, it must have drifted further south – so I scurried back south to Long Island. But to be quite fair to the Coast Guard, they were also on the same tack and got there first—"

"Did they find the wreckage then, Pete?" interrupted his wife, unable to contain herself. "Hurry up, don't keep me in suspense – what did they find – where?"

"Okay – to the point, yes, they found it first. Hold your breath – you'll never believe at Montauk. They actually made it to their destination – Montauk on Long Island – but ironically not in one piece! The wreckage was washed up all over the rocks near the lighthouse. But the fishermen must take full credit for finding the dog – make that clear to your friend."

"Of course, I understand – but go on – how in hell did you get everywhere at the right time? Don't sell yourself short."

"Well, I suppose I did play a tiny role in all of this! And the reward was a great help, too, – otherwise who would have gone out fishing a whole day for only a dog? Wouldn't fetch much at the fish auction, would it?"

"Don't joke at a time like this – you don't know what David means to poor Jen – she's absolutely broken up."

"Sorry, sorry, I meant no harm – I didn't know – I thought her husband was—?"

"Yes, of course her husband as well, naturally, but David also, he was just like a surrogate son after losing – you know in that horrendous motoring accident. But go on, let's hear more about your own clever part in the story. I can't wait to hear it."

"Well," said Peter with a quick awkward glance at the fisherman who was pretending to be far away, looking out of the window at a moonlit view of his trash containers, plus the shed where the dead body of the dog was wrapped up in a blanket. "You'll never guess the cause of the capsize – a whale!"

"A whale?"

"Yes, a whale – poetic justice, I suppose! You know this was once a famous whaling port."

"Infamous whaling port, you mean – yes I know – go on, how do you know it was a whale?"

"A piece of its fluke is still lodged in the yawl's skeg after the poor creature must have torn itself free in panic. It must have shaken *Sea Witch* till her main mast cracked and probably turned her over at the same time. That breaking up of the mast must have been the noise heard on the coast station RT. The *Mayday* call would have been transmitted with the sound in the background. To continue, if you want to hear more?"

"Of course I do."

"Well, most of the yacht in one form or another is strewn over the rocks – most pathetic – the mizzen is somehow still clinging to the smashed stern by its stays and with its sail in shreds. But that main, of course, is adrift obviously with some bits of topsides hanging from its chain plates. The main is adrift probably on its way to the Azores – and the skipper too, most likely, poor man. He didn't stand a chance in the Atlantic – unless he had one of those wonderful thermal coats and a covered-over inflatable life raft on deck."

Peter caught the fisherman eyeing the old brass ship's clock next to its twin barometer on the wall.

"Sounds like a Macbeth of the sea, doesn't it? – Very tragic! Must wrap up or this poor man will have spent all his reward money on this call – I'll tell you all about it from deck to truck when I get back. I'll stay over here in my nice little pub a couple more days, just in case anything turns up but don't hold your breath. The sea is a very cruel mistress. Look after poor Jennifer, and tell her not to worry, her dog is being well taken care of – I'm signing off – over and out – love you sweetie."

"That will be all then, sir?" said the fisherman losing his fascination, with the trash cans and taking another glance at the ship's clock. "My son will be ready to drive down with the dog while you're making out that check – Tom will get cracking right away. He's in the yard somewhere with his lobster pots."

Chapter Thirty-four

"Jennifer! It's for you," said Giselle, passing the telephone to within reach of her friend sitting reading the Bible by the light of a standard lamp beside the settee. "It's Reverend Golightly with good news about David, he says—"

Jennifer dropped the Bible and snatched the instrument with both hands.

"Is that you, Jennifer my dear? I've got good news to cheer you up."

"Yes, Reverend, it is I."

"Well, my dear, you will be very pleased to hear that the Sunningdale Memorial Parlor have done a magnificent job – fit for a president! I said they would, didn't I?"

"Reverend, thank you! Thank you! When will I be able to—?"

"You may go along to visit this evening after nine o'clock when they are closed. They are giving you a special private viewing – no mourners milling around in their other little chapels to poke their noses in. All extremely private and discreet – most important, isn't it? And don't forget the service in my church. Tomorrow morning at ten o'clock I'll be waiting to welcome you at the door. And rest assured that I haven't forgotten your chosen hymn to be sung, beginning at the second stanza: 'Run the straight race through God's good grace.' How poignantly apt! And I hope with all my heart our beloved Savior has granted your prayer."

Jennifer looked around anxiously, fearing Golightly might be over-heard as she listened, deeply moved, whilst walking towards the window out of earshot, with the instrument on its long cord.

"When I first heard the tragic news I was really shaken as you must have been. Your wonderful husband, your wonderful David, taken in their prime, cut down like a flower. Tragic! Tragic! But I am sure our all-merciful Creator has a divine purpose. We must never lose faith. I shall pray for you and for your precious loved ones that our beloved Lord has called unto His bosom."

"Oh Reverend!" exclaimed Jennifer joyfully, "how can I ever thank you enough?"

"You have already my dear, you have saved me from ruin. We Samaritans have already proved ourselves to each other in a true Christian spirit, although they were not Christians, were they, if we read our Bible – the Samaritans, I mean?

"You must be relieved about poor David being so well taken care of. How lucky for your friend to have found him like that in the great ocean. You see, God works in mysterious ways – it was meant for him to be returned to you – a pity the same could not apply to your dear husband. But have no fear, I am sure he is already in heaven. So then, take a good night's rest after your visit to the chapel and I will see you in the morning, my dear.

"Now I will just go over very briefly again with you the arrangements in place. The limousine will be picking you up from the parlor at nine thirty after you arrive there by taxi from your friend's house, to safeguard the impression that you are only going to the dog cemetery. That was your wish, wasn't it?"

"Yes, Reverend."

"I have left a veil for you at the parlor – just in case you haven't bought one. You don't want to be seen wearing a veil by Mrs. Carboni and I know you have been in no mood to get out to the shops yourself."

"Thank you, Reverend – very thoughtful of you."

"Not at all, not at all – now listen carefully. Don't forget, after the service the hearse will be on its way to the tomb where I shall be waiting to fulfill my promise to you. But there will be no mourners except yourself. The limousine, of course, will be taking you home afterwards. But one limousine is just like another. Now it is not wise for you to be seen too long in the churchyard so the service at the cemetery will be short but in fulfillment of our secret pact. Nothing for you to worry about at this most distressing time. I have given a lot of thought—"

"I know you have and I am very grateful."

"So there is nothing for you to worry about – absolutely nothing. Nobody will ever know our little secret – strictly between ourselves and in hope of our merciful God's forgiveness."

"That last word?" said Jennifer, turning to eye Giselle anxiously as the latter pretended to be solely occupied with the face forever being perfected in the mirror of her compact.

"I understand, Jennifer, my dear, but we are all sinners, are we not? Only the Catholics have saints on their register. We Episcopalians humbly concede the inequality if it is the Creator's wish."

"Can't I—"

"No, my dear, it wouldn't be wise – you trust me, don't you?"

"Of course, Reverend – of course, of course!"

"So be it, then. We need to keep all this strictly between ourselves, don't we? We need to attract as little attention as possible. Leave everything to me. All is set to run like clockwork – trust me, as I am sure you will. And remember to get a good night's rest. Most important. You need to be at your best for David in the morning, to see him off on his heavenly journey, God willing, for we must always submit to the Divine Will – we are not entities but only particles subject to the rule of the unassailable all-wise Divine purpose.

"But remember, my dear, that death is not an end but only a beginning of another voyage into new life, where goodness and mercy shall always follow as surely as night shadows day."

"Thank you, Rector, for all the trouble you have taken to see to all the arrangements and everything for my poor David at the Hartsdale dog cemetery. I'm really too distressed to do this for myself. So kind of you to offer. And thank your friend for me at the dog cemetery. And don't forget the inscription MY BELOVED PET DAVID GREYHOUND SADLY MISSED, she said into the telephone after Golightly had hung up!

Jennifer said this very distinctly for the benefit of Giselle, seen listening while pretending to be still engrossed in her omnipresent reflection.

"Jen, you were a long time with your one-sided conversation – any problems?" inquired her best friend anxiously and curious withal as to what they could be.

"No problems, darling Giselle – Reverend Golightly took care of them all for me – such a good kind man and a real Samaritan in time of need – just like you and Peter. I don't know how I could have managed without you all. He arranged everything for me at the Hartsdale Dog Cemetery. He's taken care of all my special requirements and of course, he has influence. He's been such a dear!"

"Don't tell me David's going into a tomb? Must cost a fortune?"

Jennifer gave a little start, but quickly recovered, knowing Giselle could not have cottoned on but was only fishing; a truth unwittingly spoken in jest!

"Yes, Giselle, David deserves the very best."

"Must cost you a fortune!" repeated her friend incredulously.

"Giselle – please! I don't care about money at a time like this."

"Sorry! Sorry my dear – wasn't thinking properly."

"Dearest Gizzy – so you will know, being so close to me, how I don't feel like answering a lot of questions right now. I must take a last look at my poor David. I must call a taxi."

"What, at this time of night? Don't you realize it's nearly nine twenty, Dr. Bigden's office will be closed."

"Reverend Golightly has made special arrangements for me – David will be in a shed outside and the key is being left under a flower pot."

"Why tonight? Why not tomorrow morning?" persisted Giselle, more curious than ever.

"Darling, spare me the questions please, they are collecting him very early in the morning and the Reverend has made arrangements already. I cannot alter things now – please, please let me be! If you want to be helpful, call me a taxi."

"No need, I will take you, silly thing, and we'll have Satan with us to protect you – you never know these days who's prowling about."

Giselle took her hand out of Satan's foaming, slobbering mouth to put a wet hand comfortingly round her friend's shoulder.

"You'll protect us won't you, Satan?" the mistress called to her ferocious pet guard dog and the black Doberman barked reassuringly in reply, showing teeth like a saber-toothed tiger.

"So you see, it's settled, I'll go and get the car."

"Giselle!" cried Jennifer in alarm, seizing the other's hand and pulling her back.

"Yes, darling, what is it?"

"Please try to understand – I've got to be alone with David – just this once let me be. Please! Please!"

"We'll wait in the car outside – we won't come in – I understand fully."

"No you don't! I'm afraid – I mean really alone – I would break down having someone close around me. I can just about bear the taxi driver – a complete stranger, waiting outside, but not someone close like you, Gizzy darling. Please, please, I beg you let me be!"

Jennifer was beginning to panic, desperately holding on – determined to extricate herself somehow without arousing suspicion, while her heart was thumping and with adrenaline flowing to meet each new difficulty put in her path.

Fortunately, Giselle finally gave in and reluctantly called a taxi before the Rev. Golightly's meticulous "best laid plans of mice and men" succumbed to the poet's warning.

Chapter Thirty-five

The taxi driver arrived without delay. He held open the door like a limousine chauffeur at the end of the journey. He was not disappointed in his tip, on the contrary he was delighted and helped the mourner up the funeral parlor steps, opened the unlocked door and handed her over to the funeral director.

The suave gentleman in black, sleek as a raven, was seated, reading a paperback in his imposing marble entrance hall. Immediately the man stood up and greeted the mourner most unctuously.

He was a middle-aged, stocky, well-nourished-looking individual in black coat and gray striped trousers and wearing in his lapel a flower as false as his smile and his hair.

Impossibly thick sideburns plunged to a greasy blue chin. He reeked like a plantation of hyacinths!

He quickly stubbed out his expensive cigar into an ashtray on a chromium pedestal and stretched out his well-manicured hand to greet his fashionably dressed and bejeweled VIP client.

After the greeting, his client's eyes gazed up at the exotic potted palm towering splendidly to the fan-vaulted ceiling, while potted sacred music discreetly flowed very faintly through an arch framing impenetrable gloom.

Another arch dramatically lit by candles led into a small Gothic chapel with stained glass windows, filtering moonlight atmospherically through the stained robes of apostles blessing the proceedings from between skillfully carved stone mullions.

"My deepest sympathies, Mrs. Houndsditch," said the funeral director unctuously, taking Jennifer's arm gently and leading her through the Gothic arch into the beautiful little vaulted chapel. Once inside, he stopped fastidiously to puff aerosol over the coffin, whereupon a bluebottle fly buzzed into the air. This visibly disturbed Jennifer and the man apologized, saying that the regular attendant on duty had been called to the hospital, as his wife is suddenly taken ill.

After waiting for the fly to settle and be expertly exterminated, he stepped briskly ahead to lift off the corpse's veil of mutton cloth to reveal David lying in state beneath, his beautiful head as if asleep on a white silk pillow, while the rest of his body, concealed beneath a gorgeous crimson quilt in his magnificent custom-made casket reposed in kingly fashion upon a catafalque, lit by a forest of candles.

Here indeed was the art of presentation perfectly executed to the high standard of the establishment's deserved reputation. The man departed discreetly like a shadow disappearing from vanishing light.

A voice from the gloom behind her called out before closing the door quietly, "You'll find the deceased is sleeping very peacefully; a beautiful face – simply beautiful – we've really pulled out all the stops, Mrs. Houndsditch. The casket is our classic most luxurious 'Cardinal mark two model' as you can see for yourself – wonderful quality, isn't it? Impervious lining, with simulated gold fittings and nameplate and Japanese satin quilt – fit for a king!

"It was the one picked out by Reverend Golightly and a very wise choice, if I may say so, in view of the greater width required this time for proper presentation."

Jennifer stood in awe and silence, waiting to be left alone with her loved one, hearing the mere drone of words surreally as in a dream. But she was greatly impressed with what they had done with such skill and painstaking care to please. Their so-called presentation was unquestionably magnificent.

"I'll leave you alone now – take as long as you wish and when you are through just ring the bell on the table inside by the lilies and I'll come back and lock up. But take your time – there's absolutely no rush in our profession."

Jennifer held back her overwhelming emotion until the man had closed the door gently from the outside, while the slight draft thus created sighed into the phalanx of flickering candelabra on the golden pedestals surrounding the catafalque displaying its poignant burden.

Thereupon her stoical composure disintegrated and she broke down in a squall of tears, as she hurled herself onto the torso of David, with his one glowing exposed eye not concealed by the pillow staring as if at peace to see that she had come to comfort him. He looked so incredibly alive.

No sign was there of his terrible ordeal by drowning. Nor was there the slightest trace of nibbling by fish or of bloating by sea water when she lifted the coverlet. The handsome tan and white fur looked as if it had been shampooed and then blow-dried, but Jennifer noticed that few of his short whiskers remained and there was a new small black spot on the side of his face. Otherwise, he appeared in death no different from the incredibly handsome dog he had been such a short while ago – a giant graceful greyhound that in life had made people turn their heads. After an emotional display of wetting his encapsulated smiling face with her tears, while his one visible pharaoh's eye with its corner prolonged and underlined in black glowed at her, Jennifer knelt down on the purple knee rest and prayed a very long time. Prayed for his unacknowledged right to possess a soul to enable him to accompany her into heaven.

An hour or so later, whilst she was still giving thanks to the Lord for His all-enduring mercies, she became conscious of loud footsteps pacing the tiles around the potted palms in the reception hall. Jennifer rose and bestowed a final kiss and stroked the last farewell on the velvety smooth presciently staring face as the footsteps could be heard approaching.

As she blotted her tears preparatory to leaving, the candles started collectively guttering, though she could feel no draft. It was as if St. Francis, watching over on the eve of his Feast and seeing her departing, was extinguishing them so that David would not be distressed at seeing her go.

To the funeral director's astonishment, all the wildly guttering candles were petering out most incredibly from such a faint draft as what he caused when opening the door.

Chapter Thirty-six

It was October the fourth, the Feast of Saint Francis of Assisi and the Franciscans would be receiving animals into their churches for "The Blessing of the Animals.' They would be walking up the aisle with their masters and mistresses to be sprinkled with holy water. But this was not a Franciscan church; it was Episcopal. Nevertheless, the lover of animals, St. Francis of Assisi, could have been looking down and smiling compassionately, for the bright October morning sun was spotlighting the steps of the Reverend Golightly's atmospheric Gothic church as Jennifer arrived, punctually, by the memorial parlor's immaculate limousine.

Darkly shrouded under her delicate veil of widow's weeds, her heart was thumping as with great ceremony the chauffeur assisted her up the wide steep stone steps, still dotted with confetti from the wedding of the day before.

One of St. Francis' beloved birds was singing in the pine whose shadow sloped across her path as she climbed very slowly, with her black-gloved hand upon the chauffeur's arm. But the man did not hear the bird singing because it was only David's magic pine singing in her mind.

There was an unusual silence, as if the street had turned into a graveyard, a cold cemetery of grief.

A faintly smiling Reverend Golightly, in full regalia as befitted the solemn occasion, was there keeping his promise to greet her at the door which was being held open for him by his handsome, tall, young sexton in a flowing black cassock.

Beyond, Jennifer could see the magnificent wreathed casket already waiting on the parlor's draped conveyance, just inside the aisle, with morticians standing alongside like four stiff black sentinels guarding a royal corpse. Ahead of the casket a small melancholy white-surpliced altar boy stood frozen to his long flickering candle in its ornate silver stick in the form of a cross.

The timing was perfect as if all had been well rehearsed. The little altar boy moved forward to allow the rector to take up his station a few steps behind him. The organ thundered a few bars and then stopped abruptly, so that the rector could be heard eloquently reciting the twenty-third psalm as the procession snailed up the aisle, with Jennifer tagging along behind, sobbing quietly under her delicate black veil.

She was surprised and gratified to see that the church, far from being empty was at least half filled with worshipers kneeling and whispering, or silently saying their prayers, for the Reverend Golightly was popular with his congregation. She became conscious of being surreptitiously observed and was glad of the veil to shield herself from their curiosity during her agonizingly exposed slow walk.

Her thoughts centered at first solely upon David and she could see him desperately fighting for breath as he panicked in the sea, struggling to survive. Then she saw Bernard trying just as desperately to save him until he himself went under and his lungs filled painfully with ocean brine.

She recalled Peter's dramatic description of their fine yacht wrecked upon the rocks. She recalled him saying how, among the flotsam washed up, a gull was pecking from a can of ship chandler's bully beef which had been the remains of their last supper. It reminded her of her husband's picture of the Last Supper which hung in his rectory study.

When the funeral parlor truck reached the altar steps and had to be raised over them by the morticians, Jennifer's heart missed a beat, for the wreath of lilies had slid backwards. Fortunately, it was caught just in time by an alert gloved hand, allowing the procession to be terminated safely before the candle-blazing altar without a jarring hitch.

The sexton, whispering, was in position at the foremost line of pews, having arrived by a circuitous route, ready to usher Jennifer into her front, reserved, lone mourner's pew. For her husband's relatives were to hold their separate memorial ceremony in his own church the following day. But his body had never been recovered.

As she knelt, the rector climbed slowly and solemnly into the pulpit, whereupon a fine soprano in the balcony a long way behind took her cue to begin singing the second stanza of the chosen hymn, fortified by intermittent stirring organ accompaniment. Jennifer could not hold back her tears after the profound impact made by the poignant verses so befitting the deceased:

Run the straight race through God's good grace. Lift up thine eyes and seek His face; Life with its way before us lies; Christ is the path and Christ the prize.

The hymn (FIGHT THE GOOD FIGHT) number was on the slotted board attached to a pillar, for those who wished to join in. Jennifer was touched when most of them did.

Suddenly, feeling an overwhelming desire to steal a fleeting glance backward and upward to catch a glimpse of the soprano, she finally could not resist. It thereupon warmed the mourner to perceive that the soloist's prim-glinting spectacles appeared to be focused below upon the casket before the altar. Contrary to Jennifer's expectation of the singer's physical appearance, she seemed very slim, petite and ordinary compared with the beauty and power of her voice, whose ever pure, lingering, high note wrenched tears from the kneeling mourner, whose glazed eyes were fixed on the engulfing shower of flowers on the coffin. Jennifer was strangely equivocal in her emotions, at one time being ecstatic at achieving the utmost on behalf of her beloved David and at another abysmally saddened at having to lose both him and her husband simultaneously to their mysterious divine unimpugnable Creator, whose ineffable "mercies," according to Baker in his beautiful harvest hymn, "shall endure ever faithful ever sure."

This unlimited, divine, all-embracing compassion the poor widow believed in implicitly. Her faith was unshakable. It was that kind of glorious flowering of faith which aromatized life – faith which, according to the Bible, could move mountains and make feet walk upon water.

"Knock and it shall be opened unto you, seek and ye shall find." She, the stricken mendicant with begging bowl and full of faith at heaven's gate – how could she be turned away by the All-Merciful in person, who all promises must keep? Naturally in all compassion David must be allowed to follow. In her tomb he would be patiently waiting when she in her turn came to be interred.

As soon as the singing was over, the great vaulted space began to echo with spates of suppressed coughing, whispering of voices, whispering of thin missal pages, shuffling in seats, staccato clattering of knee rests, dropping of canes and umbrellas – the disturbing pebbles of sound dropped down the echoing well of sacrosanctity momentarily broke the spell.

Jennifer slipped off the edge of her seat onto her arthritic knees, and buried her veiled face in her black-gloved hands.

She began by praying for David and then included her husband, and afterwards flitted painfully in her thoughts from one to the other like a moth singeing its wings while fluttering between two flames.

Fervently she prayed for the admission to heaven of her drowned loved ones, Bernard and David. Since the flight of a spirit departing the body occupies no space in time, she imagined they could already be awaiting her there.

Suddenly she became conscious of the Reverend Golightly's eulogy from the pulpit and she started listening with her lace handkerchief to her beautiful cougar-bright eyes.

"Dear brethren, we are here gathered to pray for the soul of our dearly beloved brother David Trewlove cut down like a flower while still in the full bloom of youth. Being an orphan, he has no family to mourn him but one, a distant and yet close relative, Jennifer Trewlove." Rev. Golightly's cherubic face beamed down on the mourner below his pulpit and his white surplice sleeves flew heavenward to command special attention from his flock for his next few poignant words. The congregation looked up; what was he about to say?

Chapter Thirty-seven

Rev. Golightly waited patiently until he had their complete attention, then began, "It is often foolishly said that lightning does not strike twice. But it hails from heaven and I assure you that it does, my dear brothers and sisters who mourn here with me today." And then to hold their interest he continued, in common everyday language, to tell a gripping, long, embellished story of how lightning struck a yacht and how the Reverend Bernard Ignatius Houndsditch was now presumed to be drowned, and, as if that tragedy were not enough for his widow to have to bear, David G Trewlove, Jennifer's beloved kinsman from Massachusetts, had been taken from her also – an ineffable double catastrophe. His voice softened as he once more began to declaim, "And he lies in peace before our eyes awaiting the Almighty's infinite mercy and to be buried in the Trewlove family grave in our own parish cemetery."

At this point the story made local news and a gasp ran out from the congregation, because Reverend Houndsditch was a well known and respected public figure. Golightly had cleverly avoided making the body in the coffin appear anything other than human!

Having achieved his goal, he reverted back to formalities with another grandiose flourish of those eloquent wings of his surplice.

"My dear brethren, our beloved sister Jennifer Houndsditch has just learned of the fate of her loving husband who was also a Good Samaritan to all in his parish as you well know by his good works among the poor, the sick and the needy.

"Therefore we perceive her bravely facing a double tragedy, as if one were not enough. So, I assure you all – brothers and sisters of this parish – that lightning *does indeed strike twice!*

"So I now beseech you to pray also for our beloved sister Jennifer and the souls of Bernard Houndsditch and David Trewlove, a blessed triumvirate.

"Who was this Trewlove whose remains lie before this altar of his Creator and at peace in hope of eternal life? And unable to plead for himself, how deserving was he of our prayers?

"Here let me say something to you about David, of whom you can know so little. Why? Because, since being rescued by our dear sister Jennifer Houndsditch, the truest Samaritan among us, he had shut himself off from the world, unable to face life itself. He was tormented by the memories of what had gone on in his workplace. The details are too horrific for me to go into but I'm sure you must be aware of them for they have been well publicized. So I don't have to go into them here – I am referring to greyhound racing, now mercifully banned by our progressive state of New York. Small wonder that David had a nervous breakdown witnessing what went on at his kennels, for it was his workplace for two long years until finally he was rescued by our Good Samaritan Jennifer Houndsditch, a distant relative."

The preacher's style changed abruptly and dramatically. His fingers clutched the edges of the pulpit. He leaned forward earnestly, turning repeatedly as if addressing every parishioner personally, while his gaze often fell lingeringly on the pew just below him where Jennifer sat.

She saw how ethereal the mundane little priest suddenly looked, as a breeze from apparently nowhere wafted the wispy white strands from his shining bald pate into the several crossing shafts of tinctured light from the lofty windows stained with the robes of biblical figures as luminous and gorgeous as sapphires and rubies. Her eyes kept straying to the alter ablaze with great silver flaming antlers of candles, half expecting them to mysteriously blow out in a spectacular fashion, like they had done the previous night in the memorial chapel. But this time, if St. Francis was looking down on his Feast with concern for his beloved animals and birds everywhere, he saw no reason to intervene. The only candles which mysteriously blew out were those in Jennifer's mind, subconsciously guttering to a phantom draft.

Hearing her husband's name mentioned, snapped her back into listening to the inspired little rector whose searing gaze she now felt upon her. Her abstracted mind cut in to hear,

"—our dear Reverend brother Bernard, whom many of you must know, was the well-loved rector of 'All Souls', nearby in Aylesford. What a tragedy! What a tragedy! The news comes as an even greater shock to those of us who knew him," (*his arms flew up*) "when we recall how recently – a mere matter of weeks – he was married to our dear sister Jennifer – truly a marriage made in heaven!

"How terrible! How terrible! He was drowned when his yacht capsized in a storm. His body was never recovered. Oh, yes – how terrible we say when it afflicts us personally. And yet our Beloved Savior tells us that we should rejoice! We should be happy for our loved one, for none of the faithful pass from this earth without passing into new life – a new and glorious life in the presence of our Heavenly Father."

Jennifer saw his arms open out, reminding her of those Catholic framed pictures of Jesus exposing the Sacred Heart. There was a dramatic pause, his hands returned to clutch the edge of the pulpit yet again. His voice became momentarily more conversational and swifter in delivery.

"A special requiem will be held in our dear brother Bernard's own parish church when the new incumbent takes over. Meanwhile, it is our compassionate duty to include Bernard and his widow, our beloved sister Jennifer, in our prayers." He now assumed a loftier manner.

"Returning to David," continued the rector, turning to face the coffin and clasping his hands together, "he sleeps before us here and before God, awaiting His infinite mercy that he may awaken into eternal life."

He turned back to face the congregation. Eloquent gestures became frequent. What his voice lacked in resonance was made up for by a wide range of inflections, dramatic pauses and emphases plus a welter of oratorical flourishes.

"Dear brethren, if our beloved brother could be some magical retrogression in time be transported into ancient Egypt, his good deeds and bad deeds would have been put onto their respective sides of divinely attested scales and weighed one against the other. What judgment could be fairer than this? If applied to David, I am certain that he would have tipped the balance in his favor and passed straight into paradise.

"On the other hand, if David had died in ancient Greece, his soul would have been ferried across the River Styx by a boatman called Charon and I have no doubt our virtuous brother would have made the divine landfall. In neither case would our prayers be a prerequisite.

"But, my dear brethren, we are neither living in ancient Egypt nor in ancient Greece. Our Christian ethos dictates that we pray for our brothers and sisters that they may pass into their future glorious Kingdom.

"Therefore I beseech you to do so sincerely and most earnestly for our dear virtuous brother David Trewlove lying in state and yet in all humility before the altar of our Heavenly Father, awaiting His forgiveness and mercy – for who amongst us is without sin?"

The Reverend Golightly, after first of all stroking his chasuble in the region over his heart, as was his habit by way of heralding rhetoric, paused to spread the wide white sleeves of his surplice, making them look like an angel's wings, while his cherubic chubby face beamed around at his spellbound parishioners. They had never heard him sound so lofty before. They were fidgeting less than usual, but instead were whispering more among themselves. Reverend Golightly saw that all faces were fixed upon him expectantly, but not until the angels' wings fluttered to rest upon the edges of the pulpit did he lean forward to repeat, "For who amongst us is without sin?" He again paused while once more soared the fluttering sleeves.

"My brothers and sisters, it is not also clearly written unto each and every one of us that we can never, never, never achieve on this earth perfection, hard though we may strive, because we are all of the flock of the Good Shepherd who professes to love all creatures great and small."

The angels' wings fluttered down slowly to alight on the ledge of the pulpit, as they had done innumerable times.

He now appeared so mild that he reminded Jennifer of pictures of the Savior depicted holding a shepherd's crook and a lamb under his arm.

"What more is there left to say of the handsome, selfless stranger from far away whom we know so little about and who in his prime was cut down like a flower? King Solomon in all his wisdom, son of David's namesake King David, has given us the Bible reports, the beauteous image and euphonious words which form part of our sad burial service.

"What more is there left for me to say? Just my own personal observation to be the last image in your minds of our dear departed brother as you kneel and he enters your prayers."

The preacher's style abruptly changed to the dramatic once more and repeated itself. His fingers clutched the edges of the pulpit, he leaned forward earnestly, revolving repeatedly as if addressing every parishioner personally, while his gaze often lingered on the pew just below where Jennifer quietly sobbed through the delicate lace of her handkerchief held to her face below her veil.

"I have met David and found him to be shy and reserved, speaking little of himself, even when adjured to do so. Therefore we must conclude that he possessed true humility. His manner was always friendly to the point of being extraordinarily affectionate. So obviously he was the most loving and caring of God's creatures of whom we are, one and all. Caring not only about those nearest and dearest to him whom it was easy to love, but even those like myself with whom he was hardly acquainted."

The white wings soured briefly and swooped, with talonish nails clawing the pulpit like a perching dove.

"Why then didn't he do his duty as a true Christian and report these atrocities to the proper authority? Did he merely wash his hands in public like Pontius Pilate who should have been named Pretentious Pilate! You will recall the perfidious Roman procurator of Judea? You know the story – be sure to wash your hands but don't lift a finger!"

The angels' wings soared high above his head and were beamed in the spotlight trained upon the casket. At that moment he could have come out of one of those holy pictures of saints levitating to be with the Redeemer! Only the luminous halo was missing.

"And what has David done about it, you may well ask? Is he another hypocritical Pilate? Most certainly our gentle stranger was not, because the truth is, my dear brethren, that in a humane, modern Christian society such as ours today, almost unbelievably, there simply is no official misnamed authority to turn to. This euphemistically misnamed sport of greyhound racing is a callous autocracy answerable on earth only to itself and the devil.

"Happily I am able to testify that David has done all he could. Through him and others like him, the public conscience has been stirred. So, one day, let us hope and pray, there will soon be a properly legislated, long overdue monitoring body that is more than just another impotent paper lion roaring through, a mouth without any teeth!

"David having been personally involved with this most worthy of charities, The Greyhound Rescue Society – who save as many as they can of the thousands of these poor, docile, defenseless innocents barbarically put to death every year – would rise if he could to plead their cause. But how can he, being that he lies before you, cut down like a flower and into our keeping placed, as is righteous, before this holy altar?

"Thus, by the authority invested in me by Almighty God, I beseech you, my brethren, to include this truly compassionate society's crusade also in your prayers and dedicate them as our candles of compassion for our dear brother David whom we cherish – candles from all our hearts lit to his memory that no evil can extinguish, for our Great Lord's mercies shall endure."

Whereupon the Reverend Golightly turned to face the altar, before which the spotlighted casket reposed on its mobile catafalque with its attendant morticians awaiting their cue to come forward and resume their stations. The rector clasped his hands in prayer and continued facing the casket while he declaimed in a voice echoing and re-echoing. His emotive words ran like quicksilver among the several moist eyes and the many hushed reverently listening ears, "I beseech thee, O Lord, to be merciful unto thy faithful repentant follower David and to forgive him his trespasses, that he may be allowed to follow thee into thy blessed kingdom, if it be thy most merciful will, through thine own son Jesus Christ our Lord, Amen."

The cherubic face thereupon turned to bestow a fleeting half smile, half pitying glance at the widow sobbing quietly under her veil, before descending magisterially from his pulpit saying, "By special request we shall now repeat singing the second stanza of our chosen hymn beginning with 'Run the straight race through God's good grace/Lift up thine eyes and seek his face'."

By the time the rector had reached the bottom step of the pulpit, the four morticians were alongside their parlor truck ready to wheel it away. The melancholy little altar boy, his face as white and waxen as the guttering tall candle on top of his cross was in position too, anxious to lead the procession as soon as his rector was behind him and the organ was thundering their cue to start snailing back down the aisle.

After the parlor truck had been gently lowered from the red carpeted steps to the tiles, with gloved hands this time holding in place the beautiful wreath of lilies, the soprano in the balcony began singing. Jennifer was profoundly moved as the soloist sang while the final slow procession glided to the door, her beloved David never to return.

She felt suddenly desperately alone and forsaken. Was there anything left behind for her to want to continue living for now that both David and Bernard had gone?

At that irrational instant, in her extreme and utter desolation she could have followed the casket into the hearse and sacrificed herself as upon a funeral pyre!

But the sight of the tall, handsome young sexton holding back the congregation, in deference to her priority as chief and only mourner so that she could follow her loved one alone, had a sobering and salutary influence upon her. It greatly helped to restore in her a determination not to abandon the human race and restore also her own suddenly disjunctive faith.

She stood frozen transcendentally in a dream world, ghosting on the threshold of the real and the surreal, hardly listening to the rector's brief comforting words, not looking into his eyes, not looking at his face, but looking into space. She gazed through glazed eyes at the blurred spectacle of the morticians easing their precious wheeled burden most reverently down the steps to the sidewalk and then sliding the coffin into the magnificent hearse. It carried a veritable flower show heaped on top of its roof – wreaths and crosses and splendiferous bouquets. The Reverend Golightly had certainly excelled himself in his role of Good Samaritan, in return for her own.

As the funeral director stepped smartly in beside the chauffeur and the hearse was ushered into the traffic being blocked by a police car with its officer in the middle of the road, the memorial parlor's immaculate limousine swept to the curb.

The chauffeur got out briskly and ran up the steps to take her arm and help her into the limousine now on its way to the cemetery. Suddenly she became anxious as to what lay in wait for her there, possibly capable of preventing David entering the family mausoleum.

Chapter Thirty-eight

But Jennifer's fears were unfounded, for in the cemetery all went off without a hitch. After the brief ceremony outside the mausoleum, the gravedigger was waiting to unlock the door and supervise the placing of the coffin on its prescribed shelf beside those of her other two Davids, father and son. Another shelf lay vacant beside it, awaiting herself.

Once inside the luxurious limousine again on her way home, it suddenly occurred to her that she would soon be having to relinquish the rectory to the new incumbent. However, her own splendid home, fully furnished, still remained unsold, and the comfortable income left to her by her rich aunt of the cranberry beds ensured that, whatever be the state of Bernard's finances, his widow was not left destitute – only desolate.

As they left the highway and began meandering down the familiar nostalgic lanes, poignant phantoms of happy days began their haunting. She saw Bernard across the buttered scones and felt his big hand on her small hand as she cut the warm breads – warm as his hand and soft as hers – in two halves, with their hands still clasped. How he had melted her with his most radiant smile, displaying such dazzling natural teeth.

These vignettes of memory kept coming while their stately stretched limousine purred slowly along. She was all alone in the back seat, lost in a world of her own. She relived that morning when Bernard had locked himself in the bathroom, too embarrassed to face Giselle; Bernard by the Christmas tree David has mistaken for a magic pine; Bernard teaching David to climb stairs; the loud creaking bed on their honeymoon; laughter at Brighton's curious royal "onion palace." A medley of memories merged into one another, with Bernard and David always together in her mind.

She saw him walk the dog that would never walk again, she saw him bandage the paw that would never bleed any more, and she rejoiced in those small, delicate cameos of remembrance – like the silver greyhound pin Bernard had bought for her in Brighton's quaint cobbled Lanes during their honeymoon in England at the hotel with a romantic view of the English Channel and sailboats as they lay in bed. This treasured grey-hound pin she was now wearing and she looked down at it repeatedly. The wearing of it felt like David leaning against her bosom!

Oh, David! Beloved mysterious David, who really were you, my darling? You could understand us so uncannily, but we were so incapable of fully understanding you. Can you possibly be some kind of a canine messiah sent down to redeem all forgotten creatures great and small? What a beautiful thought! If through your mystical intercession we could only hope for a worldwide beloved pet reunion in paradise!

Are we not promised being united with our loved ones? If pets be our loved ones, it is not merciful but cruel for us to be parted, is it not so, beloved David in heaven?

You know my wishes, you dear one who can read so well my mind. So do what you can to plead for all your sadly forgotten kith and kin.

Suddenly she was jogged out of her reverie. She became conscious of familiar trees sweeping past the limousine's windows and the sound of barking becoming steadily louder as they approached the rear of the rectory where the kitchen was situated.

The man with the blue serge cap plus a voice as softly purring as his engine would very soon once more, ever so politely, be holding open the door. The door into her lonely future with Robert, the dog left behind with Mrs. Broomworthy; because Giselle's saber-toothed Doberman Satan would have torn him to pieces if the cowardly beardie had been left in the care of Jennifer's best friend.

Now she could hear the deep cry of her vociferous Robert growing fainter as they rounded the corner and swept into the rectory driveway, saddened by the loss of the glorious blossoms of its dogwood trees. The silent surrounding wealth of shaped privet hedges, cypresses and weeping willows reminded Jennifer of the cemetery, and in her mind she pictured Reverend Golightly at the portal of the family sepulcher, supervising the coffin being carried within.

Her eye caught the roseate pink stars of Bernard's oh-so-pretty Japanese maple, shedding its poignant memories.

Three resident crows in perpetual mourning were still there sitting and looking down and appearing as if they had never moved, while the weather had moved around them. If only the happy days could have stayed as still and not moved on into memory! If only Time could reverse out of the driveway like the luxurious limousine soon must do, she would be as cheerful as the noonday sun warmly filtering through her veil of black lace as she peered through the limousine window.

Suddenly, with a brief crunching of gravel, the vehicle pulled up under the crows, causing great croaking and flapping of Apollonian-like wings among them. The immaculate chauffeur slid from his seat behind the wheel to open the door for his VIP passenger. He then stood as wooden and remote as a Buckingham Palace guard while he waited expectantly for his big tip, worthy of a sharp touch of his cap.

As the man reversed skillfully, the rectory doors opened, whereupon out ran the padding bulk of the housekeeper in carpet slippers. Jennifer raised her veil, then heard her own Christian name from the lips of the formidable woman for the very first time, while the dog barked from deep inside the dark house.

"Jennifer! Jennifer! The Reverend – your dear husband's alive. He's alive! Alive!"

"Oh Lily! Lily! I can hardly believe it – it's too good to be true! What a turn of fate – how wonderful! Who told you – are you sure? Really certain there can be no cruel mistake?" Tears began blurring her vision.

Jennifer felt suddenly the implosion of bosoms in the big woman's exuberant bear hug. The women's rejoicing was mutual, spontaneous, and ecstatic.

"No mistake, Jennifer. He's been picked up safe and sound by a Greek freighter called the Lemnos. The captain couldn't let us know sooner because of some trouble with their radio broken down. The police said they are not surprised because these tramp ships sailing under flags of convenience are always breaking down with faulty engines or equipment because they are operated on a shoestring. I only heard from the police about an hour ago – the Lemnos is docking at Cardiff in Wales – Oh! This is the happiest day of my life! And I'm so happy for you, Jennifer. The police got the message apparently relayed from a coast station somewhere."

"When is he—?"

"The rector will be flown back some time next week as soon as he can arrange a flight. When I got the news I could hardly believe my own ears! I was so overjoyed, I acted quite foolish and picked up Robert's forepaws and we did a little jig together on the kitchen tiles. He was enjoying it because his tail kept wagging all the time."

"Oh, Lily you are a dear – a softie at heart!"

"Let me finish, it's really funny. In fact when I got out of breath and stopped, he started barking till he got me to dance with him again. Jennifer, you should have been there – you would have been in stitches."

"I'm sure I would," tittered her jubilant mistress, imagining the comic scene.

"You'd be amazed too, Jennifer, 'cause surprisingly good on his hind legs is your Robert – better than some men I used to know trippin' the light fantastic in my younger days! I bet he'll be missing his buddy David now, poor dear, when he realizes he's not coming back. How did it go at the dog cemetery, Jennifer? Very sad for you it must have been – very similar to a church cemetery, I suppose?"

"Yes, Lily – very similar."

"Still, he can't complain – you've done your very best for him. Nobody could have done more. Mrs. Timmins says all dogs should be buried in a dog cemetery, not just in a backyard or left with the vet like garbage – and with a coffin and a proper grave with a tombstone and everything like they was really loved. Was your David done proper this way with all the trimmings like a funeral? I expect so – it must have been very thorough and beautiful to watch, seeing that it took so long."

"Yes, it was very beautiful – but also very sad."

Big Mrs. Broomworthy sighed a gale from her voluminous bosom, and squeezed her mistress' hand.

"I know, I know, Jennifer dear. It was the same with my Siamese a long time ago. She used to cry like a baby and so did I when she passed over. The Reverend used to have poisonous tropical fish at his pool – not anymore after my poor Sheba ate one. My poor Sheba, and she had just recovered from being bitten by a pit bull."

"I now realize, poor Lily. No wonder you had a thing about dogs ever since. Do you still miss Sheba?"

"Do you know, Jennifer, I thought I would never get over it. I missed her so terribly, then as the years passed I eventually stopped – that is until very recently when your David started leaning against me and then it all came back. I began to see Sheba in them glowing eyes – and his coloring – so like Sheba only a bit lighter – and his paws so catlike – so like Sheba."

"Did you have Sheba buried in a pet cemetery?"

"A pet cemetery," scoffed the housekeeper indignantly, "It's not conse-crated, is it? It's purely commercial. No, my Sheba is buried right here!"

Mrs. Broomworthy's finger pointed in the direction of the adjacent churchyard.

"In my husband's graveyard, Lily?" inquired Jennifer incredulously.

"Unfortunately no – under that willow tree just a stone's throw away – the rector wouldn't have her nearer. But I don't think God would have minded, do you Jennifer?"

"I'm sure God wouldn't mind, Lily."

The big housekeeper's face lit up.

"I bet millions of other pet lovers think like we do, Jennifer, only they lack the courage to speak out against the church. After all, Jesus didn't have any church – all bogged down with unnecessary rules. He was quite informal, wasn't He? In fact, Jesus was all compassion and understanding. In fact, He even let a prostitute wash His feet. So I feel sure He wouldn't deny me the last rites for poor little Sheba." She let out another deep sigh. "Still, I am very grateful to the Reverend for his weeping willow; I bet it was weeping for poor little Sheba. Anyway, it's planted on God's holy ground – 'cause it's part of our Lord's church, isn't it?"

"Of course it is – just as much as the graveyard, my dear Lily. Rest assured on that score."

"I thought so, but some say it is and some say it is not."

"Don't listen to them, Lily. They are only bigots."

Jennifer was astounded at the change that had come over the once formidable housekeeper who had become suddenly an animal lover. It turned Jennifer's withered outlook green again – greener than any rainy valley seen in England during her honeymoon! Even the crows sitting on the sacred boughs of their arboreal residence could now sound like nightingales! Especially as they could be croaking psalms for Mrs. B.'s cat which had spent its phenomenal nine lives!

The woman showed no sign of wanting to disengage herself from her mistress' side; it was as if each needed to feel the comforting contact of the other. And Jennifer remained passive, listening to the garrulous flow of Lily Broomworthy's tide of euphoria on the subject of the freighter Lemnos' heroic rescuing of the Reverend Houndsditch from drowning in the Atlantic.

Suddenly and unmistakably, Jennifer felt another contact with her own body – a firmer lower pressure this time against her legs. It could not have come, this firmer pressure, from the body of Lily, because the latter was in front of her, and this other pressure came slightly sideways from behind. As for the source of this familiar sensation of a dog leaning against her – unquestionably it identified a visitation by David!

"Jennifer!" said the astonished housekeeper, with a hand creeping down to feel her own thigh. Then, like a crayfish out of water, she began feeling the air, at knee level around her – in search of the impossible!

"Jennifer," she repeated, "didn't you feel something just then – something pressing against your legs? If I didn't know he was dead I could have sworn it was David! But when my hand went down to investigate he was gone like a ghost!"

"Yes, Lily – it really was David – you know that, dear, whatever anybody says. We know it was David, don't we, Lily? You and I know, don't we? I felt him lean against me too."

"Oh, Jennifer, I never thought I'd live to witness a miracle! The Good Shepherd must have sent David back to tell us something – I wonder what it could be?"

But Jennifer was not listening. She was in a state of great exultation, at last she felt completely fulfilled. In her heart she knew it was a sign that David was in heaven, probably leaning against his namesake, her own revered son David – both waiting for their beloved mother to join them there. And until then, happily, she felt that David (the dog) would follow her in mind all the days of her life.

About the Author

Albeit born in Bangor, Wales, yet I descend from the fourth son of Rollo the Viking, who became the first Duke of Normandy.

Twenty-one years ago, I emigrated to the USA, having wed one of Uncle Sam's remarkable daughters. She was an irresistible professional dancer, singer, entrepreneur and gifted painter in oils. Eventually, I gave up my feudal title of Baron to become a legalized American citizen of a kinder Republic than that which guillotined my ancestor and confiscated his ancient great castle estate in Gisor in Normandy. Being a friend of Marie Antoinette did not save his neck, but made it even more insecure! Thus I inherited minimal possessions apart from my title deeds (of little value to the "Reign of Terror")!

I served as a very young officer in the Norwegian and British merchant navies and survived three secular baptisms in the Atlantic due to enemy action. Subsequently, I became harbor master at Shorham, Sussex, UK—living on board my old world tall masted ketch *Roxana* for over three halcyon decades.

Having scribbled all my life, and by way of the dubious auspices of three shipwrecks, more fish than humans have swallowed my early works.

My last dramatic failed attempt at walking on water was miraculously saved by lifeboat hailing from the davits of the torpedoed Norwegian freighter *Grado*—recalled poetically in *The Sea Cries Over My Shoulder*—published by Christopher House, Boston, MA. The book got a glowing full page Oslo newspaper review (in Norwegian!) by courtesy of Otto Sorheim—with a picture of the author on board his beloved yacht *Roxana*.

The Daisy Chain, published by the controversial publisher Minerva (sued for nonpayment of royalties to numerous authors)—is based on my experiences as harbor master.

My first precocious great "masterpiece" composed in my kindergarten, was lovingly enshrined in a gold frame by my proud French mama, who inevitably mistook for genius the words she was unable to pronounce! The precocious immortal contribution to English literature is a naïve exposé of a ménage à trois between Betty the girl, a flower and a bee!

Follow Me, David is loosely based on my own late David greyhound rescued from the race track and given a happy new lease of life. The strange psychic hound is portrayed also in an epic poem, "Valhalla Hill" in *Whispers*, published by Peter E. Randall Publisher LLC, while the volume itself gained, among others, a rave review by Midwest Book Review, and appears below. Furthermore *Whispers*, in addition to numerous other extolling reviews, recently received five-star rating on Amazon.com.

Midwest Book Review of *Whispers* September 2008:

"Award winning poet and honorary doctorate of literature holder Jonathan Russell brings poetry lovers a treat with *Whispers*. Winner of the American Poetry Association's first prize two years in a row, the poems definitely show why they received such awards. The imagery is vivid and engaging, which is especially magnificent given Russell's legally blind status. *Whispers* is a must for anyone looking for the cream of the crop for poetry. "Box Car Barney": Box Car Barney, bard of the greeting/cards, sold by the railroad locomotive verse/clicking to the track's predictable signals, smooth/as iron wheels rolling to their whistle-stops./His shop was a cardboard box, the necklace of/commerce,/and the hanging Babylon of charity with hand dangling a cup-- the cash register of the homeless. Nothing/clicked in his life but coins dropped to the Muse's mart of Saccharine Art pretty cardinals/on a feeder tweeting to conscience sowing seeds/ of hope sprouting silver bell honey bee/congratulatory oratory, Christmas reindeer tinkles/and tinsel, birthday wishful sugary sprinkles/and lovers' trinkets kissed by hearts and flowers.""

Baryon Review of *Whispers* by Barry Hunter:

"This volume runs the gamut from short to long, narrative to descriptive, and covers a plethora of subjects. "The Richest Corpse in History", "Ghost Ship", "The Glowworm's Honeymoon", "The Riddle of the Middle Sex", "No Second Spring (the toxic truth)", and "The Sadness of Green" are some of the more interesting titles. "Russell has taken the poem and changed its form to meet his needs and has turned out a very interesting collection of verse. No rhyming, no iambic pentameter, just some unusual and well crafted verses to remind us that there is more out there to enjoy if we just look for it."

BookPleasures Review of *Whispers* by Lily Azerad-Goldman, B.F.A.

Whispers is a mesmerizing collection of poetry with vivid lyrics in which Russell grapples with such profound themes as existence, love and death. And his venues are wide and varied touching on topics from philosophy, love and romance to art and music and mythology. He demonstrates his vast knowledge with a cutting edge and a prickly sense of humor. Some of his poems are weighty while others tickle our funny bones.

As a poet, novelist, academic, and composer, Russell offers readers a distinctive perspective, and even though he is legally blind, he nonetheless "sees," perhaps, with more lucidity than those with sight.

The poems are written in free verse where the discrepancies and variations of meter are center stage. His cadenced verse is based on rhythmical phrases that are more irregular than those of traditional poetic meter as he follows a looser pattern than would be expected in formal verse. He does away with the structuring devices of regular meter and rhyme schemes while other elements of expression, such as diction and syntax are still prominent.

With just a few chosen words, Russell describes life's absurdities with biting drollness . . .

Whispers is definitely a book to savor a little morsel at a time, alone or with a trusted friend or small group who appreciate free verse poetry. Moreover, a collection that would find a more pulsating voice when recited aloud.